A PENGUIN MYS~

CHASING THE DEAD

Tim Weaver is the international bestselling author of the David Raker mystery series. He has been longlisted for the prestigious Dagger in the Library Award from the Crime Writers' Association and his work has been nominated for a National Book Award in the UK. He is also the host of the award-winning podcast *Missing,* about why people disappear and how investigators track them down. A former journalist and magazine editor, he now writes fiction full time and lives with his wife and daughter in Bath, England.

ALSO BY TIM WEAVER

TIM WEAVER

Chasing the Dead

PENGUIN BOOKS

PENGUIN BOOKS
An imprint of Penguin Random House LLC
375 Hudson Street
New York, New York 10014
penguin.com

First published in Penguin Books (UK) 2010
Published in an updated edition 2015
Published in Penguin Books (USA) 2016

ISBN 9780143129615 (paperback)
ISBN 9781101993323 (ebook)

Printed in the United States of America
1   3   5   7   9   10   8   6   4   2

Set in Garamond MT Std Regular
Designed by Eve Kirch

For Sharlé

"And the sea became as the blood of a dead man: and every living soul died in the sea"

REVELATION 16:3

Chasing the Dead

PART ONE

1

Sometimes, toward the end, it was like she was drowning: she would wake me by tugging at the cusp of my shirt, her eyes flickering, begging me to pull her to the surface. I always liked those moments, despite her suffering, because it meant she'd lasted another day.

Her skin was like canvas in those last months, stretched tight against her bones. She'd lost all her hair as well, except for some bristles around the tops of her ears. But I never cared about that; about any of it. If I'd been given a choice between having Derryn for a day as she was when I'd first met her, or having her for the rest of my life as she was at the end, I would have taken her as she was at the end, without even pausing for thought. Because, in the moments when I thought about a life without her, I could barely even breathe.

She was thirty-two, seven years younger than me, when she first found the lump. Four months later, she collapsed in the supermarket. I'd been a newspaper journalist for eighteen years but, after she collapsed a second time—this time on the Underground—I resigned, went freelance and refused to travel. It wasn't a hard decision. I didn't want to be on the other side of the world when the third call came through telling me that, this time, she'd fallen and died.

On the day I left the paper, Derryn took me to a plot she'd chosen for herself in a cemetery in north London. She looked at her grave, up at me, and then smiled. I remember that clearly. A smile shot through with so much pain and fear I wanted to break something. I wanted to hit out until all I felt was numb. Instead, I took her hand, brought her into me, and tried to treasure every second of whatever time we had left.

When it became clear the chemotherapy wasn't working, she decided to stop. I cried that day, really cried, probably for the first time since I was a kid—but, looking back, she made the right decision. She still had some dignity. Without hospital visits and the time it took her to recover from them, our lives became more spontaneous, and that was an exciting way to live for a while. She read a lot and she started writing a journal, and I did some work on the house, painting walls and fixing rooms. And a month after she stopped her chemo, I started to plow some money into creating a study. As Derryn reminded me, I'd need a place to work.

Except the work never came. There was a little—sympathy commissions mostly—but my refusal to travel turned me into a last resort. I'd become the type of freelancer I'd always loathed. I didn't want to be that person, was even conscious of it happening. But, with each passing day, Derryn became a little more important to me, and I found that difficult to let go.

Then one day I got home and found a letter on the living-room table. It was from one of Derryn's friends.

She was desperate.

Her daughter had disappeared, and the police didn't seem to be interested. I was the only person she thought could help.

The offer she made was huge—more than I'd deserve from what would amount to a few phone calls—but the whole idea left me paralyzed by uncertainty. I definitely needed the money, and had sources inside the Met who would have found her daughter in days. But I wasn't sure I wanted my new life to join up with my old one. I wasn't sure I wanted any of it back.

So I said no.

But, when I took the letter through to the back garden, Derryn was gently rocking in her chair with the tiniest hint of a smile on her face.

"What's so funny?"

"You're not sure if you should do it."

"I'm sure," I said. "I'm sure I *shouldn't* do it."

She just nodded.

"Do you think I should do it?"

"It's perfect for you."

"What, chasing around after missing kids?"

"It's perfect for you," she said. "Take this chance, David."

And that was how it began. I pushed the doubt down with the sadness and the anger and found the girl three days later in a bedsit in Walthamstow. Then, more work followed, more missing people, and I could see the ripples of the career I'd left behind returning to me. Asking questions, making calls, trying to pick up the trail. I'd always liked the investigative parts of journalism, the dirty work, the digging, more than I'd liked the writing. And, after a while, a few cases in to my new career, I knew it was the reason I never felt out of my depth working missing persons, because the process, the course of the chase, was exactly the same. Most of it was just about caring enough. The police didn't have time to find every person who left home and never returned—and I think sometimes they failed to understand why people disappeared in the first place. Most of them didn't leave just to prove a point. They left because their lives had taken an uncontrollable turn, and the only way to contend with that was to run. What followed, the traps they fell into after, were the reasons they could never go back.

But despite the hundreds of people that went missing every day of every year, I'm not sure I ever expected to make a living out of trying to find them. It never felt like a job; not in the way journalism had. And yet, after a while, when the money really started coming in, Derryn persuaded me to rent some office space down the road from our home, in an effort to get me out, but also—more than that, I think—to convince me I could make a career out of what I was doing.

She called it a long-term plan.

Two months later, she died.

2

When I opened the door to my office, it was cold and there were four envelopes on the floor inside. I tossed the mail on to the desk and opened the blinds.

Morning light erupted in, revealing photos of Derryn everywhere.

In one, my favorite, we were in a deserted coastal town in Florida, sand sloping away to the sea, jellyfish scattered like cellophane across the beach. In the fading light, she looked beautiful. Her eyes flashed blue and green. Freckles were scattered along her nose and under the curve of her cheekbones. Her blonde hair was bleached by the sun, and her skin had browned all the way along her arms.

I pulled the picture toward me.

Next to her, my eyes were dark, my hair darker. I towered over her at six-two, her head resting against my chest, her body fitting in against mine. If, in the years since the photograph had been taken, there had been any physical change in me, it was subtle enough for people not to notice. I worked out, I looked after myself, the same now as I did then. Yet, *I* could see the difference clearly. The version of me in the photograph lacked the weight of bereavement. I was oblivious to what was coming. I had a spark, a lustre. Grief was only a word, like any other.

Back then, I wouldn't have been able to identify with the families of the missing, because I wouldn't have understood them.

But I understood them now.

I turned around in my chair and looked up at them all, at the faces of the people I traced. Their smiles filled an entire corkboard on the wall behind me.

Every space. Every corner.

They were all I had now.

I spent most of the day sitting at my desk with the lights off, unsure exactly of why I'd come in. It was exactly a year since Derryn had been carried out of our house on a stretcher. The telephone rang a couple of times, but I left it, listening to it echo around the office. I knew I wasn't in the right state of mind to consider taking on any work, so when the clock hit four, I started to pack up.

That was when Mary Towne arrived.

I heard her coming up the stairs, slowly taking one step at a time, and then the top door clicked and creaked open. I'd known Mary for a few years. She used to work in A&E with Derryn. Her life had been tragic, just the same as mine: her husband suffered from Alzheimer's, and her son had left home six years earlier without telling anyone. He eventually turned up dead.

"Hi, Mary."

I startled her.

Sitting on the far side of the waiting area, she looked up. Her skin was darkened by creases, every one of her fifty years etched into her face. She'd been beautiful once, but her life had been pushed and pulled around and now she wore the heartache like a cloak. Her small figure had become slightly stooped. The color had started to drain from her cheeks and her lips. Thick ribbons of gray had begun to emerge from her hairline.

"Hello, David," she said quietly. "How are you?"

"Good." I shook her hand. "It's been a while."

"Yes." She looked down into her lap. "A year."

She meant Derryn's funeral.

"How's Malcolm?"

Malcolm was her husband. She glanced at me and shrugged.

"You're a long way from home," I said.

"I know. I needed to see you."

"Why?"

"I wanted to discuss something with you."

I tried to imagine what.

"I couldn't get you on the telephone."

"No."

"I called a couple of times."

"It's kind of a . . ." I looked back to my office. To the pictures of Derryn. "It's kind of a difficult time for me at the moment. Today, in particular."

She nodded. "I know it is. I'm sorry about the timing, David. It's just . . . I know you care about what you're doing. This job. I need someone like that. Someone who cares." She glanced at me again. "Do you remember Alex?"

Alex was her son.

"Of course."

"Do you remember what happened to him?"

"He died."

"I mean, the details."

I paused, looking at her, wondering where this was going.

"David?"

"Why don't we go through?" I said, and led her out of the waiting area and back to my desk. She looked around at the photos on the walls, her eyes moving between them. "Take a seat," I said, pulling a chair out for her.

She nodded her thanks.

I sat down opposite her. "So tell me about Alex."

"He died in a car crash," she said quietly.

"I remember that, yes."

"He was, uh . . . he was drunk. He drove a Toyota, like his father used to have, right into the side of a lorry. It was only a small car. It ended up fifty feet from the road, in the middle of a field; burned to a shell, like him. They had to identify him from dental records." She stopped, composing herself. "But you know what the worst bit was? Before he died, he'd just disappeared. He was gone five years before that crash. Five years. After everything we'd done as a family, he just . . . vanished. The next time I saw him . . ."

She couldn't finish the sentence.

"I'm sorry," I said.

"Five years after he disappeared, the only thing he left me with was the memory of his body lying on a mortuary slab. I'll never get that image out of my head. I used to open my eyes in the middle of the night and see him standing like that next to my bed." Her eyes glistened. "I don't think you ever met him in person—but I'm sure you heard about him through Derryn."

She took out a photograph and handed it to me. She was in it, her arms around a man in his early twenties. He was handsome. Black hair, green eyes, probably five-eleven, but broad, like he might once have been a swimmer.

The two of them were smiling.

"This is Alex. *Was* Alex. This is the last picture we ever took of him." She nodded toward the photograph. "That was a couple of days before he left."

"It's a nice picture."

"He was gone five years before he died."

"Yes, you said."

"In all that time, we never once heard from him."

"I'm really sorry, Mary," I said again, just to say something.

"I know," she said quietly. "That's why you can help me."

I eyed her. "What do you mean?"

"I don't want to sound like a mother who can't get over the fact that her son is dead. Believe me, I know he's dead. I saw him lying there with my own eyes." She paused. I thought she might cry, but then she pulled her hair back from her face, and her eyes were darker, more focused. "Three months ago, I left work late, and when I got to the station I'd missed my train. It was pulling out as I arrived. If I miss my train, the next one doesn't leave for fifty minutes. I've missed it before. When that happens I always walk to a nice coffee place I know close to the station and sit in one of the booths and watch the world go by."

She stopped, studying me.

"Okay," I said, pushing gently.

"I was thinking about some work I had on, some patients I had seen that day, when I . . ." Her eyes narrowed, as if deciding whether she could trust me—and then they glistened again, and she took a long breath. "I saw him," she said.

"Saw who?"

"Alex."

It took a moment for it to hit me.

She's saying she saw her dead son.

"I, uh . . . I don't understand," I said.

"I saw Alex."

"You *saw* him?"

"Yes."

"What do you mean?"

"I mean, I saw him."

I was shaking my head. "Wh—*How?*"

"He was walking on the other side of the street."

"It was someone who looked like Alex."

"No," she replied softly, controlled, "it was Alex."

"But he's dead."

"I know he's dead."

"Then how could it possibly be him?"

"It was him, David."

"How is that possible?"

"I don't know," she said, eyes never leaving mine. "I don't know how it could be him. But it *was* him. It was my son." She stopped, swallowed. "It was Alex."

3

I stared at her, unsure what to say.

"I know what you're thinking," she said, "but I'm not crazy. My mother, my sister, they've been gone for years, and I don't see them. I swear to you, David, I saw Alex that day. I *saw* him." She moved forward in her seat, bringing her handbag with her. "I'll pay you up front," she said quickly. "If that's the only way I can persuade you that I'm telling you the truth, I will pay you money up front."

"Have you reported this?"

"To the *police*?"

"Yes."

She sat back again. "Of course not."

"You should."

"What's the point?"

"Because that's what you do, Mary."

"My son is dead, David. You think they'd believe me?"

"Why did you think *I* would believe you?"

She glanced around the room. "I know some of your pain, David, believe me. My cousin died of cancer. In many ways, that terrible disease takes the whole family with it. You care for someone for so long, you see them like that, you get used to having them like that, and then, when they're suddenly not there, you lose not only them, but what their illness brought to your life. You lose the routine."

I didn't say anything.

"I don't know you as well as I knew Derryn, but I know this: I took a chance on you believing me, because if, just for a moment, we reversed this situation and you'd seen the person you loved, I know you'd take a chance on me believing you."

"Mary . . ."

She looked at me, half-expecting my reaction.

"You have to go to the police."

"No."

"Think about what you're—"

"Don't insult me like that," she said, her voice raised for the first time. "You can do anything, but don't insult me by telling me to *think* about what I'm saying. Do you honestly believe I've spent the last three months doing anything *but* that? I can't go to the police." She sat forward in her seat again and the fingers of one of her hands clawed at the ends of her raincoat. "Deep down, you know I can't."

"Mary," I replied softly, "how can he be alive?"

"I don't know."

"He can't be."

"You don't understand," she said.

She was pointing out the difference between us: I watched someone I love die; she'd done the same—but her loved one had somehow returned. We both understood the moment—and because of that she seemed to gain in confidence.

"It was him."

"He was a distance away. How could you be sure?"

"I followed him."

"You *followed* him? Did you speak to him?"

"No."

"Did you get close to him?"

"I could see the scar on his cheek where he fell playing football at school."

"Did he seem . . . injured?"

"No. He seemed healthy."

"What was he doing?"

"He was carrying a backpack over his shoulder. He'd shaved his hair. He always had long hair, like in the photograph I gave you. When I saw him, he'd shaved it off. He looked different, thinner, but it was him."

"How long did you follow him for?"

"About half a mile. He ended up going into a library off Tottenham Court Road for about fifteen minutes."

"What was he doing in there?"

"I didn't go in."

"Why not?"

She stopped. "I don't know. When I lost sight of him, I started to disbelieve what I'd seen."

"Did he come back out?"

"Yes."

"Did he see you?"

"No. I followed him to the Underground, and that's where I lost him. You know what it's like. I lost him in the crowds. I just wanted to speak to him, but I lost him."

"Have you seen him since?"

"No."

I sat back in my chair. "You said this happened three months ago?"

She nodded. "September fifth."

"What about Malcolm?"

"What about him?"

"Have you said anything to him?"

She shook her head. "What would be the point? He has Alzheimer's. Most days, he can't even remember my name."

I glanced at the photo of Derryn on my desk. "Switch positions with me, Mary. Think about how this sounds."

"I know how it *sounds*," she replied. "It sounds impossible. I've been carrying this around with me for three months, David. Why do you think I haven't done anything about it until now? People would think I had lost my mind. Look at you: you're the only person I thought might believe me, and you think I'm lying too."

"I don't think you're ly—"

"Please, David."

"I *don't* think you're lying," I said. "But I think maybe you're confused."

Anger passed across her eyes, and then it was gone again, replaced by an acceptance that it had to be this way. She looked down into her lap, into the bag perched upon it. "The only way I can think to persuade you is by paying you."

"Mary . . ."

"You know people."

"This is different."

"You *know* people," she said again.

"You need to go to the police."

Silence. Her hand moved to her face.

"Come on, Mary. Can you see what I'm saying?"

She didn't move.

"I know a few guys at the Met," I said.

She shook her head gently.

"This is what they get paid to do."

She looked up, tears in her eyes.

"I've got some names here," I went on, opening the top drawer of my desk and taking out a diary I used when I was still at the paper. "Let me see." I could hear her sniffing, could see her wiping the tears from her face, but I didn't look up. "There's a guy I know who works in Southwark who can—"

"I'm not interested."

"But this guy will help y—"

She held up a hand. "I'm not explaining this to anyone else."

"Why not?"

"Can you imagine how many times I've played this conversation over in my head? I don't think I can muster the strength to do it again. And, anyway, what would be the point? If you don't believe me, what makes you think your contact in the police force will?"

"It's his job."

"He would laugh in my face."

"He wouldn't laugh in your face, Mary. Not this guy."

"The way you looked at me, I can't deal with that again."

"Mary . . ."

She shook her head. "Imagine if it was Derryn."

I didn't respond.

"*Imagine*," she repeated.

And then, very calmly, she got up and left.

4

I was brought up on a farm in south Devon. My dad used to hunt pheasant and rabbits with an old bolt rifle. On a Sunday morning, when the rest of the village—including my mum—were on their way to church, he used to drag me out to the woods and we'd fire guns.

When I was old enough, we progressed to a replica Beretta he'd got mail order. It only fired pellets, but he used to set up targets in the forest for me: human-sized targets that I had to hit. Ten targets: ten points for a head shot, five for the body. I got the full one hundred points for the first time on my sixteenth birthday. He celebrated by letting me wear his favorite hunting jacket and taking me to the pub with his friends. The whole village soon got to hear about how his only child was going to be the British army's top marksman one day.

That never happened, of course. But ten years later I found a jammed Beretta, just like the one he'd let me use, on the streets of Alexandra, a township in Johannesburg—except this one was real. There was one bullet left in the clip.

I removed it, and kept it.

Later the same day, I found out that a bullet, maybe even from the gun I'd found, had ended the life of a photographer I'd shared an office with for two years. He'd dragged himself a third of a mile along a street—gunfire crackling around him, people leaping over his body—and died in the middle of the road.

Sometimes, even fifteen years on, I return to that bullet, set in a block of glass now, and sitting on a shelf in the spare room. It reminds me of my dad, and our Sunday mornings in the forest. It reminds me of the photographer who left this world, alone, in the middle of a dust-blown street. But mostly, it reminds me of the way life can be taken away—and of the distance you might be prepared to crawl in order to cling on to it.

It had just gone nine in the evening when I called Mary and told her I'd take the case. She started crying. I listened to her for a minute or so, her tears broken up by the sound of her thanking me, and then I told her I'd drive out to her house the next morning.

When I put the phone down, I looked along the hallway, into the bowels of my house, and beyond into the darkness of our bedroom, untouched since Derryn died. Her books still sat below the windowsill, the covers creased, the pages folded at the edges where she couldn't find a bookmark. Her spider plant was perched above it, its long, thin arms fingering the tops of the novels on the highest shelf.

Since she'd been gone I hadn't spent a single night in there. I went in to shower, to water her plant, but I slept in the living room on the sofa, and always with the TV on. Its sounds comforted me. The people, the programs, the familiarity of it—they helped fill some of the space Derryn used to occupy.

5

I got to Mary's house, a cavernous mock-Tudor cottage an hour west of London, just before ten the next morning. It was picture-perfect suburbia, right at the end of a tree-lined cul-de-sac: shuttered windows, a wide teak-colored front porch and empty flower baskets swinging gently in the breeze.

I stepped up to the door and rang the bell.

A few moments later, it opened a sliver and Mary looked out through the gap. "Oh, David," she said as if she'd forgotten I was coming, and pulled the door back. Behind her I could see her husband, facing me, on the stairs. He didn't move; didn't even register me. He was looking down at a playing card, turning it over in his hands. Face up. Face down.

"Would you like some coffee or tea?"

"Coffee. Thanks."

She nodded. "Malcolm, this is David."

Malcolm didn't move.

"Malcolm."

Nothing.

"*Malcolm.*"

He flinched, as if a jolt of electricity had passed through him, and he looked up. Not to see who had called him but to see what the noise was.

He didn't recognize his name.

"Malcolm, come here," Mary said, waving him toward her.

He got up, and shuffled across to us.

He was drawn and tired, stripped of life. His black hair was starting to gray. The skin around his face sagged. He was probably in his early fifties, only a few years older than Mary, but there could have been a decade between them. He might have been a rugby player once, a powerful physical force, but not any more. Here, inside these walls, his life was ebbing away, his weight was going with it.

"This man's name is David."

I reached out and had to awkwardly pull his hand out from his side to shake it. He looked like he wasn't sure what I was doing to him.

When I let go, his hand dropped away, and he made his way toward the television, shuffling slowly. I followed him and sat down, expecting

Mary to do the same. Instead, she headed for the kitchen and disappeared inside.

I glanced at Malcolm Towne.

He was looking at me with a strange expression, like my presence had registered with him but he didn't know what to say to me. Then he turned back to the screen.

Mary returned, holding a tray.

She set it down. "There's some sugar there, and some milk." She picked up a muffin, placed it onto a side plate and handed it to her husband. "Eat this, Malc," she said, making an eating gesture. He took the plate from her, laid it in his lap and looked at it. "I wasn't sure how you took it," she said to me.

"That's fine."

"There's blueberry muffins, and a couple of raspberry ones too. Have whichever you like. Malcolm prefers the raspberry ones—don't you, Malc?"

I looked at him. He was staring blankly at his plate. *You can't remember what muffin you prefer when you can't even remember your own name.* Mary glanced at me, as if she knew what I was thinking. But she didn't seem to care.

"When was he diagnosed?" I asked.

She shrugged. "Officially, two years ago. But it started about twelve months before that. Back then it was just forgetting little bits and pieces, like you or I would forget things, except they wouldn't come back to him. They just went. Then it became bigger things, like names and events, and then, the past eighteen months, he started forgetting me and, eventually, he forgot we even had a son."

I nodded, broke off a piece of blueberry muffin. "Well, I'm going to need a couple of things from you," I said. "First up, any photos you can lay your hands on. A good selection. Then I'll need addresses for his friends, his work, his girlfriend if he had one." I nodded my head toward the stairs. "I'd also like to have a look around his room if you don't mind. I think that would be helpful."

"Yes, of course," Mary said.

"Was Alex living away from home when he disappeared?"

She nodded. "Yes. But he'd come back here for a holiday for a few weeks just before he vanished."

"Where was he living?"

"Bristol. He'd gone to university there."

"And after university?"

"He got a job down there, as a data clerk." The disappointment showed in her eyes, and then she shrugged. "I asked him to come back home after he graduated; that we'd find something for him in London. The job he had down in Bristol was terrible. They used to dump files on his desk, and he'd input this data, all day, every day. Plus the pay was awful. He deserved better than that."

"But he didn't want to come back?"

"He was qualified to degree level. He had a first in English. He could have got himself into a graduate program here on five times the salary. And, if he had moved back, he'd have paid less rent and it would have been a much better springboard for finding work. He could have devoted his days to filling out application forms and going for interviews at companies that deserved him."

"But he didn't want to come back?" I asked again.

"No. He wanted to stay there."

"Why?"

"He'd built a life for himself in Bristol, I suppose."

"What about after he disappeared—you never spoke to him?"

"No."

"Not even by telephone?"

"Never," Mary reaffirmed, quieter this time.

I made her run over her story again: where she saw Alex, when, how long she followed him for, what he looked like. I took down a description of what he was wearing and the places she'd seen him too. Even with all of that, it didn't leave me a lot to go on.

"So, Alex was gone for five years before he died, right?"

"Right."

"Where did he crash the car?"

"Just outside Bristol, up toward the motorway."

"What happened with it?"

"The car?"

"No personal items were retrieved from it?"

"It was just a shell."

I moved on. "Did Alex have a bank account?"

"Yes."

"Did he withdraw any money before he left?"

"Half of it."

"Which was how much?"

"Five thousand pounds."

"That's it?"

"That's it."

"Did you check his statements?"

"Regularly—but it was pointless. He left his card behind when he went, and he never applied for a replacement as far as I know."

"Did he have a girlfriend?"

"Yes—down in Bristol."

"Is she still there?"

"No," Mary said. "Her parents live in north London. After Alex disappeared, Kathy moved back there."

"Have you spoken to her at all?"

"Not since the funeral."

"You never spoke to her after that?"

"He was dead. We had nothing to talk about."

I paused, letting her gather herself again.

"So, did he meet Kathy at university?"

"No. They met at a party Alex went to in London. When he went to uni, she followed him down there."

"So, she wasn't a student?"

"No. She worked as a waitress."

I took down her address. I'd have to invent a plausible story if I was about to start cold-calling old friends. After all, Alex had been dead for over a year.

As if reading my mind, Mary said, "What are you going to tell her?"

"The same as I'll tell everyone. That you've asked me to put a time-table together of your son's last movements. There's some truth in that, anyway."

Mary got up and went to a drawer in the living room. She pulled it open and took out a letter-sized envelope with an elastic band around it. She looked at it for a moment, then pushed the drawer shut and returned, laying the envelope on the table in front of me, and opening a corner so I could see the money inside.

"I hope you can see now that this isn't a joke," she said.

"Why do you think Alex took so little cash with him?"

She looked up from the envelope and for a moment seemed unsure of the commitment she'd just made. Perhaps now the baton had been passed on, she'd had a moment of clarity about everything she believed she'd seen.

I repeated the question. "Why so little money?"

"I've no idea. Maybe that was all he could get out at once. Or maybe he just needed enough to give him a start somewhere." She looked around the room. "I don't really understand a lot of what Alex did. He had a good life."

"Do you think he became bored of it?"

She shrugged and bowed her head.

I watched her for a moment, and realized there were two mysteries: why Mary believed she had seen Alex walking around more than a year after he'd died—and why Alex had left everything behind in the first place.

His room was small. There were music posters on the walls, textbooks on the shelves, a TV in the corner, dust on the screen, and a VCR next to it with old tapes perched on top. I went through them. Alex had had a soft spot for action movies.

"He was a big film buff."

I turned. Mary was standing in the doorway.

"Yeah, I can see. He had good taste."

"You think?"

"Are you kidding?" I picked up a copy of *Die Hard* and held it up. "I was a teenager in the eighties. This is my *Citizen Kane*."

She smiled. "Maybe you two would have got on."

"We would have definitely got on. I must have watched this about fifty times. It's the best anti-depressant on the market."

She smiled again, then looked around the room, stopping on a photograph of Alex close by. Her eyes dulled a little, the smile slipping from her face.

"I don't know if I'll ever have the strength to clear this room out."

"I know the feeling."

She nodded at me, almost a thank you, as if it was a relief to know she wasn't alone. I looked toward the corner of the room, where two wardrobes were positioned against the far wall. "What's in those?" I asked.

"Just some of the clothes he left behind."

"Can I look?"

"Of course."

There wasn't much hanging up, just some old shirts and a musty suit. I pushed them along the runner, and on the floor I found a photograph album.

"Is that Alex's?"

"Yes."

I opened up the album and some photographs spilled out. One was of Alex and a girl in her late teens: long hair, bright eyes, pretty. "Is this Kathy?"

Mary nodded. I set the picture aside and looked through the rest. Alex and Mary. Mary and Malcolm. I held up a photograph of Malcolm and Alex at a caravan park somewhere. It was hot. Both of them were stripped down to their shorts, and were perched next to a smoking barbecue with bottles of beer.

"You said they were close?"

"Yes."

"You don't think Malcolm would remember anything?"

"You're welcome to try," she said, but then stopped again, a sudden sadness washing over her. I understood why: she'd realized again, as she must have done countless times, that her son was dead, and her husband had no memory of her.

She was completely alone.

I felt so sorry for her in that moment, the loneliness written clearly in her face, but it also made me wonder what that sense of isolation might do. Would it make you believe something was true even if, deep down, you knew it wasn't?

Would it make you see someone who wasn't there?

A memory. A ghost.

A son.

I left Mary's just after midday. Once I hit the motorway, the traffic started to build; three lanes of slowly moving cars feeding back into the center of the city.

What should have been a forty-five-minute drive to Kathy Simmons's family home in Finsbury Park turned into a mammoth two-hour expedition through London gridlock. I stopped once, to get something to eat, and then chewed on a sandwich as I inched through Hammersmith, following the curve of the Thames. By the time I had finally parked up, it was just after two.

I locked the car and moved up the drive.

It was a yellow-bricked semi-detached, with a courtyard full of fir trees and a small patch of grass at the front. A Mercedes and a Micra were parked outside, and the garage was open. It was rammed with junk— some of it in boxes, some on the floor—and shelves full of machinery parts and tools. There was no one inside. As I turned back to the house, a curtain twitched at the front window.

"Can I help you?"

I spun around.

A middle-aged man with a garden sprayer attached to his back was standing at the side of the house, where an entrance ran parallel to the garage.

"Mr. Simmons?"

"Who's asking?"

"My name's David Raker. Is Kathy in today, sir?"

He eyed me suspiciously. "Why?"

"I'd like to speak with her."

"Why?"

"Is she in today, sir?"

"First you tell me why you're here."

"I was hoping to speak to her about Alex Towne."

A flash of recognition in his eyes. "What's he got to do with any-thing?"

"That's what I was hoping to ask Kathy."

Behind me I heard the door opening. A woman in her late twenties stepped out onto the porch. Kathy. Her hair was short now, dyed blonde, but a little maturity had made her even prettier. She held out her hand and smiled.

"I'm Kathy," she said.

"Nice to meet you, Kathy. I'm David."

I glanced around at her father, whose gaze was fixed on me. Water tumbled out of the hose onto the toes of his boots.

"What are you, an investigator or something?" she asked.

"Kind of."

She frowned, but seemed intrigued.

"Where's Kathy fit into all this?" her father said.

I glanced at him, and then back to Kathy. "I'm doing some work for Mary Towne. It's to do with Alex. Can I speak with you?"

She looked unsure.

"Here," I said, removing a business card and handing it to her. "Unofficial investigators have to make do with one of these."

She smiled, taking the card. "Do you want to go inside?"

"That would be great."

I followed her into the house, leaving her father standing outside with his garden sprayer. Inside, we moved through a hallway decorated with floral wallpaper and black-and-white photographs, and into an adjoining kitchen.

"Do you want a drink?"

"Water would be fine."

It was a huge open area with polished mahogany floors and steel worktops. The central unit doubled up as a table, chairs sitting underneath. Kathy filled a glass with bottled mineral water, then moved across and set it down.

"Sorry to turn up unannounced like this."

She was facing away from me slightly. Her skin shone in the light coming from outside, her hair tucked behind her ears. "It's just a surprise to hear his name again after all this time."

"I understand. I think Mary feels like she needs some closure on his disappearance. She wants to know where he went for those five years."

Kathy nodded. We pulled a couple of chairs out and sat down.

"So, you and Alex met at a party?"

She smiled. "A friend of a friend was having a house-warming."

I placed my notepad between us, so she could see I was ready to start. "You liked him from the beginning?"

"Yeah, we really clicked."

"Which was why you ended up following him to Bristol?"

"I applied for a job there. It was supposed to be a marketing position. Alex had already got his place at university, and we wanted to be close to one another."

"What happened with the job?"

"It wasn't marketing. It was cold-calling; selling central heating. I gave it a week. In the interview, the MD told me I could earn in commission what my friends earned in a year. I never stuck around long enough to find out."

"So, you started waitressing?"

"Yes."

"What did the two of you used to do together?"

"We used to go away a lot. Alex loved the sea."

"You used to go to the coast?"

She nodded.

"How often?"

"Most weekends. Some weeks too. After uni, Alex got a job in an insurance company. He had a kind of love-hate thing going on with it. Some Monday mornings he wouldn't want to go in. So we bought an old VW Camper van and took off when we wanted."

"Did his parents know about him skipping work?"

"No."

"I didn't think so," I said, smiling. "What about your job?"

"They were pretty good to me there. They let me come and go as I pleased—they sometimes even let me choose my own hours. So, if we disappeared for a couple of days, when I got back I worked for a couple of days to make up for it. The pay was terrible, but it was useful."

She began to drift, and as I waited for her to come back, I checked the notes I'd already made. "Alex didn't contact you in the five years before he died?"

"No." A pause. "At first, I just used to wait by the phone, from the moment I got home until three or four o'clock in the morning, begging, praying for him to call. But he never did."

"When was the last time you spoke to him?"

"The night before he left. We'd arranged to take the Camper down to Cornwall. He had some time owed to him at work, so he'd been back to his parents for a couple of weeks to use up some holiday. When I called him, his mum said he had gone out and hadn't come home. She said she wasn't worried, but that he hadn't phoned and he always tended to."

"Was he depressed about work at the time?"

"No," she said, seeming to consider it. "I don't think so."

I changed direction. "Did you have any favorite places you used to visit?"

She looked down into her hands, hesitating. I could tell they'd had a favorite spot, and that it had meant everything to them.

"There was one place," she said eventually. "A place down toward the tip of Cornwall, a village right on the sea called Carcondrock."

"You used to stay there?"

"We used to take the Camper there a lot."

"Did you go back after he disappeared?"

Another pause, longer this time. Eventually she looked up at me. It was obvious she had—and it had hurt a lot. "There was a place right on the beach," she said softly. "A cove. I went back about three months after he disappeared. I didn't really know what to expect. I guess in my heart of hearts I knew he wouldn't be there, but we loved that spot, so it seemed like the most obvious place to look."

"Did you find anything?"

"No," she said.

But I sensed that wasn't everything.

"Kathy?"

"That cove . . ."

"What about it?"

She eyed me for a moment. "If you go right to the back of it, there's a rock shaped like an arrowhead, pointing up to the sky. It's got a black cross painted on it. If you find it, dig a little way beneath and you'll see a box I left there for Alex. Inside are some old letters and photographs— and a birthday card. That was the last time I ever heard from him."

"The birthday card?"

"Yes."

"He went back to his parents for two weeks before he disappeared. Did he give you the birthday card before that?"

"No. He sent it from their place."

"Okay," I said. "Thank you. I'll take a look."

"I don't know what you'll find," she replied, looking down into her lap. "But the last time we saw each other he said something strange to me: that we should use the hole by the rock to store messages, if we ever got separated."

"Separated? What did he mean by that?"

"I don't know. I mean, I asked him, but he never really explained. He just said that, if it ever came to it, that was our spot. The place I should look first."

"So, did he ever store anything in there for you? Any messages?"

She shook her head.

"You checked regularly?"

"I haven't been down for a couple of years. But for a time I used to go back there and dig up that box, praying there would be something in there from him."

"But there never was?"

"No," she said. "Not a single thing."

8

Winter had rinsed late afternoon of its color by the time I left Kathy's, and as I reached Hayden Cemetery, twenty minutes later, the sun was almost gone from the sky as well. I paused briefly inside the gates, engine running, feeling guilty about not taking care of this the day before—but then I parked up and got out.

The place was deserted.

No other cars. No people.

It wasn't too far from Holloway Road, sandwiched between Highbury and Canonbury, but it was almost supernaturally quiet, as if the dead had taken the sound down with them. As I passed through a huge, black-iron arch, intricately woven with the name Hayden, I could see autumn leaves had been pushed to either side of the path, pressed into mounds and stained by rust from a shovel.

Quickly, there and then gone again, I had a flicker of déjà vu, a recollection of being in this same position, treading this same ground, a year and a half ago. The only difference then was that Derryn had been with me, gripping my hand as we wound our way deeper into this place, to the plot she'd selected for herself.

It was in a separate area called The Rest.

Tall trees surrounded it on all sides and dividing walls had been built within it, with four or five headstones in each section. As I got to the grave, I saw the flowers I'd put down a month before. They were dead. Dried petals clung to the gravestone, and others were scattered on the surrounding grass, while the stems had all turned to mush. I knelt down and brushed the old flowers away, and then placed some new ones at the foot of the grave, the thorns from the stem catching in the folds of my palm.

"Sorry I didn't come yesterday," I said quietly. The wind picked up for a moment, and carried my words away. "I thought about you a lot, though."

Some leaves fell from the sky, onto the grave.

When I looked up, a bird was hopping along a branch on one of the trees. The branch swayed gently, bobbing under its weight, and then, seconds later, the bird was gone again, ranging up left into the evening, into the freedom beyond.

I was coming down the path and through the entrance to the car park when I saw someone walking away from my car. His clothes were dark and stained, and his shoes were untied, the laces snaking off behind him.

He looked homeless.

As I got closer, he flicked a look at me. His face was obscured beneath a hood, but I could see a pair of eyes glint, and realized there was surprise in them—as if he hadn't expected to see me back so soon.

Suddenly, he broke into a run.

I speeded up, and saw that the back window on the left-hand side of my car had been smashed, the door open. Glass lay next to my tire, winking in the half-light, and my notepad, coat and a road map were on the gravel next to it.

"Hey!"

I broke into a run, trying to cut him off before he got to the entrance, and he glanced at me again, panicking. The edges of his hood billowed out as he picked up speed, and I caught a glimpse of his face. Dirty and thin. A beard growing from his neck to the top of his cheekbones. He looked like a drug addict: all bone, no fat.

"Hey!" I shouted again, but he was ahead of me now, fading into the darkness at the entrance to the cemetery.

I sprinted after him, out onto the main road, but by the time I got there he was about two hundred feet away, pounding down the pavement on the other side of the street. He looked back once to make sure I wasn't following, but didn't drop his pace—and then he disappeared around the corner.

I made my way back to the cemetery and took a closer look at the car. It was an old BMW 3 series I'd had for years. No CD player. No satellite navigation.

He must have been looking for money.

The glove compartment was open, most of its contents thrown all over the front seats. The car's handbook had been opened and left, its pages scattered. He'd checked the ashtray and pockets on the doors.

Suppressing my anger, I tidied everything up, temporarily patched up the rear window with an old rag from the boot, and then headed home.

9

I woke at three in the morning to the hum of a song playing quietly on the stereo, the TV on mute. I sat forward and listened for a while. Derryn used to tell me my music taste was terrible, and that my entire film collection was one big guilty pleasure. She was probably right about the music.

In the area I'd been brought up in, you either spent your days in the record shop or in the cinema. I'd chosen the cinema, mostly because my parents were always late with new technology; we were pretty much the last family in the village to get a CD player. We didn't have a VCR for years either, which was why I spent most nights, growing up, watching films at an old art deco cinema called the Palladium in the next town along the coast.

Derryn was different. Music was everything to her, her record collection still standing in the corner of the room, packed in a series of cardboard boxes. I'd been through them about three weeks after she died, wondering what to do with them all, and then done nothing because I realized that the one thing music had over movies was its amazing way of pinpointing memories. In the boxes were the songs that used to play in the background, without us even noticing, when we were dating; the songs she'd played at home when we'd first moved in together; the songs she'd asked me to play for her when she was weeks away from dying.

The songs that played at her funeral.

I paused there for a moment, a tremor of emotion passing through me, and then hauled myself up and headed through to the kitchen.

Out of the side window, I could see into the house next door. A light was on in the study, the blinds partially open. Liz, my neighbor, was leaning over a laptop, typing. She clocked my movement through the corner of her eye, looked up, squinted, and then broke into a smile.

What are you doing up? she mouthed.

I rubbed my eyes. *Can't sleep.*

She scrunched up her face in an *aw* expression.

Liz was a forty-two-year-old lawyer, who'd moved in a few weeks after Derryn had died. She'd married young, had a child, then got divorced a year later. Her daughter was in the second year of university at Warwick. She was smart and fun, and, while cautious of my situation, she'd made it obvious that she was interested. Some days I liked that. I didn't want to be a widower who wore it. I didn't want all the sorrow and the anger and the loss to stick to my skin. And the truth was, especially physically, Liz was easy to like: tall, slender curves, shoulder-length chocolate hair, dark, mischievous eyes.

She got up from the desk and looked at her watch, pretending to double-take when she saw the time. A couple of seconds later, she picked up a coffee cup and held it up to the window. *You want one?* She rubbed her stomach. *It's good.*

I smiled again, rocked my head from side to side to show that I was tempted, and then pointed to my own watch. *Got to be up early.*

She rolled her eyes. *Poor excuse.*

I looked at her and something moved inside me; the certainty that, if I wanted it to happen, the experience of being close to someone again, I could have it with Liz—here, now. It was clear that she was waiting for me to break free from what was keeping me back, and that conviction only made me warm to her more. I liked the fact that she respected my history. I admired her patience too. There were days—many of them— when I thought about instigating something with her. But, equally, there were others—just as many—where I didn't feel ready to step beyond the barricades I'd built. I wanted to remain inside, protected by the familiarity of how I felt about Derryn.

In the end, it came down to fear.

Everything was fear.

But I wasn't frightened of Liz's strength or intellect. I wasn't frightened about physical contact, about standing there—naked—in front of her. I was frightened of what would happen the next morning when I woke up next to someone, and it wasn't the person I'd loved, every day, for fourteen years.

10

First thing in the morning, I got the car window repaired, and then returned to the office and called the library on Tottenham Court Road that Mary claimed to have seen Alex go into.

It was an immediate dead end.

Even if Alex *had* headed inside on the day Mary followed him, it wasn't for books. She'd told me it was about six o'clock by the time he'd got to the library, and—after persuading a member of staff to check their computers—I discovered there was no record of anyone borrowing anything during the fifteen minutes he was there. After I was done, I called the company he'd worked for in Bristol, and it was just as fruitless—like talking to people who didn't even speak the same language as you. His boss remembered him, but not well, and a couple of colleagues could only give me a vague description of what sort of person he was.

Next, I phoned some old friends he'd lived with.

Mary had told me she'd kept in contact with one of them, John Cary, for a while after Alex's disappearance and that, as far as she knew, they still lived in the same place. There were three of them in all. John was working. The second, Simon, was long gone. The third, Jeff, was home, but seemed as perplexed by what had happened to Alex as everyone else.

"So, how can I reach the other two guys?" I asked him.

"Well, I can give you John's work address," he said, "but I doubt you'll be finding Simon anywhere."

"How come?"

"He kind of . . . fell off the map."

"What do you mean?"

"He had some problems."

"What kind of problems?"

A pause. "Drugs mostly."

"Did he leave the same time as Alex?"

"No. A while after."

"Is it possible Simon followed Alex?"

"I doubt it," he said. "Alex didn't get on with Simon at the end. None of us did. Simon was a different guy in those last few months. He . . .

well, he kind of hit out at Kath when he was high one night. And Alex never forgave him for that."

I put the phone down, and looked at the clock. Ten-thirty.

On the corkboard behind me, in among the pictures of the missing, was a hand-drawn map of a beach that Kathy had given me.

I removed it.

My options were narrowing already.

Winter suddenly came to life as I crossed into Cornwall five hours later, the colors of late autumn replaced by a pale patchwork quilt of fields and towns.

The village of Carcondrock was a quaint stretch of road with shops on both sides, and houses in the hills beyond, all framed by the swell of the Atlantic. The beach ran parallel to the high street, while the main road wormed out of the village and up along the edges of a rising cliff. The higher the road, the bigger the houses. Below them, against the cliff walls, the beach eventually faded out, replaced by sandy coves, dotted like pearls on a necklace along the line of the sea.

I found a car park between the beach and the village, and then headed to the biggest shop—a grocery store—armed with a picture of Alex. No one knew him. I tried the other shops without any luck and then, at the end of the high street, where the road followed the rising cliff face, I discovered a pub and a pretty church, its walls teeming with vines. Everything had an old-world feel to it: walls graying and aged; windows uneven beneath slate roofs. It was obvious why Kathy and Alex had loved it: miles of lonely beach, the roar of the sea, the whitewashed houses like flecks of chalk among the scrub of the hillside.

I got out the map Kathy had drawn for me of the hidden cove, and walked a little way along the road as it gently followed the contours of the cliff. Halfway up, leaning over the edge, I found it below me: two hundred feet down was a perfect semi-circle of sandy beach, surrounded on three sides by high walls of rock and on the fourth by the ocean. Waves foamed at the shore.

The only way I was going to get to it was by rowing around.

I returned to the village and found a wooden shack, out of which an old man was hiring boats. He was already closing up. Behind him, attached to a jetty, four row boats bobbed on the water.

"Am I too late?"

He turned and looked at me. "Eh?"

"I was hoping to hire a boat for an hour."

"It's dark."

"I reckon I've got a good half-hour of light left yet."

He shook his head. He had a red-checked shirt, yellow bib and brace trousers, green boots, and an unruly white beard. He looked like the bastard love child of Captain Birdseye and Ronald McDonald. "Son," he said slowly, as if I were struggling to understand him, "it's *dark*."

Clearly, we had different definitions of the word.

It was just after 4 p.m. at the end of November, which meant—in this part of the world—I had about twenty-five minutes before the sun set, and another ten to fifteen minutes until I was rowing back under cover of darkness. But the longer I delayed here, the less daylight I had to work with.

I got out my wallet. "How much?"

"How much what?"

"How much for an hour?"

His eyes narrowed. "Are you takin' the piss out of me, son?"

"Look," I said. "I'll double whatever the going rate is. I need one of those boats for an hour. And a torch if you've got one. I'll be back here just after five."

"You even know how to row a boat?"

"I know enough."

His gaze lingered on me. "Ain't my problem if you drown."

I nodded. "Understood."

He started opening up the shack.

Twenty minutes later, I'd found the cove and was dragging the boat up, onto the sand. The sea was benign, which helped, but the light was dwindling.

The cove was small, probably twenty feet across, the cliff walls towering above me. I flicked on the torch and swept it from left to right. At the back of the cove, in the torchlight beam, I could see a pile of loosened rocks and boulders. Some had fallen, others had been washed up. As I stepped closer, I could see the arrow-shaped stone Kathy had talked about. It had tilted, but still faced upward, and—as she'd explained—there was a tiny cross in black paint marked on it. I knelt down, clamped the torch between my teeth and started digging.

The box was buried about a foot under the surface, its bottom sitting in water, its sides speckled with rust. Kathy had wrapped its contents in thick opaque plastic. I picked at it with my fingers but couldn't break the seal, so removed my pocket knife and sliced it open. The contents were dry. I reached in and pulled out a stack of photographs and, around them, a letter. The birthday card was inside. A rubber band kept everything together.

I placed the torch in my lap and flicked through the photographs using the torch. Some of the photos were of the two of them, some just of Kathy, others only Alex. In one of the photographs toward the bottom of the pile, I noticed Kathy had short hair, meaning the picture had been taken by someone other than Alex, some time after he'd disappeared. I flipped it over and on the back she'd written: *After you left, I cut my hair . . .*

On closer inspection, I saw that they all had comments on the back.

I turned my attention to the letter. It was dated January 8, no year, and still smelled faintly of perfume. *I've no idea why you left,* Kathy had written. *Nothing you ever said to me led me to believe that one day you'd drop everything and walk away. So, if you came back now, I'd cherish you as I always did. I'd love you like I always did. But, somewhere, there would be a doubt that wasn't there before, a nagging feeling that, if I got too close to you, if I showed you too much affection, you'd get up one morning and walk away.*

I don't want to feel like a mistake again.

In the distance, thunder rumbled across the sky. I needed to get back to shore. Folding the letter up, and placing everything inside the box, I put it all into the boat and started the journey back to the village.

11

I drove out of Carcondrock and found a place to stay about three miles further down a snaking coastal road. It was a beautiful graystone building overlooking the ocean and the scattered remnants of old tin mines. After a shower, I headed out for some dinner and eventually found a pub that served hot food and cold beer. I took the box with me, ordered a pie, and sat at a table in the corner, away from everyone else. While I waited for my meal, I opened the box, removed the contents and starting spreading them out.

I focused on the birthday card first.

The last contact Kathy had ever had with Alex.

She'd kept it in pristine condition. It was still in its original envelope, the envelope opened along the top with a knife or a letter opener to avoid damaging it. When I took out the card, I could see it was homemade, but not amateurish: there was a detailed drawing of a bear in the center, a bunch of roses in its hands. Above that was a raised rectangle with *Happy Birthday!* embossed on it, and a foil sticker of a balloon. Inside the card were just seven words.

Happy Birthday, Kath. I love you. Alex.

I flipped it over.

On the reverse it was plain white, except for in the center, where—in gold pen—someone had written: *Made by Angela Routledge.* I checked the envelope again, and realized I'd missed something. On the inside, under the lip, was an address label: *Sold @ St. John the Baptist, 215 Grover Place, London.*

I wrote down the address, and then did a web search on my phone. The church was in Redbridge, east London.

Moving on to the photographs, I was able to make out a definite timeline. It began with pictures of Kathy and Alex when they'd first started going out, and ended with two individual portraits of each of them, both older and more mature, at a different stage of their lives. I sat the two portraits side by side. The one of Kathy was a regular 6x4, but Alex's was a Polaroid. When I turned them over, I noticed something else: there was different handwriting on them.

"Mind if I sit here?"

I looked up.

One of the locals was staring down at me, a hand pressed against the back of the chair at the table next to me. The subdued light darkened his face, shadows filling his eye sockets, thick black lines forming in the furrows of his forehead. He was well built, probably in his late forties. I glanced around the pub.

There were tables and chairs free everywhere.

He followed my eyes, out into the room, but didn't make a move to leave, and then stole a glance at a couple of the photographs. I collected them up, along with the letter and the card, and placed them back into the box.

"Be my guest," I said, gesturing to the next table along.

He nodded his thanks and sat, placing his beer down in front of him. A couple of minutes later, the landlady brought my meal over—and, as I started picking at it, I realized all I could smell was his aftershave. It was so strong it buried the smell of my food completely.

"You here on business?" he asked.

"Kind of."

"Sounds mysterious."

I shrugged. "Not really."

"So, where does she live?"

I looked at him, confused.

"Your bit on the side, I mean."

He erupted into laughter. I smiled politely, but didn't answer, hoping that the less I talked, the quicker he'd lose interest in this conversation.

"Just messing with you," he said, running a finger down the side of his glass. As his sleeve rode up his arm, I could see a tattoo—an inscription— the letters smudged by age. "Boring place to have to come for work."

"I can think of worse."

"Maybe in summer," he said. "But in winter, this place is like a mausoleum. You take the tourists out of here and all you're left with are a few empty fudge shops." He leaned forward, dropping his voice to a whisper. "Want to hear my theory? If you put a bullet in the head of every Cornishman in the county, no one would even notice until the caravan parks reopened."

He laughed again.

I pretended to check my phone for messages.

"So, what do you do?" he asked.

"I'm a salesman."

"Yeah?" He watched me for a moment. "Got a pal who's a salesman."

"Yeah?"

He nodded. "He sells ideas to people."

"Isn't that what everyone sells?"

He didn't reply, but his eyes lingered on me, as if I'd just made a terrible error. *There's something about you*, I thought. *Something I don't like.* He took a few mouthfuls of beer, and this time I could make out some of the tattoo—some kind of inscription: *"And see him that was possessed"*—and a red mark, running close to his hairline, around his ears and along the curve of his chin.

"Got hit with a rifle butt in Afghanistan."

"Sorry?"

He looked up. "The mark on my face. Fucking towelhead jammed his rifle butt into the side of my face."

"You were a soldier?"

"Do I look the salesman type?"

I shrugged. "What does a salesman look like?"

"What do any of us really look like?" His eyes flashed for a moment, catching some of the light from a fire behind us. He broke into a smile, as if everything was a big mystery. "Being a soldier, that teaches you a lot about life."

"Yeah?"

"Teaches you a lot about death too."

I started cutting away at some of the pie's pastry—but the whole time I could feel him watching me. When I looked up again, his eyes moved quickly from me to the food then back up. "You not hungry?"

"I seem to have lost my appetite," I said.

"You should eat," he replied, sinking what was left in his glass. "You never know when you might need the strength."

He placed the beer glass down and turned to me, his eyes disappearing into shadow again. They were impenetrable now, like staring into one of the abandoned mine shafts along the coast.

"Do you want to be left alone?"

He had a smile on his face now, but it didn't go deep. Below the surface, I caught a glimpse of what I'd seen before. A second of absolute darkness.

"It's up to you," I said.

He continued smiling. The smell of aftershave drifted across to me again. "I'll leave you alone. I'm sure you'd rather be earning commission than listening to me rant away—isn't that right?"

I didn't say anything.

"Nice meeting you, anyway," he said, standing. "Maybe we'll see you down here again some time."

"Maybe."

"I think so," he said, cryptically.

He gathered up his coat, and headed out past the locals to a door on the far side of the pub.

The evening swallowed him up.

12

That night, I had difficulty sleeping.

It had been a long time since I'd slept in a bed, a longer time since I'd been away from the house overnight, and my body had become used to the sofa, to the sounds of the television playing out in the background. Those things had become my routine. Eventually, I turned the TV on, lowered the volume, and lay on top of the sheets—and, at almost two in the morning, bone-tired, the curtains ajar and the window open, I finally began to drift, a faint breeze washing against my skin.

I stirred again an hour later.

Initially, I was unsure why. But then I heard it: *rotting autumn leaves caught beneath someone's feet*. I lay there—exhausted, a little dazed, unable to react—but then the sound came again, even louder and closer than before.

This time, I hauled myself up and stalked across to the window.

Outside, the night was pitch black, apart from tiny blocks of light from the next village, somewhere along the coastal road. As the wind came again, I could hear leaves being blown across the ground, and waves crashing against the rocky coast—but not the noise that had woken me. Not someone moving around.

I waited for a moment, and then headed back to bed.

I got up early and sat at a table with beautiful views out across the Atlantic, and a crowd of tin mines, rising up out of the hillside like brick arms reaching for the clouds. Over breakfast, I spread the contents of the box out in front of me again, and studied the photographs I'd been looking at the night before—in particular, the pictures of Kathy and Alex on their own.

Why had Alex's been taken on a Polaroid?

In the shot, he was too close to the camera, some of his features undefined, a little smudged. His hair was shorter than in the photos of him I'd seen at Mary's house, and there were dark areas around the side of his face where stubble was coming through. Behind him, there was a block of light that looked like a window, but it was difficult to see what was through it: part of a building maybe, or a roof.

I turned it over.

There were five words written on the back.

You were never a mistake.

I grabbed my phone and called Kathy, and she answered after a couple of rings. "Kathy, it's David Raker."

"Oh, hi."

"Sorry it's so early."

"No problem," she said. "I was getting ready for work."

"I've got the box here." I turned the Polaroid over and looked at Alex again. "Do you remember what photographs you put inside?"

"Um . . . I don't know."

"Just a rough idea."

"I think there's a couple of us at a barbecue . . ."

"Do you remember the one of Alex on his own?"

"Uh . . ." A pause. "I'm trying to think . . ."

"Shall I text you a picture?"

"Okay."

"I'll send two photos—one of the front and one of the reverse. Take a look at them when they come through and maybe give me a shout when you're done."

I hung up, took a couple of pictures and sent them over.

While I waited, I looked around. The owner was filling a giant cereal bowl with cornflakes, and outside, in the distance, a fishing trawler chugged into view, waves fanning out from its bow as it followed the coastline.

A couple of minutes later, my phone started buzzing.

"Kathy?"

Silence.

"Kathy?"

Gradually, fading in, the sound of sobbing.

"Kathy, are you okay?"

My question went unanswered again, and as it did, a thought came to me: "That's Alex's handwriting, isn't it?"

She sniffed. "Yes."

"Did you take that photograph?"

"No."

"Any idea who did? Or where it was taken?"

"No."

I looked at the Polaroid again, turning it over, tracing the handwriting with my finger. And then, out of the corner of my eye, I glimpsed something at the bottom of the letter she'd written him, and cursed myself for not noticing it before. *But, somewhere, there would be a doubt that wasn't there before, a nagging feeling that, if I got too close to you, if I showed you too much affection, you'd get up one morning and walk away.*

I don't want to feel like a mistake again.

"You were never a mistake," I said quietly.

Alex had returned to the box, after all.

13

When I'd called Alex's friend Jeff the day before, he'd given me a work address for their other former housemate, John Cary. As I came down the M32, into Bristol, I called directory enquiries, trying to get a phone number for him.

"Which phone number do you want?" the operator asked.

"You mean there's more than one?"

"Yes, sir. That address is a police station."

John Cary was a cop.

The station was south-west of the city center, and by the time I got there, it was lunchtime and raining hard: water ran from guttering, drains were filling with old crisp packets and beer cans, and—except for some kids further down, their cigarettes dying in the cool of the day— the streets were virtually deserted.

I parked up and headed inside the station.

There was a sergeant behind a sliding glass panel, framed by a huge map of the area. Dots were marked at intervals in a ring around the center of the city.

The sergeant slid the glass across. "Can I help you?"

"I'm here to see John Cary."

He nodded. "Can I ask what it's about?"

"I want to speak to him about Alex Towne."

It clearly didn't mean anything to him. He slid the glass panel back and disappeared out of sight, and I sat down next to the front entrance. Outside, huge dark clouds rolled across the sky. Somewhere in the distance was the snow they'd been promising, moving down from Russia, ready to cover every crisp packet and empty can, every needle and bloodstain.

Something clunked.

At the far side of the waiting room a huge man—six-four, maybe sixteen stone—emerged from beyond a security door, chiseled but not attractive. His dark skin was spoiled by acne scarring on both cheeks. I walked across to him.

"My name's David Raker."

He nodded.

"I'm looking into the disappearance of Alex Towne."

He nodded again.

"Alex's mum came to me."

"She told you he's dead, right?"

I eyed him. "Right."

"So, why are you here?"

"I was hoping I might be able to ask you a couple of questions."

He glanced at his watch, then at me, as if he was suddenly intrigued as to what I might come up with. "Yeah, okay," he said. "Let's go for a drive."

We drove north to where Alex had died. It was a picturesque spot, even though it was only a mile from the motorway, its rolling grassland punctuated by narrow roads and golden oak trees. Cary parked up and then led me away from the car, across to a field sloping away from the lane we were on. Below, a sliver of police tape still fluttered in a tree nearby—but, apart from that, there was no sign that a car had once come off the road here.

"Were you on duty when he died?" I asked.

He shook his head.

"So, you went to see him at the morgue?"

"Yeah, once he'd been ID'd. It took a week and a half to get confirmation on the dental records."

"You actually saw his body?"

"What was left of it. His hands, his feet, his face—they were all just bone. Some of his organs were still intact, but the rest of him . . ." Cary looked out at the fields. "They reckon the tank must have ruptured when the car hit the field. It was why the fire consumed everything so quickly." He glanced at me, sadness in his eyes. "You know how hard you have to hit something to rupture a petrol tank?"

I shook my head.

"That car looked like it had been through a crusher. The whole thing was folded in on itself. Old model like that: no airbag, no side impact bars . . ." He paused again. "I just hope it was quick."

We stood silent for a moment. His eyes drifted to the space where the car must have landed, and then—eventually—back to me.

"He'd been drinking," I said. "Is that right?"

"Yeah. He was four times over the legal limit."

"Did you see the autopsy report?"

"Yeah."

"It was definitely him?"

He looked at me like I was from another planet. "What do you think?"

I paused for a moment.

"What are the chances of me getting hold of some of the paperwork?"

A little air escaped from between his lips, as if he couldn't believe I'd had the balls or stupidity to ask. "Low."

"What about unofficially?"

"Still low. I go into the system, it gets logged. I print something out, it gets logged. And why would I do that for you, anyway?"

"A fresh pair of eyes might help."

"Might help who?"

"Mary. Kathy. You."

He just shook his head.

"Strange he should end up dying so close to home."

Cary looked at me. "What do you mean by that?"

"I mean, he disappears—*completely disappears*—for all that time . . . I would have expected him to have turned up somewhere further afield. By being this close to home, don't you think he risked being seen by someone he knew?"

"He didn't stay around here."

"But he died around here."

"He was on his way through to somewhere."

"What makes you say that?"

"If he'd been staying around here, I would've known about it. Sooner or later, someone somewhere would've seen him. It would've got back to me."

I nodded, but at best that seemed ambitious, at worst totally unrealistic. Cary was just one man in a local area of thirty or forty square miles. If you wanted to, you could easily disappear in an area that size and never be found again.

"So, where do you think he went?"

Cary frowned. "Didn't I just answer that?"

"You said not around here—so where?"

He shook his head and shrugged.

"Do you think there's any connection to your other friend's disappearance?"

"Simon?"

"Yeah. Simon—" I glanced at my notepad "—Mitchell."

"I doubt it."

"How come?"

"Did Jeff tell you about him?"

"He said he had a drug problem."

He nodded.

"He said he hit out at Kathy."

He nodded again. "That night, we were all there. Simon didn't know what the fuck he was doing. We got into this heated argument with him, trying to make him see that he had a problem, and Kathy was there with Alex, and said she knew someone who worked with drug addicts and could help him. Simon just flipped. The gear always made him angry, plus he always hated being called an addict. A few days later, he tried to apologize to Alex, but Alex wouldn't let it go, and then he started making promises to Jeff and me instead, telling us that he would stop—but that was why he eventually left. He couldn't. I don't think he could face us any more. So, one day he just packed his bags and he left. We only ever heard from him once after that."

"When was that?"

"A long time after Alex disappeared. Four years, maybe more. He said he'd been in London all that time, in and out of whatever place would put a roof over his head."

"Did you tell him about Alex?"

"Yeah. I don't think it even registered with him. He sounded strung out. He just kept going on about this guy he'd met who was going to help him."

"Did he say who the guy was?"

"No. He just said he'd met him on the streets and they'd got talking. It sounded like this guy was trying to straighten him out."

Cary raised his eyes to the skies as the rain started to fall again, pulling his jacket close to his body and zipping it up. "I did some asking around at the beginning," he said, glancing down at the fields below, "but I didn't get far. I think you'll struggle to find anyone who can give you a reason for Alex's disappearance. Leaving everything behind like that. . ." He shrugged. "Unless something was seriously wrong, that just wasn't how he was programmed."

14

After calling Mary to confirm I was working for her, Cary changed his mind. Once we were back at the station, I sat in an office full of paperwork and desks, most of them unmanned, while he used a computer close by to access and print Alex's case file. At the other end of the room, there were four officers with their backs to us, two of them on the phone. When he was done, he slid the printouts into a Manila folder he already had open and handed it to me.

"I'm willing to take a risk with this," he said. "But if anyone finds out I've given these to you, I'll be taking early retirement."

"I understand."

"I hope you do."

He sat down at his desk again, looked around, then removed an unmarked DVD from his top drawer. "Here," he said, tossing it across the desk.

"What's this?"

"A video one of the fire crew shot of the crash site."

I took the DVD and slipped it into the folder. "Is there anything in here?"

"In the casework?" He shrugged. "What do you think?"

"You reckon it's open and shut?"

"Alex was drink-driving. Of course it's open and shut."

I nodded, and leafed through the first few pages, but when I looked up, he was staring at me, eyes narrowed, as if he thought my silence was some kind of comment.

"Let me tell you something," he said, leaning across the desk. "The night of the crash, and for three months after, I was balls-deep in a double murder. A woman and her daughter, both raped, both strangled, left in a field in the pissing rain for five days before anyone found them. Which case do you think my DCI wanted done first? Those two women? Or some fucking drunk who couldn't even keep to his own side of the road?"

"I wasn't passing judge—"

"And since then? Take a drive down the street. I've got guys out there on PCP who think they're the fucking Terminator. I've got seventeen-year-old kids from the council estates with knives the size of your arm."

He paused, looked at me. "So, no, I haven't spent a lot of time with that file over the last year. I put in my fair share of time when he first went missing, and I got the support of some of the people in here. But as soon as he put his car through the side of a lorry, it became a zero priority case. And you know what? It's even less than that now."

I decided to redirect the conversation, removing the Polaroid of Alex that I'd taken from the box. Cary eyed me, wondering what I was looking at. I put the picture down on the desk in front him.

He came forward. "Is that Alex?"

"I think so."

Cary picked it up. "Who took this?"

"I don't know."

He went quiet again. "Where did you get it?"

"It was in among Kathy's stuff."

"She took it?"

"No."

"So, how did it get there?"

"I'm not sure."

He looked like he didn't believe me.

"All I can do is take a guess," I said.

"So take a guess."

"Alex put it there."

"After he disappeared?"

I nodded.

"Why?"

"They had an arrangement."

He frowned. "An arrangement?"

"A place where they used to hide personal items."

He didn't react this time, his face neutral, and then he opened up the top drawer of his desk again and started shuffling around inside. Eventually, he took out a notebook, virtually in tatters, the cover falling off, the pages missing their edges. He laid it down and opened it up. Words, diagrams and reconstructions of crime scenes were crammed into every space. He flicked through it, got halfway, and then looked up. "You might want to write this down," he said.

I took out my notepad.

"Like I said, I did some asking around when Alex first went missing; called a few people, set up his missing persons file. One of the things I requisitioned, as part of the investigation, was his card numbers and bank details. I basically wanted anything he could draw on. It was the best lead we'd have."

"But he didn't take his card with him."

"He didn't take his debit card, no."

He looked at his notebook. For the first time, at the top of the page, written in black and circled in red, I spotted a number.

"He left his debit card behind, but he took his credit card with him," Cary said, prodding the number with his finger. "It was valid for another five years after he went missing, so I figured it was worth keeping an eye on. I arranged with the bank to have all his credit card statements redirected to me. And they kept coming, and coming, and coming, and every time the statements arrived on my desk, I'd open them up and they'd be blank."

"He never used the card."

Cary shook his head. "Every month there'd be nothing in them. I spent four and a half years looking through his statements, and four and a half years putting them straight into the bin." He ran a finger along the number in the notebook. "Then, about six months before he died . . ." He paused, glanced at me. "The statements stopped coming."

"Because the card had expired?"

"No. The card had about six months left to run."

"So, why'd they stop?"

"I called the bank to find out. They accessed the account for me and said the statements were still being sent out."

Suddenly, I saw where this was going. "But not to you?"

"Right. I requested a duplicate set from the bank, but they didn't arrive either, so I called them up *again*, told them the duplicate hadn't turned up, and they asked me to confirm my address. I gave it to them—"

"But it wasn't the address they had."

He looked at me, nodded. "Right again. Four and a half years after Alex disappears, someone calls the bank up and asks for the statements to be sent somewhere else."

"Do you think it was Alex?"

He shrugged. "I spoke to the bank a third time, and they made the new statements available to me. Same as always—the card remained unused. But it wasn't registered to Alex any more. It was registered to a business account."

"A business account?"

"The Calvary Project."

"That was the name of the business?"

"Who knows? I spent days searching, trying to get to the bottom of who they were, and I couldn't find them anywhere. There's no Inland Revenue record of them, no website, no public listing anywhere, nothing. They're vapor."

"You mean some sort of front?"

He shrugged again.

I looked at him, trying to figure out why he wasn't more determined to dig deeper. He pushed the notebook toward me and leaned over his desk, jabbing a finger at the number. "Treat yourself," he said.

"That's part of the credit card number?"

"No. That's the telephone number the bank had listed for the Calvary Project."

It was a landline, but there was no area code in front, which was why I hadn't worked out what it was. "Have you tried calling it?"

"About a hundred thousand times."

"No answer?"

He shook his head.

"Where's the street address?"

"London."

"Did you go up there?"

"No."

"Why not?"

"'Why not?' Is that a *joke*? The card's expired, and a year ago I spent three hours picking up bits of Alex's skull from a fucking field. This case is over."

"Did you tell Mary?"

"About what?"

"About what you'd found."

"No."

"Don't you think she has a right to know?"

"A right to know *what* exactly? Even if there was something to it— and I'm not convinced there was—what difference does it make now? He's dead."

Cary had been in the field that night as Alex's charred remains had been pulled from the wreckage of his car, so I understood his reticence: the memories were still fresh, Alex was in the ground, the case was closed. He didn't know what Mary had seen three months ago—or had *claimed* to have seen, anyway—and that made a big difference too. Yet, I sensed a conflict in him: his instincts as an investigator meant he had a natural inclination to know more, about where Alex had gone, and where the Calvary Project led; but, at the same time, he didn't want to expose himself to new, possibly corrupting information about Alex. He loved his friend. He was disappointed by the way he'd died.

His memories were tainted enough already.

"So, where in London is the address?"

"Some place in Brixton. I gave the details to a guy I know who works for the Met and he pissed himself laughing. Apparently the only businesses being run out of there are from suitcases full of crack."

After I'd written down the phone number, Cary laid a thick hand across the notebook and pulled it back toward him, dropping it into his top drawer.

"I've got one more question," I said.

He didn't move.

"Basically, I was hoping you might be able to give me some . . . technical help." I held up the picture. "With the photograph."

He shook his head. "No."

"It must have been taken by someone Alex met after he disappeared, and the picture's a Polaroid, which means that person probably handled it as it—"

"No."

"I just need it checked for prints."

"*Just* need it? You realize what you're asking me to do? Get forensics involved, log it, start a paper trail. What do you think would happen if people find out I've been pushing personal work through?"

"I know it's diff—"

"I'm fucked, that's what."

"Okay. Forget I asked."

"No way," he said, but I could see that same conflict again—and, as I got up and we shook hands, I knew I still had a shot at getting the picture looked at.

15

On the way home, I called in to see Mary. She spent the first ten minutes trying to get Malcolm comfortable, settling him in front of the television, but even after we retreated to the kitchen, it was clear he was still agitated. As we began talking, he called out to her, unable to remember her name, then unable to remember what it was he was going to ask. I watched as the two of them faced each other, a glint of emotion in Mary's face, frustration in Malcolm's, and wondered if this was better or worse than what had happened to me. She hadn't buried her husband.

But she'd lost him all the same.

Eventually, once he was quiet, I followed her back through to the kitchen and then she led me down a steep flight of stairs into the basement. It was huge, much bigger than I'd expected, but it was a mess as well: boxes stacked ceiling-high like pillars in a foyer; pieces of wood and metal perched against the walls; an electrical box, covered in thick, opaque cobwebs.

"I come down here sometimes," she said. "I like the quiet."

I nodded that I understood.

She smiled. "Sorry about the mess."

"You want to see a mess, you should come to my place."

Above us, Malcolm started calling out again. Mary took a long breath and turned toward the stairs. "Now you know why I like to hide down here sometimes," she said, but then seemed to become consumed by guilt. "It's not his fault." A long pause, as if she were upset now. "I'll be back in a few minutes."

I watched her go and then started looking around the basement. On the other side, half-hidden behind boxes, was an old writing desk, an open photo album on it. Dusty. Worn. I turned some of the pages. A young Alex playing in the snow, paddling in the sea, eating ice cream on a pier. Later on, some of the pictures had fallen out, leaving only white blocks on faded yellow pages.

Right at the back, I found one of Alex, Malcolm and Mary, and someone else. The guy was in his thirties, good-looking, smiling from ear to ear. He had an arm around Alex's shoulder and the other around Malcolm. Mary was out to the side of the shot, almost detached from the group. Most of the time you couldn't read much into photographs: people put on smiles, put arms around those next to them, posed even if they didn't want to. Most of the time pictures could paper over cracks, like perfectly-formed lies. But this one said everything.

Mary was the odd one out.

Quietly, she came down the stairs. "Sorry about that."

I told her not to worry and then held up the album for her to see. "I was just being nosy. I hope you don't mind."

"No, not at all."

I picked out the man. "Who's this guy?"

"Wow," she said, coming across the basement toward me. "I haven't seen him in a while. I thought we'd managed to burn all the pictures of him." But she was smiling. She studied it for a while. "Al. *Uncle* Al. He was a friend of Malc's."

"But not a friend of yours?"

She shrugged. "I think the feeling was mutual, to be honest. Al was a wealthy guy. We weren't. He bought his way into Malcolm and Alex's affection, and the only way I could counter that was by staying close to them. He wasn't so keen to spend money on me."

"He wasn't Alex's real uncle?"

"No. Malcolm used to work for him."

"So, is he still around?"

"No. He's been dead a while now."

I put the photo back into the album. "Did Alex ever go to church?"

"Church?" She frowned, clearly surprised at the change of direction. "Not at the end, no. But when he was younger he used to come with us to the one here in town. He was part of the youth group. He always seemed to enjoy it."

"Did any of you ever attend a church called St. John the Baptist on Grover Place? That's a street in east London, near Redbridge."

"East London? No. Why?"

"It's just a loose end at the moment," I said, and moved the conversation on. "What about your church here? Anyone that Alex might have kept in regular contact with after he moved down to Bristol? Perhaps in the youth set-up?"

She paused for a moment. "He *was* very friendly with one guy there . . . Uh, I'm trying to remember his name. He used to lead worship, take the occasional service, that kind of thing. He went traveling . . . Oh, this must have been five years ago—maybe more—and he never came back to us. I'm pretty sure Alex kept in touch with him before that." She stopped a second time. "Gosh, what was his name?"

"It's probably worth following up, so if you remember, maybe you can drop me a line." I thought of the address label on the birthday card again, and then the name on the reverse. "What about Angela Routledge—does that ring any bells?"

She thought about it, but it obviously didn't. I hadn't expected it to get me far. Angela Routledge was probably just a member of the congregation recycling cards in order to raise funds for the church.

"Well, I better be go—"

"Mat," she said.

"Sorry?"

"Mat, with one tee. I knew I'd remember it eventually." She nodded. "Alex's friend from the church. His name was Mat."

16

Before I went to sleep, I opened the case file containing the printouts John Cary had given me, took out the DVD, and started it playing.

Taken with a handheld video camera, the recording was shaky and disorientating to start with, but gradually became steadier. The film began with some shots of the fields surrounding the crash site and the area the car had landed in. There was a dark, scarred trail left on the field, where the grass was scorched, and something from the car—perhaps the exhaust box—was embedded in the mud. I was hoping whoever had taken the film might zoom in on it for a clearer view, but they didn't.

Instead it cut to where the car had come off the road. There was petrol left on the tarmac and smashed glass. The light wasn't particularly good, and when I glanced at the timecode in the corner, I could see why. 17.42. It was evening.

The film cut to the car.

The roof had collapsed in on itself, one door had come off, and the boot had disappeared, pushed back into the body of the vehicle. The engine was up inside the dashboard on the right-hand side and, as the camera panned from left to right, I could see bits of windshield glinting in the grass. There was even more destruction beyond that: the grille at the front of the Toyota had been tossed free and lay in front of the car, alongside shards of colored plastic from the headlights. When the film cut in closer—with the aid of a light attachment—and revealed the inside of the car, I could see that everything was black and melted.

The film switched again to a close-up of a spot about twenty feet away. Scattered in the grass was debris that had been thrown free of the car: a burned mobile phone; a shoe; a wallet, its tan leather charred. The wallet was open, and some of the contents had spilled out. I could see part of a blackened and melted driver's license, Alex's face on it, half-obscured by blades of grass.

Finally, the film finished.

I ejected the DVD and spread some of the paperwork out in front of me. The investigators were fairly certain the crash had been caused by Alex's being drunk. There were some fuzzy photographs on one of the printouts, including a shot of the tire marks on the road, and one of the lorry Alex's car had hit. The lorry driver had escaped with only minor cuts and bruises. In his statement he said another car had overtaken Alex's and then, about ten seconds later, the Toyota had drifted across to the wrong side of the road. A third photograph showed the Toyota from head on. The right side had sustained more damage than the left. It explained why, in the film, the engine seemed further back inside the car on the right. I skimmed through the crime scene analysis, and found a technician's diagram of the crash trajectory.

I moved on to the post mortem.

Like Cary had said, the age of the Toyota meant there was no airbag, and no real impact protection. The damage was severe: teeth had been found in Alex's stomach and what was left of his throat, torn from the gum when his face hit the steering wheel. I read on a little further and then, toward the back, found two missing pages. Cary must have forgotten to pick them up when he'd printed them out. I made a note to ask him about it the next time we spoke.

A couple more pictures were loose in the Manila folder, showing Alex's body. It was a horrific sight. His hands had been burned down to the skeleton; his feet and lower legs too. His face, from the brow down to his jaw, was also just bone, and there was a huge crack in his skull, all the way down one side of his cheek, where his face had hit the wheel on impact. I turned back to the file. It got worse the more I read: his body had been pulverized, bones smashed, skin burned away, every part of him broken beyond repair. It was obvious from the damage sustained that he had died before the car caught fire.

Except, according to Mary, he hadn't died at all.

The Corner of the Room

He opened his eyes. The room was spinning gently, the walls seeming to bend as he moved his head across the pillow and rolled on to his side. Slowly, everything started to shift back into focus: the bed he was on; the dusty shaft of moonlight coming through the top window; the lightbulb moving gently in a faint breeze.

It was cold.

He sat up and pulled a blanket around him. As the edges of it brushed against the floor, dirt and dust scattering off into the darkness, a sharp pain coursed through his chest. He placed a hand against his ribs and pressed with his fingers. Beneath his T-shirt, he could feel bandages, from his breastplate down to his waist. He shifted position again, trying to get more comfortable, and the mattress pinged against his weight.

Click.

A noise from the far corner of the room. A pillar poked out from the wall, a cupboard next to it. Everywhere else was dark.

"Hello?"

His voice sounded quiet, childlike, scared. He cleared his throat, but the effort was painful—like fingers were tearing at his windpipe.

Now he could smell something too.

He swallowed, the first scent of nausea rising in his throat, and—opposite him, lit by a square of moonlight—spotted a metal bucket. The rim was speckled with dried vomit. Next to that was a bottle of disinfectant.

But it wasn't that he could smell.

Click.

The same noise again.

He gazed into the darkness in the corner of the room. No sound, no sign of movement. Shifting position again, he moved back across the bed, right up against the wall, and brought his knees up to his chest.

"Who's there?" he said.

Silence.

He pulled the blanket tighter around him and sat there, staring off into the darkness, until—finally—sleep took him away again.

He's standing outside a church, peering in through a window. Mat is sitting at a desk, a Bible open in his lap. Across the other side of the room, a door is ajar. He looks from Mat to the door, and feels like he wants to be there.

He wants to be standing in that doorway.

And then, suddenly, he is.

He places a hand on the door and pushes at it. Slowly, it creaks open. Mat turns in his chair, an arm resting on the back, intrigued to see who has entered.

Mat's face drops. "Dear God," he says gently. He gets to his feet, stumbling, his eyes wide, his mouth open. He looks like he's seen a ghost. "I thought . . ." Mat stops. "Where have you been?"

"Hiding."

Mat stops, frowning. "Why?"

"I've done something."

"What?"

"Something really bad."

He opened his eyes. A blinding circular light was above him. He tried to cover his face, but when he went to move his hands, they caught on something.

His arms were bound to the chair he was on.

Panicking, he turned his head, looking out into the darkness of the room. Immediately beside him he could make out a medical gurney, metal instruments laid out on top. Next to that was a heart monitor. Behind, obscured by the darkness, was a silhouette, watching him from the shadows.

"What's going on?" he said.

The silhouette didn't move, didn't reply.

He could see further down his body now, and realized something: this wasn't just a chair. It was a dentist's chair. He wriggled his fingers, then tried to move his hands again. The binds stretched and tightened.

"What's going on?"

He tried moving his legs. Nothing. Tried again. Still nothing. In his head, it felt like they were thrashing around. But, further up his body—where he still had feeling—he knew they weren't moving. They were paralyzed.

He looked to the silhouette again. "Why can't I feel my legs?"

Still no reply.

He felt tears well in his eyes. "What are you doing to me?"

A hand touched his stomach. He started, and turned his head the other way, in the other direction. Standing next to him was a huge man—tall and powerful, dressed entirely in black. He had a white apron on, and a surgical face mask. He lowered it. "Hello," the man said.

"What's going on?"

"You will come to understand."

"What?"

"But first we need to take care of some things."

The man pulled his mask back up over his face, and retreated from the dentist's chair, into the darkness. Instantly, a woman came forward in his place, dressed in a white coat and wearing a surgical mask, a blue medical cap tied around her dark hair. Quickly, before he'd even had a chance to react, she'd placed a hand over his eyes, over his face, and was sliding something into his mouth. A huge, metal object—like a clamp. It clicked. He tried to speak, tried to scream, but the clamp had locked his mouth open. All he could do was gurgle.

He started rocking from side to side, making a series of desperate sounds, but then his noise was drowned out by a sharp metallic buzz. He stopped, turning his head left to right, trying to see where the noise was coming from.

The woman leaned in over him again.

In her hands was a dental drill.

He woke with a jolt.

He was back in bed, in the middle of the night, when the shadows in the room were at their thickest and longest. Sitting up, he pulled the blanket around him and ran a tongue along his gums, where his teeth had once been. All that was there now were tiny threads of flesh, spilling out of the cavities.

Click.

The noise again. The same noise, every night, all night, coming from the corner of the room.

He pulled the blanket around him, and looked off into the darkness. During the day, he'd got up and examined the corner of the room, when the sun poured in from the top window. There was nothing there. Just the cupboard and the space behind it, a narrow two- or three-foot gap. In the dead of the night, when the silence was oppressive, it was easy to see things and hear things that weren't there. Darkness messed with you like that. But he'd seen it for himself: there was nothing there.

Click.

He continued looking into the shadows, facing them down. Then, even more defiantly, he got to his feet and took a step toward the corner of the room.

And then stopped again.

Out of the darkness and into the moonlight came a cockroach, its legs pattering against the floor, its body clicking as it moved. He watched it come toward the bed and then turn slightly, antennae twitching, heading deeper into the room, toward the only door in and out; the one they always kept closed. And then it was gone: under the door, into the light on the other side.

A cockroach.

He slumped back on to the bed, relieved. The mind could play tricks on you. It could make you doubt yourself; it bent reality and reason and, at your weakest, you started to question what you knew must be true. As he used a finger to wipe sweat from his top lip, wind came in through the high window, cooling him, falling against his skin, and then—very distantly—he heard the sound of the sea. He let its gentle rhythm begin to take him away.

"Cockroach."

His eyes flicked open.

"I see you, cockroach."

He scrambled back across the bed, toward the wall, bringing his knees up to his chest. And then his heart hit his throat: a hand emerged from the dark, from the spaces behind the cupboard. Slowly, the hand became an arm, and the arm a body, until a man emerged from the gloom, a plastic mask on his face.

It was the mask of a devil.

A smell came with the man as he looked up from the depths of the night, blinking inside the eyeholes. The mouth slit was wide and long, molded into a permanent leer, and—through it—a tongue slowly started to emerge.

Oh shit oh fuck oh—

"Cockroach," the man said again, moving his tongue along the hard edges of the mouth slit. It was bloated and glistening, like a corpse coated in honey, and at the very end it had been cut, sliced half an inch, cleaving the tip into two.

The devil had a forked tongue.

From the bed, he started to whimper.

The man in the mask blinked again, inhaled through two tiny pinpricks in the mask's nose, and slowly rose to his feet.

"I wonder what you taste like . . . cockroach."

PART TWO

17

The address that Cary had given me for the Calvary Project was a block of flats called Eagle Heights, about a quarter of a mile east of Brixton Road. On the way over, my phone started ringing, but by the time I'd scooped it up off the backseat I'd missed the call. I slotted the phone in the hands-free and went to my voice messages. It was Cary.

"Uh, I've thought about . . ." He paused, sounding different this time: less officious, more hesitant. "Just give me a call when you get the chance. I'm in this morning until ten, and then after lunch I'm here until four."

I looked at the clock.

Eight forty-three.

I tried calling him, but the desk sergeant said he wasn't around. Stuck in traffic ten minutes later, I tried again, and the same desk sergeant said he still wasn't around. I left a message just as Eagle Heights emerged from behind a bank of oak trees, featureless and gray, its concrete marked with grime and disrepair, as if the building was rotting from the outside in. It was twenty-five stories high, and flanked by two even bigger blocks of flats on the other side of a ringed fence.

At the front entrance, as I parked up, I saw there was a board with Eagle Heights written on it. Someone had spray-painted *Welcome to hell* underneath.

Across from me, a bunch of kids who were supposed to be in school were kicking a ball about on a patch of muddy grass. I got out of the car, removed my phone and my pocket knife, and headed for the entrance.

Inside, there were mailboxes on my left, most with nothing in. I checked the slot for the flat I wanted, number 227, but it was empty. To my right, stairs wound up and around. The further inside I got, the worse the place started to smell, and—at the entrance to the second-floor flats—I found a door with a cracked glass panel and a loose hinge.

I pulled it open.

Background noise came through from the flats: the buzz of a TV, a woman shouting, the dull thud of a bassline. There were fifteen doors on either side, all painted the same shade of muddy brown. Flat 227 was right at the end.

I knocked twice and waited.

A council notice was nailed to the door. It was almost four years old, and warned people not to enter due to health and safety violations. Some of the sticker had peeled away and the bits that remained had started to fade over time. When there was no response, I knocked again, harder this time.

Further down the corridor, two flats along on the opposite side, I heard the sound of a door opening. Someone peered through the crack, eyes darting right to left. "Who you lookin' for?" a man's voice said.

"The guy who lives here. You know him?"

"Nah."

"You seen him around?"

"What are you, a copper?"

"No."

"Social services?"

"No."

I knocked again on the door.

"You ain't gonna find nothin', mate."

"How come?"

"There ain't no one there."

I looked at him. "Since when?"

"Since forever."

"No one lives here?"

"Nope."

"You sure?"

"Am I *sure*? You can read English, can't you?"

He meant the council notice.

"So, the council cleared out the last tenants?" I asked.

"Last tenants? I been in this shithole twenty years. Ain't no one lived in that flat since the floor gave in. Hole the size of Tower Bridge in there." He opened the door a little more. He was white, unshaven, old. "No one gives a shit about us here, so ain't no one been round to fix it. Must've been five years since it went."

"No one's lived here for five years?"

"Nope." He paused. "Sometimes the council come round. Inspecting it, I s'pose. But no one's lived in there for a long time."

I started along the corridor toward him.

As I got closer he pushed the door shut. I passed his flat, walked out to the landing area, and stood away from the door, out of sight. Then I waited.

A couple of minutes passed.

Once I was definitely sure he was back inside his flat, I returned to the corridor, taking my pocket knife out on the way. Slipping the blade into the crack between door and frame on 227, I gently started to jimmy it open. The door was damp and warped, and had a curve about two-thirds of the way up. As I worked the blade, I felt some give. I removed some broken slivers of wood and started opening up a hole. On the other side, illuminated by light from the corridor, it looked stark: no carpets or furniture, no paint on the walls.

Gradually, more wood started to break, and the further down the door frame I got, the easier it came away. I tried the handle. The door moved in the frame. Glancing along the corridor, I gently used my shoulder to apply some pressure, sliding the blade back in, this time at the lock. The wood was incredibly soft, bending against my weight, and the lock was from a different time: old and hollow, its mechanisms rusted-through.

Finally, thirty seconds later, it clicked open.

I stepped inside and closed the door behind me.

18

There were no curtains at the windows, only rectangular sheets of black plastic. Thin blocks of light escaped around the edges, spilling onto opposite walls. The room smelled damp but not unpleasant, and the floorboards were dirty. Some were broken. The old man in the other flat had been wrong, though. There were small holes in the floor, but not dangerously big, and they didn't go through to the room below. They went to a concrete support. Some of the floorboards differed in color to the rest of the flooring and looked as if they had been replaced recently.

I hunted for a light switch and found one a little way along the wall, but the electrics were off. Walking across to the windows, I carefully peeled some of the plastic sheeting away, where it had been secured with gaffer tape. As I rolled it back, morning light erupted into the room in a series of dust-filled rectangles.

The flat was a skeleton, every piece of furniture removed. There were Coke bottles and empty crisp packets on the kitchen counter. In a small rubbish bin there was an apple core and two sweet wrappers. I picked up one of the crisp packets and turned it over. The expiration date was six months away.

The flat had been used recently.

Pinned to the wall was a newspaper cutting, curled at the edges. BOY, 10, FOUND FLOATING IN THE THAMES. Parts of the story had been underlined in red pen. I zeroed in on the date at the top: April 13, 2002. Nearly eight years old.

Both bedrooms were empty, dust on the floorboards and paint blistering on the walls. The windows had also been covered in black plastic sheeting. A third door led to the bathroom. The bath tub itself was filthy, mold climbing up the sides and around the taps, spreading like a disease across the enamel, and there were tiles cracked and missing, bits of them lying in piles in the bath. The sink was cleaner, and there was a bar of soap on it.

I returned to the kitchen and started going through the cupboards. With no electrics and no water, there was only food that didn't need preparation: some cornflakes, corned beef, a couple of tins of tuna, crackers, peanut butter, jam. In a small drawer, right at the bottom, was a notepad. It was empty but, on its pages, I could see the ghostly memories of things that once had been written down.

I pocketed it and moved on.

The flat was obviously used as a base of some sort; a hiding place. Maybe Alex had hidden here himself. But no one would live here for any period of time. There was no power, not enough provisions and utensils. Yet, as a place to disappear, it was ideal. The old man thought it was the council he'd heard.

But it wasn't them.

Suddenly, a telephone started ringing.

I stood completely still in the middle of the room, trying to figure out if it was coming from inside the flat. When I realized it was, I followed the sound through to the bedrooms. In the first one, there was nothing—but in the second, the noise got louder and, at the bottom of one of the walls, I spotted a phone line, a wire running up and out of it, disappearing behind one of the black sheets.

Peeling back the gaffer tape, I looked in behind: on the windowsill was a cordless phone with a digital display, sitting in a recharging cradle.

The ringing stopped.

I reached in behind the plastic and picked up the phone. On the display it said the last number had been withheld. I went to the options menu, but there were no names in the address book, nothing on the "Recent Calls" list, and no one had left any messages on the answerphone. I punched in my own mobile number, and pressed "Call." A couple of seconds later, my phone started buzzing.

On my mobile's display: PRIVATE.

Deleting my number from the "Recent Calls" list, I placed the phone back in the cradle. The fact that there was nothing on it—no history, no record of anything—meant either it was brand new, or it got wiped clean after every use.

It was time to go.

I reattached the plastic sheeting in the bedroom, and then went to the windows of the living room and started to do the same.

But then I noticed something.

Two floors down, a man was standing next to my car, a mobile phone in his hands. The handset was flipped open, as if he'd just been using it.

Had he just called the flat?

He leaned forward, cupped his hands to the glass and peered through the window into the front seat. He didn't move for a long time. Then he straightened, took in the full length of the car and looked up toward the flat.

I stepped back from the window.

Waited.

After thirty seconds, I looked again, but he was gone.

Reattaching the sheeting in the living room, I made sure I still had the notepad from the kitchen, and moved to the door, opening it a fraction.

I peered through the gap.

Shit.

The man was already inside the doors at the end of the corridor.

He's coming to the flat.

I pushed the door gently shut and backed up against the wall, just to the side of the hinge. Gripping my knife, I listened for his footsteps.

Hesitantly, the door started opening.

Through the slit between door and frame, I could see a face. He had a thick scar running toward the corner of his lips, which seemed to extend his mouth. He took another step forward. All I could see now was the back of his head. Another inch forward, and his foot came into view at the bottom of the door.

"Vee?" he said quietly.

He took a step back.

"Vee?"

Another step.

It was so quiet in the flat now, I was sure he could hear me breathing. He backed up another step and, before I realized what was happening, his eye and a thin sliver of face was filling the gap between door and frame.

He was looking right at me.

A heartbeat later, he ran.

When I got out into the corridor, the doors at the end were already swinging open and he was out of them. I sprinted after him, taking the stairs two at a time, adjusting the knife so the top of the handle faced down and the blade pointed toward my elbow. When I got to the bottom, he was looking back over his shoulder, heading out across the grass to where a length of metal fencing separated the buildings from the road. He looked younger than me, twenty-two or twenty-three. I'd run a lot since Derryn had died, pounding out the frustration and the anger, but at his age he would be naturally fitter.

Then the chase swung in my favor.

The kids I'd spotted earlier had moved their game of football further up, closer to the flats. As he looked around again, one of the kids suddenly ran across in front of him. The two of them collided. The kid went spinning, almost pirouetting on the spot, before collapsing to the ground. The man tried to avoid him, but failed, falling over him, his body hitting the ground hard. For a couple of seconds, he was dazed. He scrambled on to all fours, onto his feet, then his shoes slipped in the mud.

He went down again.

As I came at him, he jabbed a boot up into my stomach. I staggered backward, losing my footing, but managed to cling onto his coat. I pulled him toward me. He jabbed at me again with a foot, catching the side of my face. The impact stunned me for a moment. I dropped the knife, blinked, tried to refocus.

He looked between me, the knife and the fencing.

The tiny delay worked in my favor: I grasped the front of his coat and landed a punch in the side of his head—but then he pushed back and grabbed my arm, trying to snap it. Wriggling free, I pumped a fist at his face, and missed. He rolled to the left, my fist slapping against the ground, then used my weight transfer to push me off. When I swiveled to face him again, he was already on his feet, caked in mud, accelerating away.

"Stop!" I shouted.

But he didn't stop. By the time I was on my feet again, he had made it to the metal fence, and was dropping to his knees and crawling through a gap. As he straightened, safe on the other side, he pulled up the hood on his jacket so I couldn't see his face properly, and began jogging away. By the time I got to the fencing, he was halfway along a narrow alleyway, moving more slowly now to prevent himself from losing his footing again. Puddles were scattered around him, reflecting the sky. I watched him all the way to the end. When he got there, he stopped and looked back at me—and then he disappeared for good.

Frustrated, I headed back to the car, but about twenty feet from where the kids were playing football, I spotted something.

A mobile phone.

Mud was caked to it, the display face down, wet grass matted to the casing. I knelt, picked it up and wiped it clean.

As soon as I did, it started ringing.

I hit "Answer" but didn't say anything. All I got in return was silence, the sound of cars passing in the background of the call.

But then: "You're gonna wish you hadn't picked that up."

I stood, spotting my knife about six feet across the grass from me. I walked over and scooped it up, then glanced toward the fence, back to the flats, and out to the main road. *He's watching me.*

"Did you hear me?"

"Who are you?"

"Did you hear me?"

"Yeah, I heard you," I replied, and scanned my surroundings again. "Does the flat belong to you?"

"You just made a big mistake."

"Yeah, well, I've made them before."

"Not like this." The line crackled and hissed. "Listen to me: you get back in your car and you drive back to wherever it is you're from, and you forget about everything you've found. You don't ever come out of your hole again. Is that clear?"

I took the phone away from my ear and looked at the display. Another withheld number. "Who does the flat belong to?"

"Is that clear?"

"What's the Calvary Project?"

"Is that *clear?*"

"Where's Alex Towne?"

"You're not listening to me, *David.*"

I stopped. "How do you know my name?"

The line went dead.

19

The restaurant overlooked Hyde Park. At the windows were a series of booths, dressed up like an American diner, with mini jukeboxes on the tables playing Elvis on rotation. Above me on the wall was a clock showing 10.40, Mickey Mouse's arms pointing to the ten and the eight. Three booths along were a French couple and, beyond them, a group of kids eating eggs and bacon.

Apart from that, the place was empty.

On the table in front of me, I had the pad I'd taken from the apartment and the mobile phone I'd picked up off the grass outside. Just like the phone in the flat, there were no contact numbers in the address book, no recent calls, and no messages in the voicemail. Dropping the handset had been a mistake, but a mistake they could probably live with. There was nothing on it that would lead back to them. No incriminating evidence. No numbers. Nothing traceable. But whatever their connection to Alex, they were still warning me off something.

That meant I'd surprised them.

It meant I'd made inroads.

A waitress came over carrying my breakfast—an omelet, some toast and a pot of coffee—and, before she left, I asked her if I could borrow a pencil. Once I had one, I started rubbing the tip gently across the scars and grooves of the pad.

Slowly, words started to emerge.

In the top right: *Must phone Vee.* The man at the flat had asked for Vee when he'd first entered the flat. Elsewhere, less defined, were a series of names— *Paul, Stephen, Zack*—attached to messages that were hard to put together. But, at the bottom, clearest of all, was a telephone number. I dialed it.

"Angel's," a male voice said.

I waited, could hear people talking in the background.

"Hello?"

"Uh, hi," I said, deliberately sounding confused. "I'm not sure I've got the right number here, actually. Uh, this is Angel's in . . . ?"

"Soho."

I stopped. "Wait a second, this is Angel's *pub*?"

"Yeah."

Suddenly disorientated, I hung up.

Angel's was a pub on the edge of Chinatown—but I knew that even before I'd made the call. During my apprenticeship as a journalist, I was paired with an experienced reporter who covered the City. Angel's had been his local haunt at the time. He stopped going after retiring to the Norfolk countryside.

But I hadn't.

I returned, on and off, right the way up until Derryn got ill.

My car was on the other side of the park. I entered at Hyde Park Corner and headed toward the Serpentine. Everything was quiet. The trees were skeletal and bare; the water in the lake dark and still. The only movement on its surface were two model boats, gliding and drifting, their sails catching the wind. I carried on walking, taken in by the smell and sounds of the place; of the grass covered by a blanket of fallen leaves; of the oaks and elms being stripped as the depths of winter approached.

Kids ran across in front of me, their muddy footprints a reminder of where they'd been and how often. Their parents watched from the side, chatting, laughing, their breath drifting away. It made me ache with loneliness. I remembered the times Derryn and I had talked about wanting a family, about what it would be like to hold our baby for the first time—or walk, hand in hand, with our son or daughter to school. We'd started trying before she got cancer, and—after she was diagnosed, after it started taking over our lives—we never got to try again.

As I thought of Derryn, I thought of Alex. I knew, deep down, there was no way he could have died in that car crash and still be alive, in the same way I knew there was no way I could return home and find Derryn sitting in her rocking chair on the back porch. Yet, when I looked in Mary's eyes, I never saw anything less than a total conviction about what she'd seen, about her belief in what she was telling me. And I knew a small part of me—perhaps *more* than a small part—wanted her to be right. I wanted Alex to be alive, however impossible it seemed. Maybe because I thought it might bring me something: an ending, a conclusion.

Maybe some answers.

Maybe an end to my loneliness.

After days of heavy skies and biting winds, snow finally started falling as I got back to the car. I climbed in, put the heaters on full blast and started scrolling through the numbers on my mobile. When I got to the one I wanted, I hit "Call."

"Citizens Advice Bureau."

I smiled. "Oh, come on."

"Who's that?" the voice said.

"Citizens Advice?"

"David?"

"Yeah. How you doing, Spike?"

"Man, it's been ages."

We chatted for a while, catching up. Spike was a Russian hacker, here on an expired student visa, running a cash-only information service out of his flat somewhere in north London. During my days on the newspaper, when I'd still cared about breaking big stories, I'd used him a lot.

"So, what can I do you for, man?" His accent had started to become Americanized, picked up by hours of watching music videos and TV shows.

"I need you to fire up the super computer."

"Course I can. What you got?"

"A mobile phone—I want to find out who it belongs to. It's got no numbers on it, no address book. If I gave you the serial number, do you reckon you could find out where the phone was bought, maybe who it's registered to?"

"Yeah, no problem."

"Thanks, Spike."

"Give me a couple of hours, okay?"

"Sure."

I gave him all the details.

"My fee's gone up a bit since last time," he said.

"Whatever it takes, Spike."

I hung up and, within seconds, the phone was buzzing again. I looked down at the display. A Bristol number. *John Cary.* I'd forgotten to chase him up.

"John," I said, answering. "Sorry I didn't get back to you."

No response.

"I left a couple of messages," I said.

"I can't talk for long," he replied.

"Okay."

"You still want that photograph looked at?"

"Definitely."

"Send it to me at home. I know a guy at the Forensic Science Service, and he owes me a favor from a while back. I can ask him to take a look at it. Might as well make use of the labs before the government starts closing them next year."

"Thanks. I really appreciate it."

"I'm probably making the biggest mistake of my life."

I didn't know how to respond to that—so I said nothing—but I knew my instincts had been right: what had happened to Alex still ate at him.

I wasn't the only one who needed closure.

20

Angel's was a thin building, east of Haymarket. Snow was already piled up against the door when I arrived. Next to it, barred like a cell, was a small window.

I peered inside.

It was dark, a square of white light at the back all I could make out. Above me were a pair of neon angel's wings, and next to the doorway a sign that said it wasn't open until midday. I looked at my watch. It was 11.40.

"You're early."

I turned. A woman was standing behind me, looking me up and down. She was in her mid-forties, pale and boyish, her blonde hair from a bottle, her eyes gray and small. I smiled at her, but she just shook her head. She glanced from the door of the pub to the sky, then pulled her long, fake fur coat tighter around her.

"Come back in twenty minutes."

She started unlocking the door.

"I'm not here to drink."

She turned to me, disgusted. "You wanna strip club, you've—"

"I'm not here for that either."

She stepped up into the open doorway. "You wanna chat?"

"Kind of."

"This ain't the Samaritans."

She went to push the door closed, but I shoved a foot in next to it and took a step up to the doorway.

"There ain't no money here."

Her accent was strong. East End.

"I'm not here to rob you," I said.

She stared at me, then rolled her eyes. "The Old Bill. *Shit*, this must be my lucky day." She tossed her coat inside, across one of the tables near the door.

"I'm not a police officer. I just want to chat."

"About what?"

"Can I come in?"

"No."

I rubbed my hands together. "We'll just freeze to death out here, then."

She glanced up and down the street as snow settled around us, then looked at me and rolled her eyes again. "Whatever," she said, sighing, and headed inside, leaving the door open.

I stepped up into the pub.

It had hardly changed since the last time I'd been in. They'd replaced the wallpaper—but nothing else. The room was long and narrow, with a five-pointed cove at the back big enough for a couple of tables and a jukebox.

"So, what do you want?" she said, moving in behind the bar.

I removed my pad and a pen and set it down on the counter, sliding in at one of the stools. "What's your name?"

"What's it to you?"

I handed her a business card. "My name's David Raker."

She leaned against the counter and looked at it. "You're a missing persons investigator? I didn't even know those things existed."

"I'm the living proof."

She nodded. "Jade."

"That's your name?"

"Yeah."

"Pretty name."

"Whatever."

"You're not used to compliments?"

"From good-looking boys like you?" She shook her head. "No. Last time I had a man tell me my name was pretty, he was twenty stone and had a comb-over that went all the way to his chin."

I smiled. "That's my weekend look."

She went to smile and then it disappeared again, as if she'd reined it back. She looked me up and down a second time, but didn't say anything.

"So, how long you on for today?" I asked her.

"Till seven."

"That's a long day."

She shrugged. "It's a hard life."

I looked down at the notepad. A new page. A blank.

"Looks like an interestin' case," she joked.

"Could be, yeah."

"So, what's Magnum PI doin' in this shithole?"

I turned on the stool, and looked around the pub. "At least this shit-hole's got new wallpaper since the last time I came in."

"That a fact?"

"How long have you been here, Jade?"

"I don't know. Six months maybe."

I noticed a couple of photos on the wall behind me, so got down off the stool and wandered over. One was a picture of a woman I recognized. She was surrounded by a bunch of regulars on New Year's Eve, three years ago.

Her name was Evelyn.

She'd worked behind the bar back when I used to come in. I'd got to know her pretty well; well enough to tell her a little of Derryn, and for her to really mean she was sorry when I told her Derryn had cancer.

"Evelyn still around?"

"No."

I turned back to her. "When did she leave?"

A flicker of something. "Dunno."

I studied Jade. "You don't know when she left?"

"It was before my time."

I walked back to the bar and sat down on the stool again. She didn't look convinced by what she was saying, but I couldn't see a reason for her to lie.

Pushing on, I said: "I'm trying to find someone who might have had a connection with this place. If I show you a picture of him, maybe you could tell me if you've seen him in here or not."

She nodded. I took out a picture Mary had given me of Alex and handed it to her. She squinted at it, as if she was a little short-sighted. "What's his name?"

"Alex Towne."

Her eyes flicked to me across the top of the photo.

"You know him, Jade?"

She took a moment more, then handed the photo back to me. "No."

"You sure?"

"Course I'm sure."

In my top pocket I had a list of names, taken from the pad in the apartment at Eagle Heights. I unfolded it. "What about regulars with names like these?" I'd rewritten the names on a separate piece of paper, one under the other.

She read down the list and shrugged. "Probably."

"You do or you don't?"

"How the hell am I supposed to know?" she said. "This ain't exactly the Ritz, I know, but this place gets busy. Lotta people comin' and goin'."

I took the list back.

"You ask a lot of questions, Magnum."

"That's my job," I said, and looked around the pub again. Something didn't feel right about this. Either she knew when Evelyn left or she didn't, and there was something else too: the way she'd reacted to the photograph of Alex.

I turned back to her.

She looked suspicious now, unsure about what I was doing, and where this was headed. Maybe it was a natural suspicion, built up from her hours working in here, dealing with drunks and fending off come-on's from customers. Or maybe she really *was* lying to me, and was starting to think I'd seen through it.

Suddenly, the door to the pub opened.

We both looked round as a couple of old men came in talking. One of them laughed and glanced toward the bar. "Morning, Jade. Are we too early?"

She looked at me, then back to them. "No, Harry."

They shuffled up to the bar.

One of them slid in at a stool and started fiddling in his pockets for change; the other stood next to him and eyed up the beers on tap. When they were finished, they both glanced at the photograph of Alex, and then at me.

"Morning," Harry said.

I nodded at both of them. "Morning."

Jade seemed more relaxed now, her expression more defiant. *She feels like I can't get at her.*

"Is Alex Towne alive?"

A brief flash in her face.

"Jade, is Alex Towne alive?"

She moved to the back of the bar, where the pumps sat under a mirrored panel, and picked up two empty pint glasses. Without replying, she started filling one of the glasses, pulling on the pump and looking straight at my reflection in the mirror, as if trying to prove she had nothing to

hide. When she was done with the first beer, she duplicated the movement for the second.

"You okay, Jade?" Harry said.

She nodded. The old men looked between us again, trying to figure
out if I was bothering her. But they knew enough about Jade to know
that she couldn't be pushed around, and wouldn't be intimidated—at
least not while she was inside the safety of the pub.

I scooped up the notepad and the photo and left.

But that wasn't the end of it.

I'd be back at seven when she came off her shift—and this time she
wouldn't see me coming.

21

St. John the Baptist church was in Redbridge, close to the North Circular, tucked into a space behind a row of shops. Despite its obscure setting, hidden from the main road, it was an attractive, modern building—all cream walls and exposed beams. A huge crucifix hung above the door, beautifully carved from dark wood.

The main doors were locked, so I walked around to the back, and found a door marked "Office" partly open. Through the gap, I could see an empty room, a series of desks lined up, and a bookcase at the far end. I glanced along the outside of the church. Further down was a small outbuilding; wooden, like a glorified shed.

The door to that was open too.

I headed for it.

The structure was about twenty feet long by the same deep, and its exterior hadn't been treated properly, so the wood was still a raw orange color. Inside it was sparse: a couple of posters, a desk, a power lead for a laptop that wasn't there, a pad, some pens. There was a bookshelf, high up behind the desk, stacked with Bibles, biographies and reference material.

"Morning."

A voice from behind me.

It was a young guy, a silver laptop under his arm, dressed in a casual shirt and a pair of jeans. He must have been in his early thirties, with blond shoulder-length hair, parted in the center, and big, bright eyes. He was smiling at me.

"Morning," I said. "I'm looking for the minister here."

"Well, it must be your lucky day," he replied. He took another step toward me and held out his hand. "Reverend Michael Tilton."

I took his hand. "David Raker."

"Nice to meet you. You're not a Bible salesman, are you?"

I smiled. "No. Don't worry, you're safe."

"Ah good!" he said, and stepped past me into the outbuilding. "Sorry about the mess in here. We're having some work done on my office inside the church, plus I've got a youth pastor starting in a few weeks and I'm trying to get things in shape before he arrives. So this has become a dumping ground for all my stuff."

He set the laptop down and slid a small heater out from under his desk, turning the dial all the way up to ten. He closed the door.

"Pretty humble surroundings, huh?" There was only one chair, but a couple of removal crates were lying in the corner. He dragged the crates across toward me. "And sorry about the seat too. I try not to bring too many visitors in here."

I sat down. "It's not a problem."

"Thank you for being so understanding."

He sat down at his desk and glanced at his laptop. Onscreen, I could see a password prompt. I removed a business card from my wallet and handed it to him. "As I said, my name's David Raker. I find missing people for a living."

He seemed intrigued. "Oh, really?"

I nodded.

"What a fascinating job."

I smiled. "It has its moments. I'm not looking to take up too much of your day, Reverend Tilton—"

"Call me Michael, please."

I got out a photograph of Alex and handed it to him. "I'm looking into the disappearance of someone who might have visited you here at one time."

"Okay. This is him?"

"Yes. His name was Alex Towne."

Tilton picked up the photograph and studied it. "I'm trying to think," he said. "I haven't seen him around—not in the last couple of months, anyway."

"It won't have been in the last few months."

"Oh?"

"Here's the big problem: it would be more like six years ago."

Tilton looked at me, as if he wasn't sure whether I was being serious or not. "You're not joking."

"Unfortunately, no."

He looked at the photograph again. "How old is he?"

"He'll be about twenty-eight now."

"So, would he have been part of our Twenties group?"

"I'm not even sure he came here regularly. It could have been just once, it could have been a few times. But he had some connection with the church."

"How do you know?"

"I found a birthday card in among some of his things. It had an address label on the back, and the address was for here."

"I see." He frowned; gritted his teeth. "I remember most of the youth quite clearly—I mean, I used to be the youth pastor here myself—but . . ."

As he continued looking at it, I took out the birthday card.

"Here," I said, flipping it over so he could see the sticker on the back. "It says it was made by a woman called Angela Routledge. Is she still around?"

His expression dropped. "Angela died a couple of years ago."

"Anyone else who might remember selling these cards?"

"Angela tended to run the card stall on her own. To be honest, she did most of the work on her own: got the materials, made the cards, did everything herself. She was an extraordinary woman. She raised a lot of money for us." He paused again, but then something seemed to come to him. He picked up the photograph of Alex. "Can I borrow this for a couple of minutes?"

"If you think it will help."

"I used to draft in a friend of mine for the youth meetings. Let me go and call him and describe this guy, and see if he can be a bit more helpful than I am."

"You can borrow my phone if you like."

"No, it's fine. I left my mobile inside, anyway, and I should probably lock up the church if I'm going to be out here." He pointed at the picture. "What did you say his name was again?"

"Alex Towne."

Tilton nodded. "I won't be long."

He stepped past me and headed toward the main building. As I waited, I watched snow slide slowly off the roof of the church, hitting the ground with a thud.

A couple of minutes later, my phone started ringing.

"David Raker."

"David, it's Spike."

"Spike—what you got for me?"

I could hear him using a keyboard. "Okay, so the mobile phone was bought in a place called Mobile Network, three weeks ago. It's on an industrial estate in Bow. I'm guessing it's some kind of wholesaler, working out of a warehouse."

"Okay."

"You got a pen?"

I looked around the outbuilding. There was one on Tilton's desk.

"Yeah, I've got one."

"So, the phone's registered to a Gary Hooper."

"Hooper?"

"Yeah."

I wrote Gary Hooper on the back of my hand.

"I don't know whether that's any help."

"That's great."

"I've got an itemized bill here too."

"Perfect."

"Looks like the phone's hardly been used. There are very few calls and they're all to the same three numbers. Do you want me to read the numbers out?"

"Yeah."

He read them out, and I wrote them under Gary Hooper. The first two numbers I didn't recognize. The third I definitely did.

It was the number for Angel's.

"Spike, you're the magic man. I'll get you the money later."

I ended the call, and immediately tried the numbers I didn't recognize. On the first, an answerphone kicked in after three rings. "Hi, this is Gerald. Leave a message and I'll get back to you." I hung up and wrote the name Gerald down. As I was about to put in the second number, Tilton returned. He placed his phone down on the desk and turned to me. His expression said everything.

"I'm really sorry," he said, handing me the photograph of Alex. "My friend doesn't know him either. It's hard to describe how your guy looks over the phone, but I could probably list every member of our youth group over the past seven years, and . . . well, he isn't one of them. I hope I haven't spoiled your day."

"No, don't worry. I appreciate your efforts."

I glanced down at his phone. On the display it said: LAST CALL: LAZARUS—LANDLINE. He smiled at me again. "Is there anything else I can help with?"

"No, that's fine," I replied.

I shook his hand, thanked him again, and headed back to the car, letting the cold bite against my skin.

The traffic was terrible as I made my way back into the center of London. The deeper I got into the city, the slower things became, until finally everything ground to a halt. I watched the snow continue to fall, settling on chimneys and street lights, road signs and rooftops. Nothing was moving now but the weather.

After a while, I popped my phone in the hands-free cradle and punched in the final number that Spike had got me. It connected, but no one picked up. After twenty seconds, the call stopped, clicked, and an answerphone message kicked in.

It was a voice I recognized.

"Thank you for calling St. John the Baptist."

It was Michael Tilton.

22

I posted the Polaroid of Alex to John Cary, and then made my way back toward Soho. By the time I was parked, and outside Angel's, it was almost seven o'clock—and the end of Jade's shift. I bought myself a coffee, found a spot in the shadows across the street from the pub's front entrance, and waited. I didn't want to scare her, but if she saw me straight away, she'd probably disappear back inside.

That was her safety net.

Laughter sounded nearby. A group of teenaged girls emerged from my left, and stopped outside the pub, looking at each other. One played with her hair; another adjusted her skirt. They couldn't have been much more than sixteen.

From inside, probably fresh on the evening shift, came one of the barmen, emptying an ice bucket into the gutter. I backed up, further into the shadows. He registered the movement and glanced across the street, eyes narrowing, head tilting. He lingered for a second more, as if trying to satisfy his curiosity, before disappearing back inside.

The street quieted.

More snow started to fall.

The lull was disturbed by another group of women, these in their twenties, moving along the street. They were on a hen night. Behind them, a man followed close by, his boots dragging in the slush. Some of the women looked over their shoulders at him—looks that suggested, if they'd been on their own, somewhere less populated, they might have been worried—but then he started to drop back a little as they passed the front of Angel's, his face disappearing into his coat. Once he was past the entrance, he speeded up again. Some of the women at the back of the group flicked a look at him, one of them—presumably fired up with alcohol—turning and asking him, "What's your fuckin' problem?"

But the argument fizzled out when she saw his attention was no longer focused on them or where they were headed. He was looking across the street.

He was looking at me.

Our eyes locked for a split second and he seemed to hesitate. But then he tagged on to the group again, breaking into a jog and eventually passing them.

As I watched him go, something stirred in me.

A memory.

Did I recognize him?

By the time he started disappearing west, parallel to Chinatown, he was looking back again, quickening his pace—and the memory snapped into focus.

"Shit."

It's the guy who broke into my car at the cemetery.

I dropped the coffee to the ground and set off after him. At the end of the street, he turned right, then started moving through the crowds working their way down toward Shaftesbury Avenue. It was packed. Shops were still open. Restaurants were luring people in. A queue from a theater curved out and along the pavement toward me. The man glanced back again, bumped into someone and then upped his pace, disappearing into a crowd of tourists. I headed after him, quicker now, to where the group—gathering around a tour guide—were blocking the pavement. He emerged on the other side and crossed the street.

Forcing my way through the crowd, I could see him barging his way through another group of tourists further down. One of them stumbled as he pushed past, her husband calling after him. But when he looked back, it wasn't to apologize. It was to see how close I had got.

I tried to move faster, put my head down for a second, and lost him, and then decided to cross the street. There was a back alley close to another queue, black and narrow, steam hissing out of a vent high up on one of the walls. As I got closer, unable to see him anywhere, he burst out from a knot of people about halfway down, glanced at me once, and then disappeared into the alley.

The darkness sucked him up.

When I got to the mouth of the alley, at first I could only hear the echo of footsteps. But then he emerged from the shadows, partially lit by a window above. I started down the alley after him. He was a long way ahead of me, almost onto the next street already. He stopped when he got there, looking back.

And then he vanished from sight again.

By the time I'd got to the end, he was gone. I stood for a moment, looking both ways. There were crowds on both sides of the street, cars passing along it in a constant flow of noise and movement, and there were shadows everywhere—doorways to disappear in, tiny lanes and alleys, slices of night that would hide him for as long as he needed.

I looked at my watch.

Ten minutes past seven.

A sudden thought hit me: *maybe this had been the point.* Maybe they were luring me away from Angel's so I couldn't get at Jade; tricking me, manipulating me. Maybe the barman *had* glimpsed me in the shadows out front after all, and gone in and raised the alarm.

But then I stopped dead.

About a fifth of a mile down on my left, Jade was crossing the road. She looked both ways, a cigarette glowing between her fingers, and moved off in the opposite direction. I hesitated, suddenly unsure it was her.

But it was.

It was Jade.

I followed her, keeping to the other side of the street, moving in and out of the pools of light cast by the street lamps. When I drew level with the alley she'd emerged from, I looked along it and saw a big green door, partially open. Above it were a pair of neon angel's wings. She'd left through the rear entrance. Assuming she'd done that because the barman *had* seen me out front, why would they lead me back to the door that she'd been coming out of?

Because it's a trap.

I hesitated. What if the first guy had led me here and now Jade had been told to lead me somewhere else? What if that phone call outside Eagle Heights *had* been my one chance to walk away?

The one chance I hadn't taken.

She disappeared from sight at the end of the road.

I stood there, frozen to the spot, uncertainty pumping through my veins, and something flooded my chest, a sense that I'd been here before, in the first few weeks after Derryn's death: standing on the edge of a precipice, watching the ground crumble beneath my feet.

Get yourself together.

I went after her.

When I got to the end of the road, I saw her about forty yards along, on the right. She was crossing the street and heading for a thin back alley, partially lit. There was a restaurant on the corner, decorated in tinsel and Christmas trees.

Breaking into a sprint, I caught up with her quickly.

"Jade?"

She stopped and turned. She couldn't see me to start with, then I moved out of the dark and under the light of a Christmas tree.

Her face dropped.

She sunk her hands into the pockets of her fur coat: a reflex action. She felt threatened by me. I held up a hand. "I'm not going to hurt you."

Her eyes darted left and right.

"I just want to talk to you."

She didn't react.

"Were you leading me somewhere?"

Her face creased a little. "I was tryin' to get away from you."

"Why?"

" 'Cos you're trouble."

"You knew I was coming?"

She nodded. "One of the guys saw you out front."

The barman. I'd been right. "What was the point of the decoy?"

She frowned again.

"The scruffy guy," I said.

Her expression didn't change.

"The guy who led me to you. What was the point of that?"

She shrugged and looked away. But when she turned back, her expression had changed to a kind of relief, as if she'd just reached some sort of decision.

"What d'you want with me?"

"I just want to talk."

She didn't say anything for a long time.

"So, let's talk," she said.

Her eyes got darker as we walked, more opaque, harder to read. I tried to figure out whether she was scared, or confident, or both, but I gave up as we got to the car. Men were probably drawn to her suddenly and easily—but left just as quickly when they realized she'd never let them in.

"Is this what you drive?" she asked, looking at the BMW.

"This is it."

"I thought you'd have somethin' better."

"I'm not really Magnum PI, Jade."

She glanced inside, then back at me, as if anticipating the question to come. "So, what's going on?" I said.

"Can't we go somewhere?"

"Where do you want to go?"

"I'm hungry."

"Okay." We got into the car, and I started it up. "What's on the menu?"

"Cheeseburgers."

"Where?"

She looked at me. "If you're paying, there's a place I know."

23

We headed east, past the shells of old stadiums and storage yards. Everything was dark, almost decaying, as if the city were slowly dying. Tightly packed housing estates emerged from the night, lonely and deserted, windows dark, street lamps flickering on and off.

"Where are we going?"

"It's near," she said, staring out of the window.

I looked at the clock. 8.34.

She glanced at me. "You lost someone, Magnum?"

"Huh?"

"You lost someone?"

"What do you mean?"

Her eyes caught the light again. "You seem sad."

She had turned away from me now, her face reflected in the glass. I didn't want to get into this, not here, not with her—but I needed her, and what she knew. She realized that as well. She waited me out, her expression perfectly still.

"I lost my wife," I said.

"How?"

"She got cancer."

"What was her name?"

"Derryn."

She nodded. "What was she like?"

"She was my wife," I said. "I thought she was amazing."

We drove on for about half a mile more, then she told me to take a left. Out of the dark came huge blocks of flats, wrapped in the night.

"What do you miss most?"

"About Derryn?"

"Yeah."

I thought about it. "I miss just talking to her."

The restaurant was called Strawberry's and was an old carriage set inside a series of railway arches. A blue neon sign that said HOT FOOD buzzed above a serving hatch. We got out of the car and Jade led me to one of the tables out front. There were seven of them. Each one had a heater attached, their orange glow lighting the yard in front of the carriage. There was a couple on the table furthest away from us, but—apart from that—we were on our own.

"I didn't realize we were going à la carte," I said.

Jade ignored me and sat down. She reached into the pockets of her coat, trying to find her cigarettes, and laid the contents out on the table: keys, a wallet, an ATM statement, some cash, a photo which she placed face down. It had writing on the back: *This is the reason we do it.* I didn't ask her about it for now.

She found her cigarettes, removed one and popped it between her lips. "Get the burger with everythin' on," she said.

"Is this a favorite haunt of yours?"

"In a previous life," she said. "I used to come with my mum and dad. They loved places like this. Places with personality." She turned and pointed at the carriage. "They used to have a guy called Ronnie runnin' it back when it was called Rafferty's. He liked my mum and dad. Always cooked somethin' special for them."

"Your parents still around?"

A pause. Then she shook her head.

The heater was pumping out plenty of warmth. Jade removed her coat, lit her cigarette and looked at me. "So, what's your story, Magnum?"

"I'm not a PI, Jade."

She smirked. "But you want to be one."

"Do I?"

"You're actin' like one."

A woman emerged from the carriage wearing a retro waitress's uniform, a name badge that said "Strawberry's" and an expression that could turn a man to stone.

"What can I get you?" she barked.

"Two burgers with everythin' on," Jade replied. "I'll have a beer. Magnum?"

I looked at the waitress. "A black coffee—thanks."

The waitress disappeared again.

Jade and I stared at each other, light from the heater glinting in her eyes. It made her seem more mischievous somehow, as if she saw this all as a game. After a while, she started to put the things she'd laid out back into her pockets.

"That your mum and dad?" I asked her.

She followed my finger to the photo, and then turned it over. It was a picture of a young kid, perhaps five or six. The photograph was old, discolored. The boy was running across a patch of grass, kicking a football about. To the left of him was a wire fence. To the right, almost out of picture, a block of flats.

"I know that place," I said.

It was Eagle Heights.

She didn't say anything, hardly even moved.

"Who's the boy?"

She glanced at the picture. "'This is the reason we do it,'" she said.

"What does that mean?"

She smiled. "I'd tell you if I knew. But I don't. I don't know what that means. But I know what the boy represents."

"What's that?"

"Makin' a difference."

"Making a difference how?"

"What's that sayin'? Uh . . ." She took a drag on her cigarette and stared off into the night, blowing a flute of smoke out into the chill of the evening. "The end justifies the means. That's what this is."

"You've lost me, Jade."

She nodded, as if she hadn't expected me to keep up, and then took the photo and put it back in her pocket. "You ever had to keep somethin' secret?"

"Sure."

"I don't mean no birthday present."

"Neither do I."

"So what secret have you had to keep?"

"I used to be a journalist once."

"So?"

"So I worked in Israel, in South Africa, in Iraq."

"*So?*"

"I saw things in those places I'll never forget."

"What sorta things?"

I thought of Derryn, of keeping my work away from her: the things I saw, the bodies I stepped over.

"What sorta things?" she repeated.

"Things I could never bring home to my wife."

The waitress returned with our drinks.

"Come on, Magnum. You're gonna have to try harder than that."

"I'm not playing this game with you."

"It's not a game, it's a trade."

"So what are you going to trade me?"

She put the cigarette between her lips, took a drag, and then looked at it. "I shouldn't really be smokin' these," she said. "But I guess we all have our demons." She pressed a thumb against her lips, knowing and playful, and then a small smile escaped. "You follow this little project of yours any further, you're gonna have to face down a few demons of your own."

"What's that supposed to mean?"

"I'm talkin' about what you're gonna find if you get to the end . . ." She turned her beer bottle around. "I guess mostly I'm talkin' about the fact that, if you're not strong in this life, you fail. And I'm about to fail, Magnum. I'm tired."

"Of what?"

"Runnin'. Lyin'. Startin' again."

"Starting again?"

"You won't find anythin' at Angel's now. Everyone associated with it as of now will be gone by tomorrow. You askin' questions, that just makes it harder for you. You go back, it'll be new people. It'll have all changed."

"Why?"

"Why d'you think?"

I paused, thinking of something John Cary had said. "The bar's a front."

She clicked her fingers and smiled.

"For what?"

"It helps us do what we really want to do. It makes money for us. It pays our way."

"You own it?"

"Not me."

"Who?"

She picked up the statement from the table and opened it, placing it down in front of me. The bank account belonged to Angel's. There were two pages of listings, but about halfway down was a direct debit payment that caught my eye.

CALVARY PRO. 5000.00.

The Calvary Project.

Every month, Angel's was paying five grand to a company the Inland Revenue didn't even know existed.

"There's a paper trail half a mile long," she said, pre-empting the question I was about to ask, "so I wouldn't get too excited just yet. You go searchin' for any trace of that company, you'd be wanderin' in the dark, lost like a puppy dog."

The waitress arrived with our meals.

Jade didn't waste any time, biting down on the burger, juice bubbling beneath the bun. "So, where will everyone from the pub go?" I asked her.

"The others . . . I don't know. I don't make those decisions."

"What about you?"

She paused. "I'm not going back. I can't now."

"Why?"

"I'm sittin' here with you—why d'you think?"

"So, where are you going to go?"

She shrugged.

I thought of the three telephone numbers Spike had got me: one had been for Angel's, one had been for St. John the Baptist church, and one had been for someone called Gerald. "Who makes the decisions, then? This Gerald guy?"

She started laughing, almost choking on her food. "*Gerald?* No. Not Gerald. *Definitely* not Gerald. Gerald doesn't even know we exist."

"Who is he?"

"He's just some crook, livin' in a shithole in Camberwell. We just go to him for . . ." She paused. "Identity changes."

"Fake ID."

She winked. "You're good."

She took another bite of her burger.

"For you?"

"For all of us."

"Who's us?"

She smiled. "You could be a good copper."

I didn't respond this time, hoping my silence might draw her out.

"You could be a good copper," she repeated. "You ask the right questions. But you realize the whole reason we're sittin' here now isn't because you're good, but because we made mistakes. Droppin' that mobile phone like that, that was a stupid, careless thing to do. Thing is, Jason didn't expect you to turn up like that. He got jumpy."

"So who's Gary Hooper?"

"He's no one."

"The phone 'Jason' dropped at the flat is registered to Gary Hooper."

"My phone's registered to Matilda Wilkins. That don't make me her."

"So, who is he?"

"I told you—Gary Hooper ain't no one. He's a ghost. You'll be chasin' your tail all fuckin' day with that one. It's just a name. Just another lie." I watched her push some fries around her plate. "I hate to disappoint you, Magnum, but what you have here—" She gestured to herself "—is a foot soldier, not a general."

"Who's Vee?"

"Vee?"

"Jason—he asked for Vee. What's that short for? Veronica?"

She looked at me and suddenly became serious. "I'm gonna tell you what I know. I'm gonna tell you what I know because I'm tired of runnin'. I'm tired of havin' to begin again when people like you start puttin' their fuckin' beaks where they don't belong. I'm tired of lyin' to protect somethin' I don't . . ."

She stopped.

Her eyes narrowed.

"Look," she said, "first, forget Gerald—he don't know nothin'. Forget Vee too. That's just a stage name. And forget the Calvary Project. That won't lead nowhere but more made-up bullshit."

"What does it do?"

"What do you think it does?"

"I don't think it does anything. You just pass money through it."

"It's a means of protection."

"So you can launder money."

"Launder money?" She smiled. "This ain't the mafia."

"So the Calvary Project only exists in name?"

She opened a purse and took out a credit card. "All our money comes and goes through it. Our cards are registered to it. It buys our food and our clothes."

"So none of the purchases can be traced back to you."

"Right." She turned the card over. Company Barclaycard. *Miss Matilda*

Wilkins was printed at the bottom. "Jade ain't bought a pair of shoes in years."

"This Michael guy, at the church—what's he got to do with it?"

"I don't know much about that."

"So tell me what you do know."

"The church is where he recruits people."

"What do you mean, 'recruits'?"

"Helps them to start again. Sells 'em an idea."

I stopped. *Sells 'em an idea.*

Suddenly, from the darkness of my memory, a face emerged: the guy who had come and sat next to me at the pub in Cornwall; the guy with the tattoo.

My friend's a salesman, he'd said. *He sells ideas to people.*

I looked at Jade. "Who's the guy with the tattoo on his arm?"

She shot me a look—a sudden, jerking movement like she'd just been punched. Her eyes widened, her face lost color. She was trying to work out how I'd made the connection. "Walk away from that," she said quietly.

"From what?"

"From him."

"Who is he?"

She paused, ran her tongue around her mouth, then jabbed a finger at the photograph of the boy. "He'll protect what that represents above all else. He will go to the ends of the earth to do it. If you can get what you need and get the fuck out without him seein', then you should do that. Because the only other way to stop him would be to bring the whole thing down."

"Bring it down?"

"The whole house of cards."

"You mean your organization?"

She nodded. "But I think it might be too late for that."

"Why?"

"They know who you are. They warned you off once. That's what they do. They give you a chance. But you comin' to the bar this mornin', going to the church like you did . . . They only give you one warning."

"So what happens next?"

"What happens next?" She paused, looked at me, and we both understood the silence. I felt my blood chill. *You know what happens next, Magnum.*

"Why?"

"Why d'you think?"

"Alex?"

She took a sip of beer, didn't answer.

"Jade?"

I could hear myself getting impatient. She was still protecting the cause, still dancing around my questions, even while she was telling me she wanted out. She was scared about walking away—but not from whatever support system she had in place here. She was scared of the people who were running things.

"Why help me?" I said.

"Because this whole thing's outta control." She looked at me, brushing food away from her mouth. "We've been careless."

"Who's we?"

She didn't reply.

"Jade?"

"We. Us." She paused. "Him."

"Who?"

She glanced at the photograph of the boy, still out on the table.

"The boy?" I asked her.

"No," she said quietly.

"The man with the tattoo?"

She was teetering, unsure whether to commit.

"Jade?"

"No. Someone else." She looked at me, and—for the first time—something glistened in her eyes. "I think, in some ways, he's the worst of them all."

"Who?"

"You've pissed him off."

"*Who*, Jade?"

"You've really pissed him off. But maybe it's happenin' for a reason. I'm not sure I believe in him any more, in what he's fightin' for and the way he's fightin' it." She stopped, eyes looking up to the sky. "And I'm not sure He does either."

I followed her gaze.

"He? What is this—some sort of mission from God?"

She didn't reply, but I could tell I'd hit on something. "Jade?"

"I need to pee," she said, pushing her plate aside, and heading off toward a toilet block next to the carriage. She looked back once, and then she was gone.

The thought that she might try to escape crossed my mind the instant she left the table, so I gave her five minutes, then slid out and headed to the toilets.

It was a dumping ground at the back: drinks cans, carrier bags, a shopping trolley, needles. Beyond, the railway arches continued, gradually melting into the night. I could see one of the windows was open on the female side, and there was a crack in it, top to bottom.

"Jade?"

The door to the women's toilet was closed, so I pushed at it gently. Inside, the light was on—and, within seconds, I clocked blood on the floor, at the far end of the space. I stepped up, and inside.

Jade was slumped against one of the cubicle doors, her head tilted sideways. She was already dead. Her fingers were wrapped around the steak knife that had come with her burger, the blade streaked in blood. The cuts in her wrists were deep, her lifeblood chugging out of them, on to her hands, her clothes, the floor.

Reality hit home: *she'd rather take her own life than walk away from whatever she was involved in.* The idea sent nerves scattering down my back.

It meant she was terrified of the consequences.

And of the people who ran it.

As the breeze picked up again, faintly I heard a noise, like paper flapping. Beneath one of her hands, half-hidden by her balled fingers, was a piece of card. I moved across to her again, took it from her grasp and pocketed it.

Then I got out my phone and called the police.

24

The police arrived at Strawberry's ten minutes after I called them.

There were two officers: Jones and Hilton. Jones was in his early sixties, while Hilton was much younger, nervous, reeking of inexperience. He held up pretty well when Jones beckoned him to the toilet block, both of them kneeling down to look at Jade's pale body.

Later on, they drove me to a station in Dagenham.

It was obvious from the start that Jones didn't believe I'd killed her. Witnesses at the restaurant backed up most of what I told them had happened, in particular the timings, and when he asked me why we were there I told him the truth, or a version of it. I knew her, wanted to talk to her and she'd agreed as long as I drove her to her favorite restaurant.

"You get what you wanted?" he said.

"I don't know. Maybe."

Jones shook his head. "Hope she paid for the petrol."

I got the feeling he was so close to retirement he could smell it. Any case that wanted to stick around wasn't going to be one of his. That suited me fine. If he'd been a couple of years younger, I might have got a rougher ride. Instead, he told me they'd want to keep my BMW for a couple of days, as well as my clothes, and that they'd want to speak to me again once the body had been examined.

"That might take forty-eight hours," Jones said, "but I wouldn't bank on it. More likely you won't be hearing anything from us until the new year."

After that, he showed me the door.

Liz arrived about forty minutes later. She was the only person I knew who would be up at one in the morning; perhaps the only person I could turn to in an emergency now. After Derryn died, people stuck close to me for a while, cooked things, offered advice, sat with me in the still of the house. I had no family left, no brothers or sisters, so I relied on people from my newspaper days, on friends of my parents, on people Derryn had known. Most of them were very good to me—but most of them eventually grew tired of having to babysit me. I think, in truth, my sadness started to weigh on them and bring them down.

By the end, Liz was the only one left.

On the phone I told her where she could find the spare key, and asked her to get some clothes for me. Jones lent me a pair of police-issue trousers and a training top while I waited. When she arrived, she handed me a pair of jeans, a T-shirt and a coat and I changed in an empty locker room at the back of the station. She waited next to the front desk, dressed in tracksuit trousers and a zip-up training top.

"You okay?" she asked when I finally emerged again.

I nodded. "I'm fine. Thanks for coming."

We walked to her Mercedes, parked around the corner, and grabbed some takeaway coffee from a petrol station on the way there. Inside the car she turned the heaters on full blast.

She pulled out, and we drove for a while.

"I appreciate this, Liz."

She nodded. "You going to tell me what happened?"

I glanced at her, and she looked back. She had a dusting of makeup on. Maybe she hadn't taken it off after work, or maybe she'd just put it on before she came out. Either way, she looked really good. And, as her perfume filled the car, I felt a momentary connection to her. A buzz. I looked away, out into the night, and tried to imagine where the feeling had come from. It had been a long day; a traumatic one. Perhaps it was just the relief of going home—or perhaps, for a second, I realized how alone I was again.

"David?"

I turned back to her. "Things got a bit messy today."

"With a case?"

"Yeah."

"Are you in trouble?"

"No."

"Are you sure?" We stopped at some traffic lights, red light filling the front of the car. It reflected in her eyes as she looked at me. "David?"

"I'm fine," I said. "Honestly."

Her gaze moved across my face. "I can help you."

"I know."

"If you're in some sort of trouble, I can help you. I'm a lawyer. It's my job. I can help you, David."

Something passed between us; something unspoken. And then the feeling came again, an ache in the pit of my stomach.

"Whatever you need," she said quietly.

I nodded again.

"You don't have to do everything on your own."

I looked at her. She leaned into me a little, her perfume coming with it. The fingers of her hand brushed against my leg, her eyes were dark and serious.

"I can help you," she said again.

My heart shifted in my chest, like an animal waking from hibernation, and I found myself moving toward her. "I need . . ." But then I thought of Derryn, of her grave. *It's too soon.* Liz was so close to me I could feel her breath on my face.

"What?" she said.

The lights changed.

I looked at them, then back to her. The roads were empty. Behind us there was nothing but dark, cavernous warehouses. Her eyes were still fixed on me.

"I just . . ."

She studied me—and something changed. She nodded slowly, and then she shifted back, slipped the car into first, and took off.

"I'm sorry," I said.

"You've got nothing to apologize for."

I looked at her, my eyes wandering down her body. Her breasts. Her waist. Her legs. When I looked up again, she was staring at me.

It's too soon.

"I don't know what I think," I said quietly.

She nodded. "I understand."

"Some days . . ." I paused. She turned to me again, her face partially lit in the glow from the streets. "Some days it's what I want."

She didn't say anything.

"But some days . . ."

"I'm not going anywhere," she said gently. "I can help you, David."

"I know."

"When you're ready, I can help you."

When I got home, I took out the card Jade had left for me.

It was headed with the Strawberry's logo. Blood was spattered across it, her fingerprints marking the corners. I thought she'd taken a napkin as she'd left the table, but she'd picked up one of the restaurant's business cards instead. Inside the b of the name was a burger; the lines of the t were fries.

And in the middle, in shaky handwriting, she'd written: *Jade O'Connell, March 1, Mile End.*

25

I fell asleep at three and woke again an hour later. The TV was on mute, an empty coffee mug sat on the floor next to the sofa, and the remote control was resting on top of it. I switched off the TV, picked up the mug and took it through to the kitchen.

That was when I noticed the security light was on.

I stepped up to the kitchen window and looked out into the night. There were footprints in the snow, one after another, all the way up to the front of the house. As I moved closer to the glass, I could see they were at the side too.

None of them were mine.

I put the mug down on the counter and walked back through the house to the bedroom. The curtains weren't quite drawn. Outside, I could see a trail of footprints right in front of the windows, running parallel to them, tracing the circumference of the house before coming back on themselves.

Then: a noise.

Swiveling, I looked across the darkness of the bedroom. *What was that?* All I could hear now was snow dripping from the gutters. I edged toward the bedroom door and peered down the hallway.

Had it been the front door?

I tried to remember what the front door sounded like when I opened and closed it, tried to remember anything about any of the noises the house made. But as I looked along the hallway and waited for the sound to come again, there was nothing. Just silence.

Maybe it's an animal.

Liz had a cat. It set the light off all the time. But what about the footprints? I tried to think logically: had I been out in the garden, or around to the back of the house, since it had started to snow?

As I cast my mind back, the noise came again.

A soft tap.

Edging out into the hallway, I started moving toward the living room again—and then stopped.

The handle on the front door was moving.

For a split second, it felt like the soles of my feet were glued to every fiber in the carpet, but then I shuddered out of the moment, and the handle moved again: slowly, quietly, tilting downwards until it couldn't go any further.

The door started to come away from the frame.

If I'd been asleep, I wouldn't have heard a thing.

It opened all the way up, the security lamp leaking a square of yellow light across the hallway, but nothing else: no movement, no shadows, no sounds.

Then a man stepped into the house.

He was dressed head to toe in black, looking into the darkness of the living room, his back turned toward me. On the top of his head was a mask. He pulled it down over his face, before I had a chance to identify him, and then felt around in his belt for something.

And then he turned and looked down the hallway toward me.

I stepped back into the bedroom, my heart racing. He'd removed a gun from his belt, silencer attached, and his face was a plastic Halloween mask—eyeless, mouthless, unmoving. I tried to process what I'd just seen, and then it hit home like a punch to the throat: an armed man was inside my house.

A devil.

I quickly looked around the bedroom. Two stand-alone wardrobes, full of clothes and shoes. A bookcase. A dresser. The door into the ensuite.

No hiding places.

No weapons to hand.

Another noise from the hallway. *He's coming.* The door into the bedroom swung back into a tiny cove, about two feet deep, cut into the wall. It was my only option. I slid behind it, pulling the door as far back toward me as it would go. I could only see in two directions now: right, through the narrow gap between the door and the frame; and left, to the far edge of the bed and the dresser.

I looked left.

As I turned, the sound seemed immense; every noise amplifying in my ears, every beat of my heart, every blink of my eyes. I expected to be able to hear the man as he approached, hear *something*, but the house was silent now.

No footsteps. No creaks.

In the mirror on the dresser, I could make out all of the bedroom. The bedside cabinets. Derryn's books. Her plant. The bath, basin, shower. The door—and, beyond it, into the blackness of the hallway. Nothing moved.

But then, suddenly, he was there.

A flash of red plastic skin.

The toes of his boots, dark but polished, shone in the glow from the security light at the other end of the house. More of the mask emerged as he came further into the room, consuming the darkness. Halfway in, he stopped, scanning the bedroom, his body turning. But he made no sound at all.

I didn't move.

Didn't breathe.

I had nothing to compete with a gun, and only one way to protect myself: make him believe I wasn't home.

Another step.

He brought the gun up slightly, his finger wriggling at the trigger gently. It sounded like he was breathing in—sniffing—like a dog trying to pick up a trail. He glanced toward the dresser, into the mirror, seeming to look right at me—and then he moved again, past the bathroom, and along the edge of the bed.

I could smell something then.

A horrible, degraded odor, like decaying compost, trailing the man as he moved. I swallowed, felt like I had to, just to try to get the smell out of my throat and nose. But the stench didn't go away. It was coming off him like flakes of skin. I swallowed again, and again, and again, but couldn't get rid of it.

The man in the mask bent slightly and scanned under the bed, then came up again and leaned forward to look at Derryn's bedside cabinet. I heard the gentle slide of drawers opening and closing, then another noise: a small picture frame being picked up. When he turned around, his hands were down at his side again—one holding the gun, one suddenly empty—and the picture frame was gone. In it had been a photograph of Derryn and me on our last holiday together.

He'd pocketed it.

It took everything I had not to make a sound.

Whoever was behind the mask had crawled beneath my skin—violated me, my wife, our memories. A bubble of anger worked its way up through my chest, then fear cut across it as the man approached, the gun slightly raised in front of him. Faster, more determined, as if he now realized where I was.

He stopped in the doorway, scanned the bedroom a second time, and then breathed in through the mask again; a long, deep intake of air, whistling through the holes in the plastic.

I could smell him.

His decay. His stink.

He headed across the hallway, into the spare bedroom opposite, nothing visible of him in the shadows except the red plastic of the mask, searching for any sign of me, for anything that might look out of place. I stood motionless, soundless, staring through the gap between the door and the frame, into the black of the mask's eyeholes, praying he didn't return.

Finally, he left the bedroom.

And then the devil was gone.

The Program

He was sitting on the edge of the bed, looking across at the door out of the room. It was open. Beyond was a living area, stripped of all decor. The only furniture he could see was a table in the middle, and a single chair pushed under it.

It was a trick. Had to be.

He tried to work out how long they'd kept him, how long he'd been waking in the middle of the night and staring into the corner of the bedroom. Two or three weeks. Maybe a month. Maybe more. And during that time the door had never been open.

But now, all of a sudden, it was.

He leaned forward a little. He could make out more of the living area, without having to move: a second door to the right of the table, closed. A bookcase, empty, next to that. On top of the bookcase was a book. It had gold lettering on it and a Post-It note attached to the front.

Hesitantly, he got to his feet, dropped the blanket onto the bed and slowly shuffled to the bedroom door. Now he could see what the book was.

A Bible.

Looking ahead of him, behind him, ahead of him again, he took another couple of steps forward, into the living area. The floorboards were cold against his bare feet.

"Hello."

He started.

A man was standing next to the door to the bedroom, leaning against the wall, dressed entirely in black. Tall, broad, well built.

"How are you feeling?"

I recognize you, he thought, looking across at the tall man, trying to find the tail of the memory. But it wouldn't come to him. Memories were starting to swim away, disappearing every day—and they weren't coming back again.

"Have you lost your voice?" the tall man said, and stepped away from the door. "My name is Andrew."

"Where am I?" he said, his words indistinct as they passed through his toothless gums.

Andrew nodded. "Ah, so you do speak."

"Where am I?"

"You're safe."

"Safe?" He looked around him. "From who?"

"We will get to that."

"*I want to get to it now.*"

Andrew paused. Something flared in his eyes, and then it passed again. "*Do you remember what you did?*"

He tried to think, tried to grasp at another memory. "*I, uh . . .*"

"*You made a mess of your life, that's what you did,*" *Andrew said, his voice harder now.* "*You had nowhere else to go, no one to turn to. So you turned to us.*"

"*I turned to Mat.*"

Andrew smirked. "*No, you didn't.*"

"*I did.*"

"*No, you didn't. Mat doesn't exist.*"

"*What?*" *He frowned.* "*I want to see Mat.*"

"*Are you deaf?*"

He looked around the room, toward the door. "*Wha—where is he?*"

"*I told you,*" *Andrew said.* "*He doesn—*"

"*I want to know where he—*"

In the blink of an eye, Andrew was on to him, clamping a huge hand onto his throat. He leaned right into him and squeezed with his fingers. "*You have to earn the right to speak. So, don't ever speak to me like that.*"

Andrew shoved him away.

As he stepped back, fingers massaging his throat, the memory finally formed: bound to the dentist's chair, looking up at a man in a surgical mask.

Andrew.

"*You . . .*" *he said quietly, running his tongue around his gums.*

"*Don't say anything you're going to regret.*"

"*You took out my teeth.*"

Andrew just looked at him.

"*You took out my teeth,*" *he said again.*

"*We saved your life.*"

"*You took out my teeth.*"

"*We saved your life,*" *Andrew spat. He took a big step forward again, his hands opening and closing.* "*I'm willing to help you here, but I can just as easily feed you to the darkness.*"

The darkness.

He swallowed, looked at Andrew. He knew what that meant.

It meant the devil.

"*Is that what you want?*"

"*No,*" *he replied, holding up a hand.*

Andrew paused, steel showing in his face. "*I don't care about your teeth. There are*

things going on here more important than your vanity. Soon you will come to under-
stand the situation you are in—and the situation you were pulled out of."

He stared blankly at Andrew.

"I don't expect you to understand. That's why I've left something there for you to
read." Andrew nodded at the Bible. "I suggest you study the passages I've highlighted.
Process them. You'd better start to appreciate that you're standing in the middle of this
room with your heart still beating in your chest."

Andrew stepped closer to him.

"But if you cross us, we will kill you."

He's in a flat, numbered 227, two floors up. There's no furniture, and
holes in the floor. He's sitting at a window, facing Mat. He feels scared.

"What am I going to do?"

"I have friends who can help you," Mat says. "They run a place for
people like you."

"I don't want to run any more."

"You won't have to. These people—they will help you. They will
help you to start again. The police will never find you."

"But I don't know who I can trust."

"You can trust me."

"I can't trust anyone any more."

"You can count on me, I promise you that. These people will help
you to disappear, and then they will help you to forget."

"I want to forget, Mat."

Mat shifts closer, places a hand on his shoulder. "I know you do. But
do me a favor. Don't call me Mat from now on."

"I don't understand."

"My friends, the people who are going to help you, I'm not Mat to
them. Mat is dead now." He pauses, looks different for a moment. "You
can call me Michael."

When he woke, Andrew was sitting at the bottom of the bed. He brought his knees
up to his chest, glanced at Andrew, and then looked out through the top window.
Early morning. Or maybe late afternoon. He wasn't sure any more.

"Have you read the book I gave you?" Andrew said.

The book. He tried to remember a book he might have been given, any book, a
spark that would lead him there—but it wouldn't come.

"I can't remember," he said quietly.

"It was a Bible," Andrew replied, ignoring him. "The book was a Bible. You remember I gave you a copy of the Bible, right?"

"No."

Andrew paused, studied him. "That's a shame."

"Why am I losing my mem—"

"We've been treating you differently from the others, you know that?"

He looked at Andrew. "The others?"

"Your program is different."

"I don't understand."

"Your room, the food we give you, the way we've been with you—it's not our normal way of working. I don't think you realize how lucky you are." Andrew's eyes shifted left and right, suspicion in them. "But I worry about you, you know that? I worry that you think the best way to get better is to fight us."

He didn't say anything.

"Am I right?"

He shook his head.

"Normally, that doesn't concern me. On our regular program, we have ways of dealing with problems. But with you here, among this luxury, it's more difficult." Andrew studied him for a moment. "Do you want to fight us?"

He shook his head again. "No," he said. "No, I swear."

But this time Andrew just watched him, saying nothing.

He lifted his head.

He was sitting in the corner of a different room, pitch black. He couldn't remember how he'd got here; didn't have a clue how long he'd been out. His arm was raised to head height and locked to something. Knotted maybe, or clamped. It pinched his skin when he moved, and pins and needles prickled in his muscles.

Where the hell am I?

He could see a thin shaft of moonlight bleeding in through a window further down the wall. And as his eyes started to adjust to the darkness, other shapes emerged: a door on the far side, slightly ajar; and a white shape, like a sheet, at a diagonal from him. There was a breeze coming in from somewhere, and the sheet was moving, billowing up as the wind passed through.

Something specked against his skin.

He turned. The wall beside him was wet, almost glistening. There was a liquid on it, dribbling down. He brushed it with his hand. Water. It was running down the walls, all the way along the room.

Next to him, at his eyeline, was a square metal plate, bolts in all four corners, with an iron ring coming out of it. Water was on that too—and something else as well. Darker.

Blood.

"Shit."

He tried to move his arm away from the wall—but something glinted and rattled. He felt handcuffs pinching his skin. One loop was attached to the ring, the other clamped around his left wrist. He couldn't move, couldn't escape, couldn't even get to his feet without being pulled back down again.

Then he realized something else.

The sheet had moved; edged a little closer to him, parallel to the wall. This time, he could make out something beneath the sheet: a shape.

"Hello?"

The shape twitched.

"Hello?"

It twitched again.

The sheet slid a little, falling toward the floor, and from beneath the white cotton, a face looked out at him. A girl. Maybe only eighteen.

"Hello," he said again.

She was thin, her mouth flat and narrow, her skin pale. In the darkness of the room, she looked like a ghost.

"Where are we?"

She looked toward the door—a slow, gradual, prolonged movement—and then back to him. But she said nothing.

"Are you okay?" No reply. Her head tilted forward a little, as if she was having trouble holding it up. He tried edging away from the wall, as far across the room as he could go. "Are you okay?" he repeated.

And then he felt something soaking through his trousers. He looked down at the floor. A pool of vomit was under one of his legs. He backed up, away from it, and slipped. The handcuffs yanked at him as they locked in place, and pain shot through the top of his arm, like his shoulder had popped out of joint.

"Keep quiet."

The girl.

She was staring at him now, her eyes light like her skin, her hair matted and dirty. The sheet had fallen away. Beneath, she was wearing only a bra, some panties and a pair of socks.

"Are you okay?" he asked.

She didn't reply.

"Can you hear me?"

She twitched, as if someone had jabbed her with the point of a knife, then turned to look out to the landing again. She stared into the darkness beyond.

"*What's your name?*"

She finally turned back to face him. "*Keep quiet.*"

"*What's going on? Where are we?*"

She shook her head.

"*What's your name?*"

She looked at him. "*Rose.*"

He edged away from the wall again, careful to avoid the puke this time. The smell in the room was starting to get to him.

"*Listen to me, Rose. I'm going to get us out of here—but you're going to have to help me. You're going to have to tell me some things.*"

She stared out through the doorway, and didn't turn to face him again this time. Her spine was dotted down the middle of her back, and there was a bruise, big and black, on her left side, just next to her bra strap.

She said something, but he didn't pick it up.

"*What did you say?*"

She pulled the sheet around her again, and faced him. Her arm was also handcuffed to the wall. He noticed there were more rings running the length of the walls on both sides of the room, equal distances apart.

And something else.

A sharp piece of tile, maybe from a bathroom wall, or a roof, about four feet in front of him. It was shaped like a triangle, jagged on one side. He moved as far away from the wall as he could get, the handcuffs locking in place again, and swept a leg across the floor.

"*What are you doing?*" *Rose whispered.*

He tried to get to the tile again. His boot made better contact this time, and the tile turned over, the noise amplified inside the stillness of the room.

"*Stop it,*" *she said.* "*He will hear you.*"

He looked at her. "*Who?*"

"*The devil.*"

He stopped moving, a shiver passing through him, throat to groin. "*Who is he?*" *he whispered.*

She shrugged. "*A friend of the tall man.*"

The tall man. He fished for the memory, but it wouldn't come. He stared at her blankly.

"*Andrew,*" *she said quietly.*

Andrew.

Then the memory formed: the man who dressed all in black; the one who had been there when they'd taken his teeth.

He looked at Rose. "I can't . . ."

"Remember anything?"

He paused, a part of him scared to admit it. "Yes."

"Yeah, well, that's what they do," she said. "That's how they make you forget about what you've done. You want my advice?" She glanced at the doorway again, and then back to him. "Hang on to what you can, because once it's gone, it's not coming back."

"What do you mean?"

"I mean, eventually, you'll forget everything."

"Forget everything?"

"Everything you've done."

"What do I need to forget?"

"I don't know," she said.

She watched him for a moment, as if trying to figure out the answer for herself, and then turned her attention back to the doorway. The sheet had slipped again. Against her pale skin, the bruise on her back looked dark, like spilled ink. He imagined it was painful right down to the bone.

"Did the devil give you that bruise?"

Rose looked down at herself and brought her free hand around to her back, running her fingers across the surface of her skin. "Yes."

"Why?"

"I tried to run."

"Run from what?"

"What do you think? This place. The program."

"The program?"

A creak outside the room.

"Rose?"

She put a finger to her lips and studied the darkness beyond the door. "Seriously, you need to be quiet," she said eventually. "He likes to surprise you. He likes to watch. Give him an excuse and he will hurt you." She paused, felt for her bruise again. "The people who help run this place, I've watched them. Most of them still believe in something. They still seem to have rules. But the devil . . . I don't know what he believes in." Rose stared at him. "He will hurt you—and he will hurt me. That's what he does for them." She paused, blinked. "Sometimes I think he might actually be the Devil."

Click.

They both looked toward the corner of the room, into the darkness. The one corner where no light reached.

"*Cockroach.*"

Instantly, Rose started to sob, moving quickly back against the wall, her hand-cuffs rattling above her. She dropped to the floor and curled into a ball.

"*Are you going to save her, cockroach?*"

A voice from the blackness of the night. He shuffled across the floor on his backside, moving in as tight to the wall as he could get. Water soaked through to his back. And even from across the other side of the room, he could smell the man in the mask now: an awful, decaying stench, like a dead animal.

From the corner of the room, a sliver of a horn emerged, sprouting from the top of a red mask. "What are you going to do, cockroach?" the voice continued, fleshy and guttural. "Escape and take her with you?"

Laughter, the sound muffled by the mask.

"*You're a mistake. You don't fit in. Do you think there can be one rule for you and one for everyone else? Is that what you think, cockroach?*"

More of the mask emerged from the darkness: an eye hole.

"*Is that what you think?*"

Half the mask was visible now.

"*You're not special.*"

He looked at the devil and tried to reply. But the words crumbled in his throat, his breath barely able to pass out through his lips.

"*You die, just like everyone else.*"

Deep underground, in the bowels of their compound, was another place: the biggest room they had, split into two and divided by a set of double doors.

The largest part of the room was once used as an industrial fridge, but there was nothing in it now. It sat empty, its strip lights buzzing, its walls stained brown and red with rust, its floor dotted with blood. Next to it, on the other side of the double doors, was a second, smaller room.

When they came for him at dawn four days later, unexpectedly, violently, that was where they took him. They dragged him to a solitary chair in the middle of the room, and they made him face what awaited.

The final part of the program.

PART THREE

26

The only evidence the devil had ever existed was a tiny piece of dirt on the carpet immediately inside my front door. As the sun came up, I wandered through the house, trying to see if he'd left anything behind, any evidence of who he was.

But there was nothing.

Shortly after, my phone started ringing. On the display: ETHAN CARTER. Ethan had been in South Africa with me during the elections, and was now the political editor at the *Sunday Times*. I'd phoned him when I got in from the police station the night before, and left a message, giving him the name Jade O'Connell, the date of March 1 and the keyword "Mile End." I asked him if he could look into the information, and to give me a call back.

The truth was, though, I didn't feel much like a conversation, especially after the events of the night before, so I left it to go to voicemail, and then retrieved his message a couple of minutes later.

"David, it's Ethan. I e-mailed you what I could find. Enjoy."

The computer was in the spare bedroom.

I booted it up, and went to my inbox. There was a message waiting from Ethan, with three attachments. The first was a copy of a *Times* front page. It was dated March 2, 2004. At the bottom was a story about a shooting at a bar in Mile End. Three dead, five injured. I read a little way, then opened up the other two attachments. One was a second-page story, dated March 3, a column with a photograph of the bar and a caption underneath that read: "The scene of the shooting." The third, dated March 7, was smaller, a "News in Brief" piece, with no picture. Each of the attachments were high resolution. I clicked on the first.

THREE DEAD IN EAST END SHOOTOUT

03/02/04—Three people were killed and five injured during a shootout at a bar in London, yesterday.

Police couldn't confirm the names of the dead but did say they believed all three victims were members of the Brasovs, a violent splinter group previously affiliated to notorious Romanian gang, Cernoziom.

Witnesses reported hearing gunshots go off inside the Lamb, a pub on Bow Road, Mile End, as well as shouting and screaming, before two gunmen exited the building, eventually escaping in a white van. Police said they were interviewing witnesses, but are appealing for anyone who thinks they might have seen anything to come forward.

I closed the attachment and opened up the second one.

MILE END VICTIMS NAMED

03/03/04—Three gunshot victims, killed on Friday at a pub in Mile End, London, have been named.

Brasov gang members Drakan Mihilovich, 42, his brother Saska Mihilovich, 35, and Susan Grant, 22, were all murdered when two gunmen walked into a pub on Bow Road and opened fire on them.

The Mihilovich brothers are widely thought to be responsible for the recent murder of Adriana Drovov, wife of George Drovov, a leading member of Brasov rivals, Cernoziom. The third victim, Susan Grant, was reported to be Saska's girlfriend.

Four others were injured during the shooting. Two are described as being in a critical condition.

I went to the next story.

MILE END VICTIM FOUND DEAD

03/07/04—In a bizarre twist, a woman injured in the so-called "Mile End Murders" on 1 March has been found brutally murdered at home.

Jade O'Connell, 31, thought to be an innocent victim of a violent gang war in the Tower Hamlets area, was only released from hospital on March 5, after suffering cuts and bruising during the shooting. Neighbors discovered O'Connell's front door open, and her body inside. Her skull had been crushed, and her teeth and hands had been removed—"to make identification harder," according to investigators—injuries that are consistent with victims previously targeted by Romanian gang, Cernoziom.

"This is one of the most sickening crimes I've ever seen," Detective Chief Inspector Jamie Hart, the officer leading the hunt for the killer, said yesterday.

Ms. O'Connell had no surviving relatives.

At the bottom, Ethan had added something else: *P. S. I was covering Home Affairs at the time, so I remember this story. Cernoziom are vicious bastards: the removal of the teeth and hands like that—it's part of their ritual. They see it as "cleansing," like some kind of symbolic act. Everyone knew it was them, even though— officially—the police could never find out who killed her.*

Except she hadn't been killed.

Someone else had.

Jade was supposed to have been murdered in 2004, and yet—until yesterday—she was walking around, living and breathing.

But it was a lie.

Everything was a lie.

Or, perhaps, everything except Mary's account of having passed Alex in the street. Because the longer I spent looking for him, the more I started to wonder if her memory of that day might be the only true thing I could hold on to.

27

Gerald, Jade's fake ID contact, lived on the third floor of a dilapidated four-story townhouse in Camberwell. The police still had my BMW, so I hired a rental car and headed south of the river, finding a space opposite the front of the building.

I switched off the engine and waited, watching a cat trying to get into the middle of a big pile of bin liners, the contents spilling out across the dirty snow.

Ten minutes. Twenty.

Thirty.

Forty minutes later, an opportunity arrived.

A woman was walking toward the house, digging around in her handbag for keys. I got out, set the alarm on my car, and crossed the road, catching the door just as it was about to close behind her. She eyed me for a second, but then seemed to lose interest, and headed off into the belly of the building. When she was gone from view, I pushed the door shut behind me, and started heading up.

The building smelled old and musty, but not unpleasant, and on the third floor, I found two doors, one facing the other. Gerald lived in the one to my right.

I knocked a couple of times.

After a brief pause: "What?"

A voice from inside the flat.

"Gerald?"

"What?"

"I need to speak to you."

"Who are you?"

"My name's David. I'm a friend of Jade's."

"Who's Jade?"

"Jade, Melissa—whatever you prefer."

A thud. His feet hit the floor on the other side of the door. He was looking through the spyhole at me. I looked back, into the eye of it. A moment's silence, and then the door creaked slowly out from the frame. He had it on the chain.

"How you doing, Gerald?"

He was forty, pale and fat, his brown hair disappearing fast. He looked like he hadn't seen daylight since he was a teenager. His eyes moved past me, out into the hallway. "How did you get inside?" he said in a sharp south London accent.

"Someone let me in."

He looked me up and down. "What d'you want?"

"I need to talk to you."

"About what?"

"About some IDs."

"Keep your fuckin' voice down."

"How about it?"

"I don't know what you're talkin' about."

I smiled. "Of course you don't."

He eyed me again, then closed the door. I listened to the chain fall from its runner and swing against the door. When he opened up again he waved me in.

The flat was a mess. Clothes strewn across the back of chairs and sofas; packets of crisps and burger cartons dumped on the floor. Curtains had been pulled most of the way across the only window I could see, leaving a sliver of a view across the street. On one wall was a painting. On the others were shelves full of books and equipment. Toward the back of the room was a guillotine, rolls of laminate and a pile of large silver tins containing different colored inks.

"Welcome to the penthouse," he said.

He picked up a couple of sweaters and a pair of trousers and tossed them through the door to the bedroom.

"I need something from you," I said. I reached into my pocket and took out a roll of banknotes. "A little help."

"Help?"

"A few names."

He raised an eyebrow. "What are you, the Old Bill?"

"No."

"My snitchin' days are over, mate."

"I'm not a cop. I'm a friend of Jade's."

"Bollocks you are."

I held up the banknotes. There was two hundred in the roll. "How much to lose your newly developed conscience?"

He looked at the money. "How much you got?"

"Two hundred," I said.

He nodded. "That's a start."

I deliberately didn't say anything else. Two hundred was as much as I had on me, and I wasn't about to leave and come back. I stepped toward him, and for the first time I could feel the kitchen knife tucked into the back of my trousers.

"Jade told me you provided her and her friends with IDs," I said. "I want to know who you spoke to, who came here. Specifically, if you're sending IDs out, I need to know where they're going. You tell me that and I give you this money."

He looked at the two hundred, then at my pockets, where I presumed he thought I might be keeping some more. "Okay," he said eventually.

"Did you only deal with Jade?"

"Mostly her."

"What does 'mostly' mean?"

"Her, yeah."

"She came to pick up IDs for herself?"

"No," he mumbled. "Some others too."

"Speak up."

"Some others too."

"Who else's?"

"I don't know. She never told me. I don't work for her, or whatever the hell she's a part of. I work for myself. I'm independent. She just gives me the photographs, and the names and addresses she wants on the IDs, and I make them for her."

"You make IDs for the same people every time?"

"Yeah, mostly."

"You keep any records of their real names?"

He laughed. "Oh, yeah. I keep a record of all of them, so when the pigs raid me I can make it easy for them. Of course I don't keep a list of fuckin' names."

"Did Jade ever tell you who she worked for?"

"No."

"She ever mention a guy called Alex?"

"How the fuck am I supposed to remember?"

I pushed on. "How many IDs did Jade pick up?"

"In four years?"

"You've been doing this for her for four years?"

"Yeah."

"How many?"

"Fifty. Maybe more."

"When does she come round?"

"Whenever she needs something."

"She doesn't have particular days?"

"No."

"When was the last time she came around?"

"I dunno. Week ago maybe."

I processed what he was telling me. *A week ago.* "So that means that you're doing IDs for them at the moment?"

"Yeah."

"For delivery when?"

"Friday."

"Day after tomorrow?"

"Congratulations, you know the days of the week."

"Is Jade supposed to be picking them up?"

"Not any more."

I stopped. "Do you know why?"

He looked at me, shrugged. "No. Someone just called this morning."

"And said what?"

"That I'd have a new contact. Some guy called Michael."

I nodded. "How many IDs are you doing for this new guy?"

"Five."

I fished around in my pocket for the photo of Alex and held it up. "You recognize him?"

"I can't see."

"So take a closer look."

He shuffled forward and squinted at the photograph. "No."

"His wasn't one of the IDs you're doing?"

"No."

"You ever done an ID for him?"

"Dunno."

"Be more specific."

"I dunno. Don't remember if I have or haven't."

"You better not be lying to me, Gerald."

"I ain't lyin'."

He looked like he was telling the truth. He was staring straight at me, barely flinching as he spoke. "How long does it take you to make up these IDs?"

"Depends."

"On what?"

"On what it is. If it's a driver's license, I can do it in a few hours. A passport takes longer. You gotta get the marks right, everything in the right place."

"They ever ask for passports?"

"No."

"Do you ever source anything else for them?"

A shrug. "A few guns."

He studied me, watching my face for any reaction to the mention of guns. I just nodded and stepped closer. "Do they come and collect their stuff from here?"

"No. I drop 'em off."

"Where?"

"It changes every time."

"So where are you dropping them *this* time?"

"A deposit box."

"In?"

He held up both hands and walked through to the bedroom. While he was in there, I reached around to the back of my trousers and repositioned the knife so I could get at it more easily. A minute later, he came back out, a piece of paper in his hands, and held it out to me. I took it from him and glanced at the address.

It was in Paddington, close to the station.

I slid it into my back pocket. "Did he give you a drop-off time?"

"He said he'd be leaving his place at 6 p.m. on Friday," Gerald replied. "He said I needed to make sure they're dropped off at the box before then."

28

At ten-thirty, I stepped out of the shadows, and made my way around to the back of St. John the Baptist church. The main building was alarmed. I could see a box high up next to the crucifix, winking on and off—but there was no alarm on the outbuilding. They wouldn't have had the chance to wire it up yet.

There were two locks requiring two different keys, but the flimsy wooden door meant that it could only ever act as token security. I'd brought a crowbar from the car, so slid it into the door jamb, and began prizing away at an opening. Some of the door split straight away, coming off in thin strips. I kicked them out of the way, and took a quick look around me, then started levering some more.

It was freezing cold—colder than at any point in the past few days—and my hands numbed quickly, but the more I could feel the door giving way, the less aware I was of the temperature. Eventually, a whole panel started to come loose, falling away like a sheet, and with a sharp tug I managed to tear it off completely.

It landed in the snow with a thud.

I waved a hand inside the outbuilding, double-checking for an alarm that I might have missed, but the place remained silent, so I reached inside, flipped the lock on the handle and pulled what was left of the door open.

Removing a penlight, I went for the desk first.

There were three drawers. I put the penlight between my teeth and started digging around inside. Pens, some envelopes, a church newsletter—nothing of any interest. The second drawer was empty. In the third were four empty files.

Beside that were the crates.

I stopped for a moment, checking outside for any sign of life. The weather would help me: snow would crunch under foot, signaling any approach—but, as I was in the middle of an illegal act of breaking and entering, I wanted to be sure.

Satisfied, I turned back to the first crate and flipped the top off it. It was a mess, crammed with books, magazines, and folders full of notes and photos.

I picked up the photos.

Michael Tilton was in all of them: with his mum and dad; with what could have been a girlfriend or a sister; with some friends at a twenty-first birthday party. One was taken at a service, him high up in the pulpit, one hand on a Bible. Right at the bottom, half sliding out of a separate, faded envelope, was another picture: a boy running around on a patch of grass, chasing a football.

Jade had the same photograph.

I flipped it over. Written on the back was exactly the same message as had been written on hers: *This is the reason we do it.*

Placing the photos back in on top of the books, I pulled the top crate off the one below. It landed on the floor with a thud. Inside, it was more of the same.

But then I found an address book.

I opened it up, every page full of names and addresses. Most were local— Redbridge, Aldersbrook, Leytonstone, Woodford, Clayhall—but others were further afield, in Manchester and Birmingham. I flicked through from beginning to end, stopping briefly under each letter to see whether I recognized any names.

I didn't.

Until I got to Z.

Right at the back of the book I found an entry for a "Zack." I got out my notes and flipped back through to the names I'd collected from the flat in Brixton. Using the nib of a pencil, I'd managed to bring old, missing pages of their notebook to life, and had found three names.

Paul. Stephen.

Zack.

The listing for him didn't have a surname, only an address—for a house somewhere in Bristol. Coming off his name and the address was a separate line.

It led to yet another name.

This one I recognized too.

It said *Alex.*

29

It took three hours to get to Bristol. By the time I came off the motor-way, it was two o'clock in the morning and I needed rest desperately. I drove for a while, heading deeper and deeper into the deserted city, until I found a dark spot next to a railway yard. I backed in, under a bridge, and kept the heat on for an hour, the stark reality of my situation hitting home: a man had come into my home, in the middle of the night, to kill me. They were hunting me. I was a fugitive; on the run. I was out of options.

All I could do was fight back.

All I could do was try and make it out alive.

I woke suddenly.

It was light, almost midday, fresh snow on the ground, and on the hood and windows of the car. For a moment I felt disorientated, unsure of where I was, pulled too quickly from sleep and chilled to the bone. When instinct started to kick in, I suddenly became panicked, looking out into the spaces beyond the car for faces I didn't recognize. But there was no one around. Once I settled, once the heaters were on again, I put the car into gear and headed out into the morning.

The address was for a house in St. Philips.

It was a street full of gray, pebble-dashed terraced houses, bordered by the former foundations of a factory, now just a swathe of broken concrete, riddled with weeds. I did a circuit in the car, along the road, into an adjoining one, and then back down past the house. The curtains were drawn, with no sign of life.

Parking within view of the house, I waited, low in my seat.

After a couple of minutes a bus wheezed to a stop at the end of the road. An old couple got off. Behind them, a mother and her children, huddled together, their jackets zipped up to their chins. The family veered off left, into a road about halfway down, but the old couple continued down the street toward me, breath gathered above their heads. When they got to my car, they looked in, eyeing me.

Another ten minutes passed.

A second bus pulled up, and then a third. More people got off—young families and pensioners mostly—all disappearing into houses on the street, or passing the car and moving on somewhere else. Once it got quiet again, I fired up the engine and turned up the heaters. The temperature readout said it was −2°C.

About thirty minutes later, an Astra entered the street from behind me. I watched it approach in the rear-view mirror, pass my car, brake, and then start reversing into the space in front of me. It bumped up on to the pavement and then off again, stopping about a foot from the front of my hire car. A woman moved around inside, the hood up on her jacket. She glanced in her rear-view mirror, picked something up, and then got out. She was carrying a shopping bag and her keys.

Wind carved up the road, fierce, unflinching, and tendrils of hair escaped from the woman's hood, whipping around her face. She pushed the door shut with her backside, trying to juggle her shopping bag, and on the keyring I could see a silver crucifix, dangling down, brushing against the side of the door.

A crucifix.

I sat up, suddenly interested in her as she headed up the street. Her hood ballooned out as the wind came again, even stronger this time, forcing her into a side-step. Momentarily, she lost her balance, her foot drifting away from the edge of the pavement into the road—and, as she did, the shopping bag dropped from her grasp. It hit the ground hard, fruit scattering everywhere: apples, grapes, pears.

She bent down and started picking them up.

When the wind came a third time, swaying her, she put a hand flat to the ground to balance herself and her hood whipped back off her head, a tangled mop of black hair revealing itself. This time she paused and stopped picking up the fruit, half-glancing in my direction. There was something in her expression, a sudden nervousness, and as she began grabbing hold of the fruit again, more of it rolled away, spilling out of the bag a second time, or dropping from her grasp entirely.

Then something strange happened.

She stood up—and she walked away.

She left the fruit rolling around in the gutter, the shopping bag too, half its contents lying in the middle of the slush-soaked street. As she started searching through her keys, she quickened her pace, almost jogging away from me now.

I inched open my door, cold air rushing in.

And then she reached her house.

It was the one I'd been watching.

I got out of the car, and started heading down the street toward her. She clocked the movement instantly, but didn't tilt her head in my direction. Instead, her eyes swiveled to meet mine, as if trying to disguise the angle of her gaze.

All of a sudden, I felt a jolt.

Wait a second.

I recognize her.

Her hair was a different color, longer and more unruly. Her face was pale and serious—older, more weathered. And her nose looked different: it was more tapered, thinned out, as if she'd had work done on it. Before, when I'd seen her serving behind the bar in Angel's, it had been wider, less shapely. But it was definitely her. It was the same woman I'd seen in photographs on the wall of the pub.

It was Evelyn.

As I got closer, her movements became frantic.

"Evelyn?"

She couldn't unlock the door.

"Evelyn?"

From behind me I heard a voice, distant at first, then louder. I looked back and saw a black guy coming toward me, shouting, "Oi! You can't park here!"

I ignored him.

When I turned back, Evelyn had opened the door, and was heading inside. It was on a slow spring, creaking as it swung back in slow-motion. I made a dart for it, and managed to catch it just as it was about to connect again with the jamb.

I looked into the hallway.

It was half-lit and dark, warmth spilling out onto the front step. I couldn't see Evelyn now, and started to hesitate, tension swirling around in my guts. But then I heard a creak on the stairs to my right and I realized I wanted an answer.

I had to know what was going on.

So I headed inside.

30

She had disappeared upstairs.

I went after her, taking two steps at a time, and heard a series of creaks on the landing, more movement, and then a thud. At the top, there were three doors.

One of them was closed.

"Evelyn?"

No response.

I tried the handle: locked.

"Evelyn," I said. "It's okay." I placed a hand on the door. "It's David Raker. I know you saw me out there. I know you remember me. All I want to do is talk."

From inside: the sound of a window sliding along its runners. I tried the door a second time and realized, this time, that it wasn't locked— something had just been wedged under the handle. With a shove, I managed to get it far enough open to see her leaning half-in, half-out of the window, one foot on a snowy roof, one on the floor of the bathroom.

"Evelyn," I said softly. "I just want to talk."

She looked at me once, then swung herself through the window and out onto the roof. Beyond it, I could see a narrow alleyway running parallel to the street I'd parked on. She slid, arms outstretched either side of her, trying to take careful steps but failing on the ice and snow—and then she jumped off, disappearing out of sight. For a moment, I couldn't see her, only hear her: the thump as she landed in the alleyway; a splash; gravel kicking up—and then the sound of her running.

I headed back downstairs.

The front door was still open, but doors on my left and right were closed. *Had they been like this when I'd come in?* Unsure, I found myself drawn deeper into the place, reminded of the flat in Brixton: the plain walls, probably only painted once; no carpets on the floor, only the original boards. Along the hall I could see a kitchen, plain and unremarkable, a rear door opening out onto a small garden full of rubble, broken outdoor furniture, and thick, twisted weeds.

"*Uuhhh . . .*"

I stopped.

What the hell was that?

As I processed the sound, I began to realize it had come from the door on my left—and I started to be able to smell something too. Swallowing, I glanced back along the hallway to the front door. Snow powder blew in from windowsills and scattered across the carpet. There was no one outside, Evelyn was gone, the house was quiet, all the doors shut—and, yet, I still couldn't shake the sensation.

It felt like I was being watched.

The left hand door opened in to a living room. No television, no DVD, just a few books scattered across the floor and a blanket in the corner. There was one window, the curtains pulled, and a small archway leading to an adjacent room.

I looked through to it.

From where I was standing, I could see the edge of a leather sofa. Someone was lying on it.

I inched forward.

I could see the head, the chest.

An arm.

This time I stopped. The arm was locked in place, hanging off the side of the sofa, the knuckles brushing the floorboards. Inches from the fingers was a needle. It had rolled away, out of reach. Some of the liquid had escaped, pooling on the floorboards next to an ashtray over-run with cigarettes.

It was a man—a boy, really.

His trousers were wet, a dark patch flowering from his groin and tracing the inside of one leg. At the end of the sofa was a bucket, half full of vomit. It was the smell I'd picked up in the hallway, except here it was totally overpowering.

I covered my face with my sleeve.

He couldn't have been older than eighteen, but his arms were dotted with track marks, veins puffy and enlarged, visible like a road map through the skin. He was as white as the snow outside, his eyes half-closed, dull yellow patches smeared below his eyelashes like badly applied makeup.

The sound of a door closing.

I looked back through the arch. From where I was, I could see the kitchen, the light shifting, shadows changing, as someone approached it.

A second later, he appeared.

It was the black guy who had shouted after me in the street.

He was in his early thirties, five-ten, but wide: muscles moved beneath the skin at his neck and shoulders, and a vein wormed its way out from the corner of one eye, up onto his shaved head. He was looking out through the kitchen door at the garden, his breath steaming up the glass.

I looked back at the kid on the sofa.

His eyes were closed, but his jaw had dropped open, his tongue slipping out, over his lips, almost slapping against them. He seemed to be struggling with it, like it was too big for his mouth, choking sounds juddering in his throat. As he rolled further in my direction, I realized something else: his gums were bleeding.

But it was worse than that.

Much worse.

Because his teeth had been removed too.

Reeling, I moved quickly, back through the arch, into the living room. The guy in the kitchen was still looking out at the garden, distracted, distant. Quietly, I moved behind him and along the hallway, checking behind me. He was starting to turn now, as if he'd heard me. I upped my pace, reaching for the front door.

But then it opened in at me.

Evelyn stepped in, her cheeks flushed, anger streaked across her face. A split second later, she brought her hand up from her side. She was holding a gun.

The barrel drifted across my face and I instinctively stumbled back, my hands coming up to protect me. She walked toward me, the gun out in front of her. I hit a wall, and stopped, looking along the body of the weapon. It was new, in beautiful condition, as if it had never been fired.

I held up both hands. "Evelyn, wait a second . . ."

She stopped about two feet from me. The gun was level with one of my eyes, incredibly still. "What are you doing, David?"

I didn't speak. I had a horrible feeling she would fire as soon as I did, even though she'd asked me in a gentle, almost admiring way; even though I'd known her since before Derryn died, talked with her, laughed with her, shared with her.

"What are you *doing?*" she said again.

I didn't move.

"You should have left us alone," she said.

She moved toward me again—my body tensing, my head automatically lowering, angling away from the gun. But then I felt the weapon at the back of my neck, and realized Evelyn was still in front of me. She'd handed the gun across.

"You should have left us alone," she said again.

"I don't want you, Evelyn. I don't want this."

She didn't say anything. I turned slightly, and could see the guy from the kitchen, the weapon in his hand, his finger at the trigger.

"I just want Alex."

"Alex doesn't—"

"That's enough, Vee," the man said.

Vee.

Vee was what they called Evelyn.

Before I had a chance to react, in words, in actions, I felt the gun smash into the side of my face, close to the temple.

I staggered sideways and hit the wall.

And then I blacked out.

31

I opened my eyes.

The first thing I saw was the crumbling skeleton of a red brick building. It was what remained of the factory that I had seen earlier, when I'd first parked up. I was on its foundations, surrounded by a tangled web of weeds and overgrowth. To my right, I could see the street the house had been on: it was about a hundred and fifty feet away, the row of terraced homes reduced to windows of pale light.

They'd gagged me.

I was on an old wooden chair. When I moved, I could feel my hands had been bound, and I'd lost most of the sensation in my feet. I looked down. I had my jeans and T-shirt on, but they'd removed my coat and taken my shoes and socks. I was sitting barefoot, my soles flat to the floor, toes embedded in snow. The cold was making my bones ache.

I listened.

I could make out cars passing on the street, the distant sounds of the city beyond that. To my left and in front of me, there was nothing: no sound, no view. It was just an endless concrete base, rolling off into the darkness of the evening.

That was the point.

No one came here.

No one would find me.

A moment later, I heard movement—birds flapping their wings, arcing up to my left and into the night sky—and then, fading in, the sound of footsteps. Rubble scattering, the crunch of snow. Someone was approaching out of sight.

I waited, shivering, my whole body throbbing.

And then I could smell something: saccharine, like boiled sweets. A wind picked up, carrying the odor in again, and when it died away, I became aware of another change: warm air, close to my ear. What *was* that?

Then I realized.

Someone's breathing on me.

I flinched, angling my body as far to the other side as I could go, and there was the sound of a retreat: footsteps fading off and then disappearing entirely.

Silence.

I thought about screaming through the gag, about making as much noise as I could, but I was too far away from the street for anyone to hear me, and it was obvious it would make no difference anyway: why leave me out here if it put them at risk?

More wind, louder and colder.

"Evelyn?"

The gag muffled my voice, reducing it to a series of animal sounds, and as I tried to lift my feet up out of the snow, to find some respite from the cold, I felt it again: breath at my ear. This time I stayed still, even though it was harder: they were so close to my ear now, I could feel their nose glancing the ridge of my jaw.

It's a game to them.

I jabbed my head sideways.

A sharp, painful impact—and then the sound of footsteps staggering back, crunching against snow. I started to turn my head, despite pain needling behind my eyes, but then I heard them come forward again—closing the space—and a hand grabbed me under the chin, the thumb digging in against my cheek.

"Don't do that again."

A man.

He let go of my face and pushed my head forward so my chin touched my chest, holding it there. I could see blood running off my face, into the snow.

"Stay like that," he said. "And close your eyes."

He cleared his throat, and then there were more footsteps in the snow, crunching, fading away, and coming back again. He'd been to collect something.

I moved my head, discomfort forcing me to lift it up, and felt his hand spread across the back of my skull and a gun slide in under my chin.

"What did I say to you?"

"I can't hold it there," I tried to say to him through the gag.

"Move again and I'll put a bullet through your brain."

I stayed still, trying to come up with some sort of plan. But I was finding it difficult to concentrate. It was the pain in my face—but mostly it was the cold.

"I'm going to remove the gag," he said, "but if you make any sound louder than a whisper, my people will be picking bits of your face up off the floor for a week." He paused and, in the silence, a thought came to me: *I recognize his voice.*

Was it the man with the tattoos?

"You listening to me?"

I nodded, letting him know that I understood, and as he removed the gag, something else registered: . . . *my people will be picking bits of your face up . . .*

My people. He was in charge.

He tossed the gag past me, and it landed in the snow a couple of feet in front of me. As he leaned in again, I picked up the same scent as before: sweet, sugary. "I'm going to ask you some questions," he said, barely a whisper now, "and you're going to tell me the truth. Hold anything back, and I'll rip out your throat."

I could feel him at my ear again.

"What are you doing here?"

"Alex," I said quietly.

"Oh, I see." A dismissive grunt. "I'm sure during your cozy little chat with Jade, she must have warned you off this . . . I'm not sure what you would call it. A quest? A mission?" He spat out the words like they tasted sour in his mouth, and I could feel flecks of saliva on the side of my face. "You going to answer me, David?"

I shrugged.

"A shrug? That's all I get?"

Again, I didn't respond.

"What did Jade say to you?"

"Nothing."

He sighed. "Don't lie to me."

"I'm not."

I was absolutely chilled now—I couldn't feel my arms, my hands, my feet—and I was finding it hard to stay focused. When he shoved the gun in against my jaw, I barely reacted: not because I wasn't alarmed, but because I was drifting off.

"Are you awake?"

"I'm cold."

A snort of derision. "*Listen* to me, David: you'd better start dancing with me, or I guarantee I'll be putting you in the ground next to your wife."

They knew all about me.

They knew my name.

They knew about Derryn.

"Jade told me I was in danger," I said.

"Well, she was right. Do you know why?"

I nodded. "Alex."

"Oh, *please*. You think this is all to do with him?"

I shrugged.

"Don't shrug at me."

"I don't know."

"Well, at least you have the humility to admit that." A pause. "I'm guessing that little mess at the church was yours. Breaking and entering is a crime, David."

"What the hell do you call this?"

The man laughed. "The difference is, you don't know who I am. I know who you are. I know all about you." He pressed the gun in against my cheek, and I could feel the outline of the muzzle. "Was the address for the church in that box?"

The box.

He was talking about the box Kathy had directed me to; the box with the birthday card and the Polaroid in it. He'd seen me with it that night at the pub.

"David."

"Yes."

"The address for the church was in the box?"

"On the back of a birthday card."

"What else was in there?"

I thought of the picture I'd given to Cary. "Nothing. Just photos."

"Just photos?"

I nodded.

"Don't lie to me."

"I'm not."

His hand dropped away, the gun with it. "I know about you, David," he said. "I know about your background, where you come from, what you do. It's my job to know all of that, because it's my job to ensure people like you don't fuck up what I've built. And you know what? Reading about you made me wonder: this quest, mission, whatever it is, is it about the kid— or is it about your wife?"

I looked up, turned, and he held up a hand, grabbing the side of my face and forcing it back down. He pushed me further this time, until my head was past the level of my knees; until I was almost doubled over. Bile burned in my throat.

"You're a big man, David," he said, "but your wife's death makes you easy to control. When people die, it hurts. It sucks you dry. You feel so hollow inside, you wonder if you're ever going to be normal again. But you've got to let them go—they're not coming back. Your wife, the kid you're trying to find, they're gone."

"If he was gone, I wouldn't be here," I said.

He placed his spare hand on the crown of my head, fingers spreading, and then paused. For a moment, I wondered what he was going to do—but then, in a flash, he'd whipped the butt of the gun around and struck me hard on the chin.

The chair rocked on the concrete.

I started to drift again, in and out of consciousness.

"What else do you know?" he said.

I twitched, trying to roll my chin.

"What else?" he said again.

"You recruit people."

"Is that what Jade told you?"

I nodded.

"What do you mean, 'recruit'?"

"I don't know."

"Are you lying to me again, David?"

"No."

"Okay. What else?"

"Some of you are supposed to be dead." I paused, tasting blood in my mouth, waiting for a comeback. But he didn't say anything—just pushed down on my neck again, indicating he wanted me to continue. "You've got a flat registered to a company that doesn't exist, and a pub you're using as a way to make money. A front, full of your people, who rotate when questions start getting asked. When a hole starts to appear, you shift them somewhere else and the hole closes up."

"What else?"

"That's all I know."

"Bullshit. What else?"

I stopped, tried to think.

"What else?"

He thought I knew more than I did, and—as I tried to form a plan—I realized I could play on that. Maybe it would be the only way out: pretend I knew more than I did and he'd have to find out what; see how far I'd dug my way in.

"You think whatever you're doing is a mission from God."

He released his grip ever so slightly, and leaned in closer to my ear. "What did you say?"

"You think it's a mission from God."

I felt him shift his weight.

He stepped away, the gun going with it—and then I heard a series of beeps. *What's that?* Seconds later, I found out: he was using a phone.

"Zack, it's me. You can take him now."

Silence.

"And make sure you bury him where no one will find him."

32

I spent an hour rolling from side to side in the boot of a car, and then—finally—we came to a stop. As the engine silenced, I felt dread curdling in my stomach.

Bury him where no one will find him.

My wrists were bound behind me, my ankles too, and my top, my coat, my socks and shoes, had all been left behind. All I had were my jeans and a T-shirt.

The boot opened.

Before I had a chance to try and place where we were, the black guy from the house reached in and pulled me out. As soon as I was standing, he shoved me hard against the side of their car—the Astra that Evelyn had been driving—and spun me around, so I was facing away from him. Then he cut the binds at my ankles.

I looked around me.

We were on a mud track, black and sodden, trees looming overhead on both sides. It was deathly quiet. We must have been miles from the nearest road.

Behind me, the passenger door opened and closed, and from my left came a second man: Jason, the guy I'd chased at the apartment in Eagle Heights. He moved around to the front of the car, a gun in one hand, a torch in the other, and zipped his coat up to his chin. A half-smile broke out on his face as he looked at me, as if he'd figured out what I was thinking: *They're going to kill me out here.*

And no one's ever going to find my body.

"You don't have to do this," I said to them.

Jason pushed me forward, away from the car.

"Why are you doing this?"

He pushed me forward again. "Walk."

I started moving, staring along the track.

As I looked at the forest on either side of me, full of snow and dead leaves, full of disturbed earth, an image came back to me of Derryn standing next to her grave, looking down into the darkness herself. How had she felt in that moment?

Did she tell me the truth?

Or did she lie to protect me?

My thoughts shattered as I felt a hand on my shoulder, pushing me to the right, in beyond the treeline. Jason's hand clamped on to my bicep, tightening as we started the ascent through gently sloping ground. Snow was everywhere—in the branches, on the forest floor. I looked at him. "Why do you have to do this?"

"Shut up."

Behind him the guy from the house was scanning the woodland. His torch was sweeping from side to side, illuminating a dense clutch of trees to his right.

"Jason," he said from behind me. "Wait a sec."

Jason told me to stop, and then looked back at his partner. Further up the slope, deeper into the forest, moonlight carved down through irregular gaps in the canopy, forming pale tubes of light. Where it couldn't penetrate the foliage, the woods were as black as oil. Between my toes I could feel grass poking through the snow and hard, uneven ground that you could break an ankle running across.

I looked back.

Jason was closer to the other guy now, whispering. It was incredibly still; so still their whispers carried across the night: "You know what he told us to do."

The black guy didn't reply.

"He said take him to the usual spot."

"This is a better spot."

"Come on, Zack. Let's just do what he said."

Zack.

"This is a better spot," Zack said again.

"It's right on the fucking road."

"Look how dense it is here."

"Who gives a shit?" Jason said, his voice rising.

Then he quieted as Zack stared him down. Zack was the senior partner, clearly. Jason nodded his apology and leaned in closer. "All I'm saying is, I don't really wanna piss him off. He told us to take him up to the top and do it there."

"I know what he said."

"That's where we put the others."

The others.

There were more like me; more that had got too close. My heart gripped in my chest and I felt my stomach contract. Subtly, I tried to wriggle free of the duct tape at my wrists, but the movement registered with Zack, and he looked over.

Run.

My face burned, even in the cold.

You have to run.

I glanced up the slope, then back to them. They were still talking. Jason was gripping the gun tightly, his finger moving at the trigger. Zack glanced at me, eyes narrowing, as if he sensed I might be on the cusp of doing something stupid.

Run.

I felt the binds at my wrist again. How the hell was I going to run with my hands tied behind my back? I scanned the woodland in front of me again, and more doubts kicked in. *They know the terrain. They know the path. They know where to force me to go, and where to head me off.* But then I started to think of the alternative: the two of them leading me through a maze of trees to a dumping ground full of skeletons. Making me beg for my life. Putting a bullet in my chest.

Watching me die in the snow.

Do it now.

I looked back once—right into Zack's eyes.

And then I made a break for it.

I almost fell before I'd even started, my toes grazing a tree stump. But then I was away, pushing through the darkness, heading up the snow-covered slope.

"Hey!"

Zack's voice.

It echoed after me, suppressed by the canopy of the trees, bouncing off the bark. My feet slid on the snow, my gait unbalanced by my hands still being at my back, but—as I gained more speed—I heard the sound of them starting to panic.

"I'll take the road," Zack said.

Something punctured the underside of my foot—a stone, maybe a sliver of glass—but I didn't stop. I tried to make my strides as long as possible, tried to swallow up as much ground as I could. Huge trees lurched out of the night, almost knocking me off balance, and as I arced further right, deeper into the forest, I finally stole a look behind me: Jason was about forty feet further down.

Our eyes met.

He lifted the gun, ready to fire, and then lost his footing, adjusting himself almost instantly. He was quick and fit, used to running. I knew that from before.

He was probably closing on me already.

I passed through one pool of light, and headed for the next. As I did, I tried to up the pace, every bone in my body aching, every nerve prickling, and saw that the foliage thickened about twenty feet ahead. It got dense quickly, most of it hidden from the moonlight. *I'll get caught in there*, I thought, but—as I looked behind me again; Jason close, but partially disguised from view—I knew I didn't have time to back out. Bracing myself, I ducked and headed inside the knot of branches.

Thorns scratched my skin, snow flecked against my face, and the darkness seemed to close in. I moved through the foliage as fast as I could, big branches clawing at me, weeds and vines grabbing at my feet. Beyond the noise of the branches cracking and splintering against me, I expected to hear Jason following me—but there was nothing. He wasn't following me. He'd gone a different route.

I stopped, dropping to the ground.

Something cracked to my right, as I faced up the hill. I turned, narrowing my eyes, willing myself to see into the darkness. They'd both had torches—but they'd both switched them off. There was no light close to me now—and I realized, in some ways, that this was worse. They knew this area. They knew the hiding places, the holes. They could be right on top of me and I wouldn't even see them.

I leaned back, slowly, searching the ground behind me for anything I could cut through the binds with. Just off to my left was a thorn bush. I pressed myself against it, shredding the skin on my lower arms, and felt the pop of the duct tape as the bush's spikes punctured it. The ground beneath my fingers was covered in a layer of snow, hard and crystallized. As I concentrated on my wrists, I started to notice the pain in my feet: it felt like there were cuts on the arches of both, and the ankle on the right felt a little tender. A light sprain, almost certainly bruised.

I felt the duct tape shift.

I'd loosened it.

Pushing my wrists away from one another, in opposite directions, I felt the binds start to give—and then they popped free. I ripped them away and dropped them to the ground, looking out into the dark around

me. Thorns were embedded in my skin, and blood trails ran from cuts
on both arms. I went to wipe them away.

And then stopped.

Over on my right, I saw a flash of color: pale blue—the color of Jason's
jacket—catching in the moonlight. I waited, watched. Another flash of
blue. My heart was banging so hard against my ribs, it was hard to concentrate. I saw him a moment later, lithe and quick—no crunch of snow,
every footstep landing where it was supposed to. More blood ran from my
arms, and then a trail broke from my hairline, over the bridge of my nose,
down to the corner of my mouth.

I didn't move.

Didn't wipe it away.

He was about ten feet to my right now, up the slope from me, coming
around the edges of the area I was in. His jacket was a bad idea. If he'd
taken it off, he could have been standing next to me and I wouldn't have
even seen him. Instead, the jacket reflected back what little light there was.
He turned where he was, then swung back round in my direction, the gun
out in front of him, and stared straight at me. I gazed back, looking at him,
frozen, conscious of moving. But then his head swiveled—facing further
up the slope—and he took a step up.

The higher up he went, the more obvious my escape route became:
down the slope, back toward the track. Except I didn't know where the
hell Zack was.

He said he was going to take the road, so presumably it wrapped
around the forest, and came back again at the top in a rough semi-circle.
But I didn't know how close the road was. It could be a way off. Perhaps
if I waited for Jason to disappear up the slope, and then ran, Zack would
be even further behind me.

Or maybe the road was so close to me here that, when I got up and
made a run for it, they'd both see me instantly and put a bullet in my
back. Either way, whether Zack was close or not, I'd still be running
blind. The best I could hope for would be to get back to the car and head
down the track the way we'd come in.

Eventually it would lead somewhere.

Jason continued to climb. He was about fifteen feet up, at a diagonal
from me, but slowly coming back around in my direction. He stopped,
looking down the slope again. Then, out of nowhere, something flashed—
a blue light—and I saw him take a mobile phone out. He had it on silent.

He looked at the screen, then back toward my spot. *They're communicating by text now.* I glanced back in the other direction. Had Zack spotted me? Was he telling Jason where I was?

Jason's eyes were fixed on my position now, the gun in one hand, the phone in the other. I held my breath as he took a step closer, and then another.

He can see me.

He edged even closer, padding across the snow and the leaves, until he was about three feet from me, looking across the tangle of bushes I was hiding in.

The gun drifted across my face.

He gazed across the top of my head, his eyes fixed on something beyond, and then raised a hand and pointed at himself. *Zack.* He was signaling to him.

Jason was in front of me, up the slope.

Zack was behind, below.

I was surrounded.

Jason scanned the forest, left, right, into the darkness of what was around him. He didn't move, just stood there, listening to the sounds: the movement of the leaves, the creaking of the earth, the faint drip, drip, drip of water. A thought came back to me then of my dad, standing in the middle of the woods close to the farm, doing exactly the same thing. He'd been an amateur tracker. He'd listened to the noises, took in the smells, knew what footprint belonged to what animal.

But Jason was the real thing.

I could see that, instantly.

He knew enough to separate the sounds of nature from the sounds of what had encroached upon it. He knew I was close by. I couldn't have got clear of him in the time available to me. He knew that. Now it was a question of finding me.

Do something.

Slowly, I guided my hand to the ground and felt around again, my palm flat to the ground. There was nothing: just frozen mud and hard snow. Jason took a step forward. I reached further out into the undergrowth, and my fingers brushed something. *Rocks.* There was a pile of them but only a couple felt big enough. One was larger than the other. I picked it up and brought it into me, then did the same with the second. My sleeve brushed against a branch, but the sound didn't carry.

I wrapped my hand around the smaller one.

Wait.

Wait.

Slowly, I opened up my body and tossed the stone as hard and as far as I could to my left. It hit the forest with a thud, snow spitting, brambles crackling.

Jason spun around.

And then Zack appeared to my right.

Zack was quicker off the mark, moving forward, around the thorns I was in, toward the noise, gun primed. Jason seemed more reticent—as if he knew it might be a trick—but followed at a distance, walking rather than running.

I reached down behind me and picked up the thicker stone, moving up onto my haunches. The hardest, sharpest end of it poked out of the top of my hands.

Jason was about six feet away from me now, the gun still at his side. In his face I could see he hadn't been fooled by the diversion. As Zack, facing away from both of us, looked off into the forest beyond where the rock had landed, Jason was half-turned to the right, looking down the slope.

Do it.

I squeezed the stone.

Do it now.

I launched myself at Jason. He turned even further toward me, his eyes widening, but it was too late by then: I'd already jabbed the stone's point into the top of his skull. It made a hollow, splitting sound, like a ruptured watermelon.

He hit the ground.

Zack turned, eyes frantically searching the darkness.

Beside me, Jason's gun was lying on a patch of snow. I scooped it up and peered at it. I didn't recognize the make, didn't have time to check it was loaded.

I just gripped it—and I ran.

Firing a couple of times in his direction, trying to give myself a head start, I headed back down the way I'd come. A shot rang out, a puff of bark spitting out of a tree about six feet away. I kept running. A tree loomed out of the dark and I grazed my arm against the trunk, an ache shooting up through my muscles, into my shoulder. I pushed it down with the rest of the pain, and carried on running.

A second shot, a third.

A fourth narrowly missed me, hitting a tree as I passed it. My lungs felt like they were compacting. I knew I was losing ground. I knew I was slowing down. I couldn't keep this pace up—my feet were torn to shreds and there was still no sign of the road. I wasn't even sure I was heading in the right direction.

Then I fell.

My left foot clipped the grasping arm of a tree root, and I tumbled head first, hitting the ground hard. I collapsed onto my front and cried out in pain.

It felt like I had broken my arm.

Looking up, I could see Zack, about twenty feet away to my left. He hadn't spotted me yet, but he'd heard me and he was heading in my direction. I glanced around. *Where the hell was the gun?* I spotted it a second later, wedged against the foot of an oak tree, its gnarled bark closed around the weapon like a mouth.

I scrambled to my feet.

Zack, almost on top of me, fired, the bullet fizzing past me into a tree about a foot from my left shoulder. I reached down, grabbed the gun, and fired back.

Once. Twice.

The second bullet hit him.

He jolted sideways, his gun tumbling away from him, making a metallic clang as it bounced across the frozen mud. Stumbling, his legs gave way—like a light flickering out—and he hit the ground, cracking his head on an exposed root.

I moved across to him.

Blood oozed from a wound in his chest. He was dying and he knew it, the expression in his face almost acquiescent—as if, sooner or later, whatever he was involved in was bound to catch up with him. This wasn't chance, or bad luck.

It was providence.

"I'm sorry," I said to him.

He blinked once.

And then he didn't blink again.

I felt around in his pockets for the car keys and then, once I had them, I headed back down to the track. The sky was starting to lighten, just faintly, and as I got to the car, opened up, and slid in at the wheel, I realized it had been a week since Mary had come to me. What had I allowed myself to become in that time?

I looked in the mirror and saw a thin gash right on the hairline where Zack had clocked me with the gun at the house. There was a bruise high up on my cheekbone too, but neither my shoulder nor my arm, thankfully, had been broken.

I stared at myself. Who *had* I become?

Would Derryn even recognize this version of me?

This fugitive.

This killer.

I pushed all the doubts down, and looked at the clock. 7.49. They all thought I was dead now, so I had to use that. We must have been gone a couple of hours, and burying a body would probably take another couple on top of that.

That gave me two hours, maybe three if I was lucky, before they realized Zack and Jason weren't coming home.

33

A mile and a half down the track, I reached a country lane with sign-posts to Bristol. I was twenty miles from the city center, in the middle of the Mendips.

In the glove compartment there was a phone, empty like the last one of theirs I'd found. No names in the address book. No recent calls. I sat there for a moment, deciding what to do next, then used the phone to dial into my voicemail.

I had one message.

It was John Cary.

He'd rung the previous day, at 5 p.m. "I've got something for you," he said. "Call me." He left a number. There was a pen in one of the side pockets on the door. I scrawled his number on the back of my hand, and then called him.

He answered after two rings.

"John, it's David Raker."

"I've been trying to get hold of you," he said. It was over twelve hours since he'd made the call, and he didn't hide his annoyance. "You ever answer your phone?"

"I've been . . ." I paused. "I've been tied up. Sorry."

"Yeah, well, that makes two of us. Let me transfer you." I waited. Two clicks and he was back on, whispering this time. "I got your stuff back from the lab. If you get anything out of this, that's great. You take it as far as you want. But whatever you choose to do with it, I don't want to be kept informed. Understood?"

A bizarre start.

"Understood?" he said again.

"Understood."

"Okay," he continued, "so the lab lightened the Polaroid for you. Alex is in the middle of the shot, in what looks like the front bedroom of a house. The whole background is a little out of focus, but there's clearly a window behind him, and on the other side of that, some kind of veranda. To me, it looks like the type of thing you'd get on the front of a farmhouse."

"Anything else visible through the window?"

"Just grass and sky."

"No recognizable landmarks?"

"No. It's taken from a weird angle. Kind of shot from below. Alex is looking down. The window and the veranda, they're both on a slant because of the angle."

"Okay."

"You on e-mail there?"

I gave him my address.

"You asked about fingerprints before," he went on, but then there was a hesitant pause. "Well, there's two sets on the photo."

I felt a charge of adrenalin.

"You know a Stefan Myzwik?"

"No."

"What about a *Stephen* Myzwik?"

"Is that a Stephen with a ph?"

"Yeah."

Something sparked. The name was on the pad I took from Eagle Heights. *Paul. Stephen. Zack.* "Maybe," I said.

"Stefan Myzwik, aka Stephen Myzwik, aka Stephen Milton."

"Who is he?"

"Thirty-five years of age, born in Poland, moved to London in 1995, served ten years for stabbing a sixty-year-old man with a piece of glass. After he got out, he violated the terms of his parole, and, under the alias of Stephen Michaels, used a fraudulent credit card to rent a vehicle in Liverpool."

I could hear him turning pages.

"Wait a minute . . ."

"What's up?" I asked.

"There's stuff missing here."

I thought of something. "There were pages missing in Alex's file as well."

"What do you mean?"

"I was going to ask you about them."

"What was missing?"

"Some of the forensic stuff."

More pages being turned. "Where the fuck have they gone?"

"Has someone deleted them?"

"Deleted information from the *computer*?" A long silence came down the line. I could hear him flicking through the file, faster this time. "This file's fucked."

Something had got to him.

Something more than just pages missing from a file.

"Do you want me to call you back?" I said.

"No," he replied. "I haven't got time for this shit. I'll look into it later. Let's just get this over and done with." More pages being turned. "He's dead, anyway."

"Who, Myzwik?"

"Yeah."

Somehow another dead body wasn't all that surprising. First Alex, then Jade, now Myzwik: all of them dead—or supposed to be.

"How'd he die?"

"Looks like his body was dumped in a reservoir near here in July 2008."

"Near Bristol?"

"Yeah. Divers dredged him up about two months later. He must have made some dangerous friends."

"How come?"

"He was missing his head, and both his hands were found on the other side of the reservoir." Cary paused. "The head was never found, apparently."

Instantly, I saw the parallels with Jade's "death" in 2004, and then recalled the boy in the house in Bristol: he'd been missing teeth.

They were trying to prevent identification.

Or, at least, add some confusion.

"You said there were a second set of prints on the photo?" I asked.

"Yeah," he replied, but then there was a long drawn-out pause. "The prints we pulled off the photograph match some pulled off the wheel of a silver Mondeo used in a hit-and-run six years ago." More paper being leafed through. "Witnesses recall seeing a white male about Alex's age and description having an argument in the parking lot of a strip club called Sinderella's in Harrow. I'm quoting direct from the police report here: 'At eleven twenty-two p.m. on November ninth it is alleged the suspect drove the silver Mondeo—'"

"Wait a minute. November ninth?"

"Yeah."

"That's the day before Alex disappeared."

"Correct. 'Suspect struck the victim—Leyton Alan Green, 54, from Fulham—as he was coming out of the bar, causing critical internal injuries. The victim died a short time later. Witnesses recall seeing a silver Mondeo with a Hertz sticker in the rear window depart the scene shortly after.' The silver Mondeo was recovered in a long-term parking lot at Dover, five months later, on April twelfth."

"You're suggesting Alex *killed* someone?" I said.

"*I'm* not suggesting it. It's here in black and white."

We both stopped to take the information in.

"This Green guy—has he got a record?"

"No. He's clean."

"And the car was a rental?"

"Yeah."

"What did Hertz say?"

"Alex took advantage of the kid they had serving in there. Paid cash, using a fake ID, managed to register everything under the name Leyton Alan Green." Cary grunted. "Very cute."

I paused, trying to take it in. Things were changing fast. "Can I get a copy of those files?"

He didn't reply straight away.

Then, quietly, he said: "I sent them to you yesterday."

34

It took me three hours to get home. I parked at the end of my street and sat and watched the house. A biting wind pressed at the windows and snowflakes blew across the street, and—without the engine on and the heaters off—the car cooled down quickly. Almost as quickly, my body reacted: adrenalin passed out of my system, and the cold began to get at me. I still had no coat, no shoes, no socks. I'd driven one hundred and twenty-five miles in bare feet. As I reached down to the ignition and fired up the engine again, heaters bursting into life, I was shaking.

I slowly thawed out, eyes on the house.

The road had always been quiet, so anything out of place would stick out a mile. Even so, I knew from the night before that they weren't just barmen and priests—they were trackers and marksmen. They were killers. They could fade in and out, and they could disappear. The advantage was still with them.

I looked at the clock.

11.27.

They were probably starting to realize that Zack and Jason weren't coming home. The likelihood that they were already here, watching the house, waiting for me to arrive, was remote. But I wasn't about to take any chances. I needed basic provisions. I needed a shower. I needed to patch myself up. I needed shoes, a laptop, some extra clothes. Mostly, I needed to be sure I wasn't being followed.

I got out of the car, locked it and headed up the street toward the house. They'd removed everything from my pockets the previous day, including my keys, so I headed straight around to the back of the house and took the spare key out of one of the hanging baskets next to the rear door.

Inside, it was cold.

I approached each room carefully, checking them over just in case, but no one was waiting and nothing had been touched. The files Cary had sent the day before were on the floor, under the letterbox, handwritten but otherwise anonymous.

Washing off the dirt and the blood in the shower, I dug out the warmest clothes I could lay my hands on—a pair of jeans, a thermal training top, another zip-up and a coat—and grabbed an old laptop from the second bedroom. There was a spare phone in the bedside table, and some cash there too. They had my wallet, so I'd need to cancel my cards, but I'd worry about that once I was back on the road. Adding the gun I'd taken from Jason, the files that Cary had sent me, as well as some bandages and plasters to make running repairs, I locked up the house and headed back down the street to where I'd left the Astra.

I stopped.

There was someone leaning in against the passenger window, the hood up on his coat, cupping his hands against the glass. I backed up and crouched down behind the nearest vehicle. He glanced along the street toward the house, didn't see me, and moved around the front of the car to the driver's side. He tried the door. When he stepped away from the car a second time, I caught a glimpse of his face and recognized him straight away: the man who had broken into my car at the cemetery; the man I'd followed outside Angel's. He was scruffy and unkempt, and looked more meager in the daylight, and that immediately set off alarm bells.

This was the type of trap they liked to lay.

They made you believe they were one thing, that they were weaker than you, and then they turned everything on its head.

He looked back at the house and fixed his gaze on the front door. I could see his eyes narrowing, as if he knew something was up. It was like he'd studied the street before my arrival—had seen which cars were where, and who they belonged to—and had now found a piece of the puzzle that didn't fit properly.

I unzipped the carryall, getting ready to grab the gun—but then the man took another look at the car, turned, and headed the other way. I watched him go, reaching the end of the road. He looked back once— and was gone from view.

It was a trap.

It had to be.

He knew the car belonged to them, and if it was parked in my street, he knew I was home. He could have gone to make a call—maybe because he didn't want to come at me alone. By now, he'd have heard what I'd done to the others.

But he didn't return.

The road remained quiet, unmoved.

I got to my feet and sprinted across the street, flipping the locks on the car with the remote and sliding in at the wheel. I looked in my rearview mirror, half-expecting to see them entering the road, and jammed my foot to the pedal. I got to the bottom of the road, paused there, and checked again. No sign of the man.

No sign of anyone coming after me.

But it wouldn't stay that way for long.

35

I left the Astra in a supermarket car park in Hammersmith. There was a satellite tracking sticker on the front windshield, so if they were smart—which they were—they'd call the tracking company and locate the car. Afterward, I found a coffee shop about a quarter of a mile further on, connected to their Wi-Fi, and logged into my e-mail. Cary had already sent a copy of the Polaroid—brightened and altered by his contact at the FSS—to my phone, but the file had been too large to open.

The e-mail's subject line was *Pic*. Underneath, he had written: *This doesn't exist on the server any more—if you want another copy . . . tough. It's gone.*

I dragged the attachment off, onto the desktop, and opened it up.

At its default size I could just about make out the side of Alex's face and some of the window in the background. It was clear what a good job the forensic tech had done the second I downsized it. The face was more defined, the scar on his right cheek visible for the first time. His hair too: it wasn't shaved, as it had been when Mary had seen him, but it was cut close to his scalp, the dome of his skull reflecting light coming in through the window—which was, itself, much clearer.

Cary was right about the angle of the shot.

It was odd.

It looked like Alex might be on the bed while the photographer—perhaps Stefan Myzwik, whose prints were *also* on the Polaroid—was on the floor below.

I zoomed in slightly, concentrating on the view out of the window behind him. The veranda was clearly visible now—an ornate, handcarved wooden railing running its entire length—and there was the hint of a grass bank, just as Cary had suggested, as well as a vast expanse of blue sky. But Cary had missed another tiny detail: a speck—no more than half an inch in the corner of the photograph—which was a different shade of blue. I moved closer to the screen and zoomed in.

Water.

The room overlooked the sea.

As I examined that, something else caught my eye. I dragged the picture across, zooming in even further onto one of the window panes on the left side.

There was a reflection in the glass.

Vague, ghostly.

I could see a hillside covered in heather, and a sign nailed to the railing at the front of the veranda. Even reversed, I could make out what was printed on it.

Lazarus.

Immediately my mind spooled back twenty-four hours: I'd seen the same name on Michael Tilton's mobile phone when he'd returned to the outbuilding at the church.

LAST CALL: LAZARUS—LANDLINE.

He'd gone inside to ask a friend about whether they recognized Alex. But it wasn't a friend he was calling. It was a place, a house, somewhere Alex stayed.

I grabbed a second coffee, kicking everything around my head, and then called Terry Dooley, an old contact at the Met from my days as a journalist, to tell him the car I'd hired the day before—still parked in Bristol—had been stolen. It was a lie, of course, but I wasn't about to head back down the M4 to pick it up.

"So?" he said. "Why is that my problem?"

It sounded like he was having lunch.

"I need you to file the paperwork for me, Dools."

He laughed through a mouthful of food. "Davey boy, you and me used to have an understanding. You scratched my back, I scratched yours. But since you jacked in the day job to do . . .. whatever *this* is, you ain't got anything I need."

"You owe me," I said.

"I don't owe you shit."

"Look, Dools, let me make this really easy for you: I'll e-mail you the details of where I last saw the car, you fill out the form for me and liaise with the rental company, and I'll carry on pretending I don't know where Carlton Lane is."

He stopped eating.

Carlton Lane was where Terry Dooley and three of his detectives were one night about four years before I left the paper. In a house at the end was a brothel. One of Dooley's detectives ended up having too much to drink and punched a girl in the face when she told him he was getting a bit rough. She got revenge the next day by e-mailing enough details to the newspaper to protect her income and the brothel while landing Dooley and the other detectives in serious trouble. Luckily for Dooley—and his marriage, and his kids—the e-mail ended up in my inbox.

Silence on the line.

"Is that a 'yes,' Dools?"

He sighed. "Yeah, whatever."

"Thank you."

I hung up and e-mailed him all the information he'd need to complete the paperwork, and then called the rental company to fill them in. Next, I dialed my phone network and told them my phone had been in the car when it was stolen.

I asked them to redirect all calls to my new mobile.

After that, I grabbed the files that Cary had given me—Stefan Myzwik, and the death of Leyton Alan Green—and laid them out on the table in front of me.

Myzwik's casework detailed his record before he went to prison in 1995, aged just twenty-one, and picked up again after his release in 2005. In July 2008, his headless corpse was discovered in the reservoir on the edges of the Mendips.

The file confirmed that Myzwik's body was brought ashore by police divers after part of his coat had been spotted floating on the surface of the water. They'd found his credit cards in a wallet on the other side of the reservoir. Forensics had worked on the recovered hands, but a definitive fingerprint match couldn't be made, owing to the amount of time the corpse had been underwater. Instead, they determined that the body most likely belonged to Myzwik due to loose teeth they'd recovered nearby, which matched up with dental records. The rest of the head remained missing. There was a black-and-white photograph of him from his last arrest, his thick black hair in an untidy side parting, his dark eyes looking out from a face dotted with acne scars.

Likewise, identification of Alex had also been less than definitive. Personal belongings had been found scattered around the remains of the vehicle he crashed, including his driver's license and a wallet containing photographs of Mary and Malcolm, and enough had remained of Alex's face for the pathologist to find what appeared to be the scar that he carried on his cheek, consistent with pictures that Mary had given Avon and Somerset Police. An odontologist was drafted in to work from dental records too, but most of the teeth left in the skull had shrunken and malformed in the intensity of the fire, becoming impossible to identify with absolute certainty. Once again, investigators had relied on loose teeth—knocked out when Alex's face hit the steering wheel on impact with the field—found in his windpipe and stomach. They *did* belong to Alex—seeming to confirm that the body was his.

But I was starting to think differently.

I'd shared a meal with Jade, five years after a series of newspaper stories claimed she was killed by Romanian organized crime. Stefan Myzwik's corpse had been found in a reservoir with its head missing and its hands on the opposite side of the water, but just happened to have a scattering of loose teeth close by. Alex was ID'd the same way—except the teeth left in his skull were deformed, and the ones that did manage to survive weren't in his mouth, but in his throat and digestive tract.

It wasn't just that either.

In Myzwik's file, two pages were missing, not part of the printouts I had on me, and not part of the printouts John Cary had made from the computer either.

That meant they'd been removed.

Why?

I switched to the second file—the murder of Leyton Alan Green. It was much thinner. He'd owned two electronics stores in Harrow, and a third in Wembley. The night he died, he'd been driving a dark blue Isuzu Trooper. It was new, bought the week before from a dealership in Hackney. The police had done some background checks on the vehicle, toying with the idea of the murder being related to the purchase of the jeep. But, like everything else, it was a dead end.

The report detailed the night Green was hit by the Mondeo, but eyewitness accounts were thin on the ground. A couple of people identified the Mondeo.

No one could identify who was driving it.

Toward the back were some photographs. The biggest was of the murder scene. Green's body was under a white sheet, only the sole of his shoe poking out. Blood had stained the sheet. Little circles of chalk were dotted around the body, ringing pieces of the Mondeo. The next pictures confirmed this: shots of pieces of the bumper, and even a chunk of the hood. *He must have been hit hard.* Close-ups of his face followed, bloodied and battered. Another one of his left hip—black with blood and misshapen—where the Mondeo had made the initial impact.

I was about to return both case files to the carryall when, at the back, close to a description of Sinderella's strip club, I found another photo of Leyton Green.

He was in a suit, at some sort of event.

My stomach tensed.

I know him.

His ginger hair parted, a familiar smile creeping across his face, it was the same man I'd seen in an old photograph in Mary's basement. Malcolm. Him. Alex.

And Mary out to the side.

Leyton Alan Green was Alex's Uncle Al.

36

Michael Tilton left the church at six o'clock.

The night was cold, steam hissing out of vents, warm air rising out of the ground as Tube trains rumbled through the earth. I waited for him in a darkened doorway outside the station, and then followed him inside. He went through the turnstiles and down the steps to the platform.

A train had already pulled in.

I stepped into it a couple of doors down from him, half-turned, the top and sides of my face obscured by a ski hat, and watched as he sat, a satchel on his lap.

With a jolt, the train took off.

Tilton looked up, around at the other passengers, so I ducked my head, conscious of him seeing my reflection in the windows of the carriage. After about thirty seconds, I flicked a look at him again: he was sitting cross-legged, reading.

The drop-off for the fake IDs was in Paddington. It was a place called Store "N" Pay, a facility of about a thousand lockers. People paid a daily or monthly rate for a unit and got a swipe card that gained them access to the building any time they wanted. I'd called them before leaving the coffee shop: they reeled off prices and unit sizes—you could go as big as a garage, or as small as a sports center locker.

We changed at Oxford Circus, and I kept my distance on escalators, but it was easy enough: central London was packed, full of commuters and tourists, the crowds making it simple to keep out of sight. The only danger was losing Tilton in the crush. When we got to the Bakerloo line, I waited on the concourse, out of sight.

Eight minutes later, we were in Paddington.

Out of the mainline station, he headed southeast. We were moving in the direction of Hyde Park, residential streets running like capillaries either side of us. I maintained a distance from him, following from the other pavement where I was better hidden. After a couple of minutes, he veered right into a narrow road with cars parked on either side and a shop front at one end. A sign hanging above the door said STORE "N" PAY. I hung back as he climbed the steps up to the front, swiping a card through a reader beside the door. It buzzed, and he headed inside.

There was a big window at the front, a blue neon SECURE LOCKERS sign at the top. Through the glass I could see an unmanned front desk, a series of regular red lockers, and then an arrow directing customers along a corridor in the center. That was where the bigger units were. A ramp led down to the lower ground floor and a pull-up garage door, which was presumably how customers unloaded their bulkiest items. Tilton wouldn't need that door, though: he was already standing in front of a locker on the left hand side, close to the glass, removing the IDs.

They were in a small brown envelope.

I looked down the street.

Parked about fifty feet along was my new rental car—a non-descript gray Ford Focus. I'd hired it in Acton, driven it over here, parked it up, and then got the Tube back out to Redbridge. I'd need the vehicle close by—for when we left.

Tilton was done.

He pushed the locker shut, slid the envelope into his satchel, then swung the satchel over his shoulders. As he started moving, so did I. I crossed the street—closing the distance between us as quickly as possible— and headed up the stairs.

He pulled the door open.

Instantly, I pushed him back inside, moving into the store, and shoving the door shut behind me. He stumbled back, anger in his face—and then he saw who it was. Anger became shock: his mouth dropped a little, the color draining from him. As he quickly tried to pull himself together, a hand went to his satchel.

"David."

I backed him into the corner, where it was harder to see us from the street, and looked along the corridor that led to the bigger units at the back of the facility. There were the edges of a counter poking off, but I couldn't see any staff.

"I've got to admit, I didn't think we'd see you again."

I turned back to him. "I'll bet."

His hand was still on the satchel.

"Where's Alex?" I said.

He acknowledged the name, but only with a slight nod of the head.

"Do you need me to speak up?"

"No, I heard you. Why do you want to know?"

"Where is he?"

"Why is this so important to you?"

"*Where is he?*"

I took another step toward him.

His eyes narrowed. "You're making big problems for yourself—"

"You can save the threats, Reverend. I've heard it all before. In case you forgot, your friends already tried to kill me once."

"That was nothing to do with me."

"Oh, of course," I said, nodding at the satchel, at the identities contained within it. "You've got no idea what goes on outside the walls of your church."

"A name means nothing, David."

"So, you came all this way for nothing?"

He shook his head. "I don't understand what drives you. I mean, *why?* Why come this far? This has nothing to do with you. You could have turned back at any time. But you didn't and now . . . now you're going to get torn apart. Why?"

I didn't reply.

"I don't believe it's the money. You've probably earned enough already. Are you a completist, David—is that it? You want to finish what you started. I respect that. I like to finish what I start. I don't let anything get in the way of finishing—"

"Enough bullshit. Where's Alex?"

I could see exactly where this was heading, which was why I'd cut him off: the same place it had gone before. *This quest of yours,* the man with the tattoos had asked me in Bristol, *is it about the kid—or is it about your wife?* They'd hit on something, and now they were going back to it again. Derryn was my weakness.

She was the chink in my armor.

"Did you think there was any hope for your wife, even at the end?"

I eyed him.

"There's always hope, right? If there wasn't, you wouldn't be here."

"Shut up."

He held up a hand to me, as if apologizing, but then carried on. "Death's not something you can fight. It's not a *tangible* thing. It's an undefeatable enemy, an unfair battle, an adversary you can't see coming." The corners of his mouth turned down: a sad expression, but only skin deep. "I know how you feel. I know about the fear of death, David; what comes after. You were scared for her, right?"

He took a step toward me.

"You *must* have been scared for her. A man of no religion, of no beliefs—weren't you scared about what came next for the person you loved above all else? Wouldn't you like to find out?" He paused, taking another step closer. "That's why you're still interested in this, isn't it? That's why you're here." Another step. "You want to find out where she went. Why she had to be taken from you when she was still so young." Another step, bigger this time. "As hard as it is to hear, only God knows when and why our time comes to an end, David. And when He sees some of the people we have in our world, some of these young people getting out of their depth, walking a tightrope between life and death, deciding for themselves how close they want to brush with the afterlife, He is disappointed. I'm sure of that. He is *angry*. Because you and I, we don't get to decide when our time is up."

He paused, and started to reach out for me.

"God is the person who chooses—"

I slapped his hand away, and reached out for his neck, driving him into a space between two banks of lockers. He hit the wall with a thud. Reaching around to the back of my trousers, I removed the gun—taken from the place I was meant to die in—and shoved it hard, up into his jaw. He flinched and started to panic.

"David, wait a min—"

"Don't tell me what I believe in," I said to him through my teeth. "You've got no idea what I believe in. I *want* to think that she's somewhere better than here, no longer sharing oxygen with scumbags like you. But when I listen to you, when I listen to *all* of you, all I hear is lies. You're talking out the side of your mouth the whole time. So don't tell me what I believe, and don't talk to me about my wife."

"David, I—"

"I'd think about saving your breath for the next couple of hours." I pushed the gun into his face even harder, his body rigid. "Because, one way or another, you're telling me everything you know."

37

It was almost ten by the time we got to Tilton's flat, part of a new development on the banks of the Thames between Deptford and Greenwich. We stopped at the entrance, a narrow foyer with a glass roof, connected to the main building by a corridor on the other side, and he let us in. I checked both ways, just to make sure we were alone, and then shoved him in through the doors. Immediately inside, on the right, was a communal garden: stone flagging among a sea of pebbles, and a covered area where cream awnings stretched out across sets of wooden benches.

"Nice place," I said to him.

He didn't reply.

I followed him along to a set of lifts. Doors to our right and left led through to the ground-floor apartments. He called one of the elevators, then turned to me. I was carrying his satchel over my shoulder and his phone in my hand. The phone had been empty—just like the others—and the laptop was almost out of battery.

We rode the elevator up.

At his apartment door, he eyed me, an act of defiance, but I nodded to the lock and he wilted again, letting us both in. A decent-sized living room bled into an open-plan kitchen; two doors led from that into a bathroom and a bedroom.

"Do the Calvary Project bankroll this?"

Again, he didn't respond.

I locked the door and told him to sit in the corner of the room with the lights off, then took the sofa opposite him. There was enough light from outside.

Undoing the buckles on the satchel, I took out the book he'd been reading and dropped it onto the floor, and then removed the laptop. "Where's the lead?"

"At work."

"Where is it?"

"At work."

"I don't believe you, Michael. Where is it?"

"At work," he repeated.

I sighed. "You really want to do this?"

He just looked at me this time.

I got up, moved across the living room, and punched him hard in the side of the face. He jerked sideways, off the edge of the sofa he was perched on, and then automatically scrambled away from me on all fours. "*Shit*," he said, clutching his face, looking up at me. There was no blood, but his left cheek was marked.

"It doesn't have to be like this."

He looked shocked.

"Where's the lead?"

He glanced around the room, clearly trying to come up with some way of delaying me, but then I took another step toward him, my same fist clenched. I didn't want to have to do things this way, but I was sick of being lied to, of being boxed in and pushed around. Tilton glanced from my fist to my face, and then out beyond me, toward the television. He was looking at a low cabinet full of sliding drawers.

"The third one down on the left," he said.

I retrieved the power lead and plugged it into the laptop. The machine had 3% battery. As soon as it started charging, a password prompt kicked in onscreen.

"What's your password?" I asked him.

"Eleven, forty-one, forty-four."

I put in the code and the laptop began whirring into life. As it booted up, I turned back to him. "What's the significance of the numbers?"

He shrugged.

He was still nursing the side of his head, and looked a little woozy. I took the gun from my belt and laid it down on the glass table next to me with a clunk.

Tilton looked at it, then to me.

The desktop finally appeared, loaded with folders. There were four on the right of the screen—Monthly Budgets, Twenties Group, December Sermons and December Scripture—and a further two on the left, Pictures and Contacts.

I clicked on Contacts.

A second password prompt appeared. I tapped in the same code as before. This time the prompt box juddered and told me I'd put in the wrong password.

"What's the password for the folders?"

I tried Monthly Budgets and it opened. The others—Twenties, Sermons,

Scripture—all opened up as well. So it was just the Contacts folder that was locked.

"What's the password for the Contacts folder?"

He just stared at me.

I rubbed at my forehead—annoyed, tired of this already—and then picked up the gun. "What's the password for the Contacts folder?"

"Are you going to shoot me in my own home?"

"You don't think I'm capable of it?"

He eyed me. "You're not a killer, David."

"Tell that to Zack and Jason."

A flash of something in his face—fear, panic—and then it was gone again. He gestured at the laptop. "Humor me, and go to the folder marked 'Pictures.'"

"What's the password for the Contacts folder?"

"Just humor me. Please."

My eyes lingered on him, and then I double-clicked on the Pictures folder. There were thirty documents, all jpegs, with filenames like "thelast supper.jpg" and "jesusandpeter_water.jpg." I opened up a couple. They were paintings of biblical scenes: the virgin birth; Jesus being tempted by the Devil; the parable of the two sons; Jesus on the cross.

"Open 'widow-underscore-nain,'" he said.

"I haven't got time for a sermon."

"It might answer a few questions for you."

I looked for the file and found the name halfway down the list. It was a painting of Jesus standing over an open coffin, a widow beside him.

A man was sitting up in the coffin.

"You asked me about the numbers," he said.

I frowned. "What?"

"The password—for the laptop."

Eleven, forty-one, forty-four.

I studied him. The expression on his face worried me for the first time: he looked like he'd worked out some sort of plan, a strategy, a way to get back at me.

"Come on, David," he said. "We both know why you're here, why you didn't turn around and walk the other way the moment we gave you the chance."

"What the hell are you talking about?"

"You know what that painting is of? It's the raising of a man in Nain.

Jesus and his disciples visited there after leaving Capernaum, and they came across a funeral procession. When Jesus saw the widow weeping for her dead son, he felt compassion for her. He understood her torment, experienced it, almost as if he'd experienced the loss of the boy himself. And he felt so much compassion for the widow that he raised her son from the dead. He *raised* that boy from the *dead*."

"What's the password?"

"There are three accounts of Jesus bringing someone back to life in the Gospels. The young man in Nain, which is in Luke; the daughter of Jairus, which is in all except John; and, of course, the most famous account of them all—"

"What's the password?"

"—the raising of Lazarus."

I looked at him, a hint of a smile on his face, and remembered the Polaroid of Alex. In the background had been a reflection of a sign, *Lazarus* printed on it.

I'd seen reference to it on Tilton's phone too.

"Where's Lazarus located?" I said.

"Some scholars," he went on, "argue that the story of the young man in Nain and the raising of Lazarus are in fact one person. If that were the case, that would reduce the number of people that Jesus resurrected from the dead, down to two."

"Enough. Where's Lazarus located?"

"I guess, in a way, that's what you've been hoping for—isn't it, David? You want to believe that Alex has somehow come back from the dead . . ." He paused, smiled. "Because you want to believe it might be possible for your wife as well."

I stared at him: swallowed, took a breath.

"Am I right, David?"

I was burning up inside, livid at him for using Derryn to get at me. It took all I had not to go on the attack. I wanted to put the gun in his throat. I wanted to see him choking on it. But, instead, I picked up my phone, and started scrolling through my Address Book. In a reflection, in the window to my right, I could see Tilton shift forward on the sofa— off balance now, unsure of what was I doing.

"The thing with you, Reverend," I said calmly, quietly, "is that you still have something you care about." I pretended I'd got to the name I

wanted, and looked up at him. "The only thing I ever cared about, I had
to bury twelve months ago."

"What are you doing?"

"I'm making a phone call."

"To who?"

"To the media. I'm going to destroy your reputation."

"What? What are you talking about?"

"I used to be a journalist, remember. So I'm going to call everyone I
know on every paper I ever had any dealings with, and I'm going to tell
them who you are. Not the fantasy you deliver every Sunday morning
from the pulpit. But *this*. These people you're involved with. These things
you've done. The bodies you've helped to bury. In an hour, your life will
be worth absolutely nothing."

He came forward, to the edge of the sofa. "Wait a second . . ."

I pretended to dial.

"Wait a second, wait a second . . ."

I killed the call.

It had been the right play: he was prideful, self-centered, arrogant. I
didn't doubt he believed in the organization, in whatever it was they were
doing, and whatever his part in it was. But even if he wasn't prepared to
admit it to anyone but himself, he enjoyed the trappings of his church even
more: the way people treated him, the way they hung on his every word
once a week, his status, his standing.

"Start talking," I said.

"Eleven, forty-one, forty-four," he replied, emotion tremoring in his
voice.

"No more riddles."

"John, chapter eleven, verse forty-one to forty-four. The raising of
Lazarus. When we recruit people, when we help them out, that's what
we promise them."

I frowned. "To raise them from the dead?"

"To give them a new life. A new start."

"Is that what you did to Alex?"

"We helped him."

"Is that what you did to him?"

"Two, five, one, five."

I stopped. "What?"

"That's the password for the Contacts folder."

I watched him for a moment, getting a sense of where his thoughts were at: he was giving up what he knew, because he figured it wouldn't matter anyway. Tilton was just the tip of the iceberg. If I went hunting deeper into the swamp, I'd find things much worse than him. He probably figured I'd be dead before I got a chance to tell the world what was going on. Maybe he was right, maybe he wasn't.

But it was too late to back out now.

I put the code into the password prompt and the Contacts folder opened. Inside was a Word document. After loading it up, I found a long list of addresses and telephone numbers, including some I recognized: Jade, Jason, Zack, Evelyn.

This is the Calvary Project.

There must have been forty names, dotted all around the UK, including a couple without street addresses. They had e-mails instead. One of them worked at the Met. Another had an NHS suffix. *They're in the police, in the hospital system.* I remembered the two missing pages from Alex's file, and suddenly it started to make sense. They removed anything incriminating; an act of self-preservation.

Then, at the bottom, another entry caught my eye.

There was no name attached to this, just an address: *Building 1 (Bethany) / Building 2 (Lazarus), Stevenshire Farm, Old Tay, near Lochlanark, Scotland.*

"Go to the farm," Michael said, as if reading my mind. "Go up there and see what's *really* going on." He stopped, watching me, and—for the first time—I saw something new in his face: pity, unease. "But don't expect to come back again."

"Why, what's up there?"

He nodded at the laptop. "Go back to the Pictures folder."

"Tell me about the farm—"

"This *is* about the farm."

I returned to the Pictures folder. "Now what?"

"You see that file halfway down?"

I looked at the list of .jpgs again, and saw what he was referring to. I hadn't taken note of it the first time: a picture without a filename like the other ones.

It was just called 2-5-15.

"The one with the numbers?" I asked.

He nodded.

I clicked on it, and another painting started to load. It was a man knelt in front of Jesus, his face lifted to the sky. He was tormented, his eyes like fires, his mouth like an open tomb. Something snapped into place, but I wasn't sure what.

"The second Gospel, Mark," Tilton said. "The fifth chapter; fifteenth verse. 'And they come to Jesus, and see him that was possessed with the Devil . . .'"

And see him that was possessed.

It hit me like a sledgehammer: the man in Cornwall, the man who I'd felt at my ear down in Bristol—the same inscription had been tattooed onto his arm.

"I tried to help you, David," Tilton said softly, almost mournfully. "I tried to tell you to turn around and walk the other way, but you didn't want to listen. You wanted to see what was hidden in the shadows. Well, now you'll get to find out."

"Who is he?"

Michael didn't reply.

"Is he in charge?"

"No, not in charge." Michael looked at me. "We got him in at the start, just for one thing. His . . . experience helped us. But then we started needing him more and more, and slowly he became more powerful. He maneuvered himself into a position of power. And, after that, he started bringing his own . . . ideas." He stopped, shook his head. "So, no, he's not in charge. A man called Andrew is in charge up there. But that man—there's no one there who can stop him. The God that I know, the God that has your wife, isn't the same as the God he works for."

I frowned at him. "What are you talking about?"

"'And they come to Jesus, and see him that was possessed with the Devil, and had the legion, sitting, and clothed, and in his right mind: and they were afraid.'" Michael glanced toward the laptop, to the painting on it. "I don't know what his real name is. I think maybe even *he* has forgotten it. I just know what he calls himself."

"Which is what?"

"Legion," he replied. "'Because many devils were entered into him.'"

Legion

Legion came out of the darkness and clamped a hand onto the man's face. The man shifted in the chair, trying to wriggle free, but every effort to lean away from the hard plastic of the mask saw the devil move in closer, eyes darting, breath crackling through the tiny nose holes. The man's wrists and ankles were bound to the chair; the chair was bolted to the floor. Legion's fingers dug deeper into his skin. Slowly, he turned the man's head, forcing him to look directly at the mask.

"Do you know where you are?"

The man shook his head.

"You're at the door to your next life."

Legion smiled inside the plastic mouth slit and then pushed his tongue out through it. The two ends wriggled like worms breaking the surface of the earth.

"Do you believe in God?"

"Please . . ."

"Do you?"

"I don't kn—"

"Do you believe in God?"

Alarm flared in his chest, and he closed his eyes, trying not to look at the mask, trying to imagine what the right answer might be. Then, something Rose had said came back to him: Sometimes I think he might actually be the Devil.

He kept his eyes shut and tried to force his arms up, hoping the duct tape might tear. But the harder he tried, the harder Legion pressed his nails into his face. When he stopped trying to fight, the pressure released. He felt blood run down his cheeks, and a slight residue on his skin where Legion's hand had been. He wanted to touch his face, wanted to wipe himself clean, but he couldn't move.

Finally, he opened his eyes.

In front of him, Legion placed a hand on the mask and lifted it, up past his chin, his nose, his eyes, until it was on top of his head. His real face was angular and taut, his skin pale, his eyes dark, blood vessels running across the top of his cheekbones where the skin appeared almost translucent. He looked in his late forties, but he moved with the purpose and efficiency of someone much younger.

"I never joined this cause because I believed in what they did," Legion said, his fingers touching a scar running along his hairline and down to the ridge of his chin. "The people here, they believe this is some higher calling. A mission." Legion moved

in closer, putting a finger playfully to his lips. He smiled again, but this time there was nothing playful in it; only darkness and menace. "Ssshhhhh, don't tell anyone, but I just saw this as an opportunity. They needed me to do some dirty work for them. And after I left the army, I needed somewhere to hole up."

He pulled the sleeve up on his right arm.

"That doesn't mean I'm not a believer," he went on. "I just don't believe in the same God as them. Most of them here, they believe in a God that forgives; a God that will bend to whatever mistakes we make, and sanction a second chance. I don't. I suppose you could say . . . I'm more of an Old Testament kind of guy."

He turned his arm so the tattoo was visible. It was bluey-black, smudged by age, and ran in horizontal lines, from his wrist to the bend in his arm.

"'And they were afraid,'" he said.

Legion stood there, almost transfixed by what was written on his skin, and then he reached down and touched a finger to the last four words of the tattoo.

"I've seen the wrath of God," he continued, but more quietly now, his voice distant. "I've watched people being blown to pieces. I've seen men bleeding out of their eyes. I've seen floods and earthquakes. I've seen destruction. And you know what? We should be afraid. You should be afraid." He paused, pulling the sleeve of his shirt back down. "Because God doesn't forgive. He doesn't believe in second chances. He punishes. He tears apart. He consumes. So, the question I always ask myself when I see Andrew preaching about the power of redemption is: if God doesn't care about me, why the fuck should I care about you?"

Legion stepped aside. Beyond him, a double door opened up into the next room. It was semi-dark, but the dull glow from a strip light showed what awaited.

"No. No, please."

"This," Legion said, "is my contribution to this place."

As the man looked from the next room to Legion, all he could hear in his ears was his heart crashing against his ribcage, battering against the walls of his chest. When he tried to swallow, he realized his throat was closing up. Sweat had soaked through his clothes. He looked at Legion, then ahead again, into the room where they were going to take him next.

At the device standing in the middle.

He gagged.

His throat forced up whatever he had left, and he leaned forward and let it fall from his lips. It hit the ground and spread, filling the cracks in the concrete, his breathing heavy now. The panic, the dread, were starting to get on top of him.

Then he realized something.

Legion was gone.

He glanced left and right, but around him nothing moved. Nothing made a sound. There was no sign of the devil. He swallowed. Tears started filling his eyes.

"Do you know who Lucifer was?"

A voice, right behind his ear, fierce and violent, like shattered glass.

He whimpered.

A pause. "Are you crying?"

He tried to hold the tears back, but then he looked at the device standing in the other room—a harrowing shape in the shadows—and imagined himself being dragged across the floor toward it. Quietly, he started begging for his life.

Out of the corner of his eye, he saw Legion loom out of the darkness, about six feet away. The mask was in place again, eyes blinking in the eye holes, tongue moving in the mouth slit. "In Ezekiel," Legion said, his voice crawling with power, "it says, 'Thou art the anointed cherub that covereth; and I have set thee so.' It's talking about Lucifer. It's talking about the origins of Satan. 'Thou wast upon the holy mountain of God; thou hast walked up and down in the midst of the stones of fire. Thou wast perfect in thy ways from the day that thou wast created, till iniquity was found in thee.'" Legion paused. "Do you know what that means?"

He shook his head, tear tracks on his face.

"It means Lucifer had everything he could possibly want. He had God's ear. But even that wasn't enough for him. So, God cast him out of heaven." The devil glanced to his left, to the room with the device. "Do you think a God that cast out one of his own angels can hear you when you beg for your life? Do you? He doesn't hear anything you say. Nothing. God wants you to be scared of him. And he wants you to be scared of me." Legion leaned into him. "Because you know what? I am the real Lucifer. I am God's right-hand man. I am His messenger."

"Please," he sobbed.

Legion stepped away. "And His wrath moves through me."

PART FOUR

38

Lochlanark was a small town halfway between Oban and Lochgilphead. It looked out over the islands of Scarba, Luing and Shuna, to the Firth of Lorn, and to the misty, gray Atlantic beyond. It took seven hours to drive up from London, and I stopped only twice the whole way. Once to fill up the car, and once to call in at a petrol station to make sure I was on the right track. They told me Old Tay—where the farm was located—was a one-street village about seven miles north.

When I got there, I found five cottages and a sloping village green that dropped all the way down to the sea. Inland, there were woods, and the rising peaks of Beinn Dubh beyond, streaked black and green, small streams of snow in every fold. Right at the end of the village, I finally found the entrance to the farm.

I parked in a frozen field, about a hundred yards from the entrance. The sun clawed its way up past the mountains behind me just before 8 a.m., and as I sat there, watching the place—no one coming or going—I realized how long I'd gone without sleep. Two days ago, I'd had a disrupted night in the front seat of my car, down in Bristol. Last night, I'd driven five hundred miles, only stopping for petrol. I was exhausted, and I could feel it: my bones ached, my eyes were gritty, my head was swimming with static. Whatever I planned to do here, whatever my approach was going to be, I knew I was taking a risk. Tilton would have let them know what had happened down in London. They'd know about Zack and Jason.

Maybe that was why it was so quiet here.

Maybe they were already waiting.

I cleared my head, gathering myself, and took in what awaited. Wire-mesh fencing circled the property, and the main gate—about six feet high—seemed to be electrically operated. A CCTV camera was positioned on a post to the left of it, to see who came and went. Using binoculars, I could pick out the two buildings.

One, the smaller, was closer to the road, about twenty yards from the entrance. A path, footprints frozen in the mud, led down an incline and around to the back of it. There was another CCTV camera on the front, pointing up toward the gated entrance to the farm. I had no idea if this one was Bethany, or Lazarus.

The second building, the farmhouse, was large enough to incorporate at least five bedrooms, and was much further down an uneven gravel track. Its windows were blacked out. The walls were peeling. If snow hadn't been brushed into neat piles either side of the front door, it would have looked as if it had never been lived in. A third CCTV camera was bolted to the roof, pointed at the front.

The track that ran between the two buildings, rolling down the incline of the hill, was uneven. Old, disused barns were perched on either side of it, full of frozen hay bails and rusting chunks of machinery. Beyond the farmhouse was the sea, crashing onto sand scattered with sheets of ice. Every time a wave reached for the shore, it pushed the smell of the place toward me: manure, sea salt, rust.

I leaned over and flipped the glove compartment.

Inside was a pair of wire cutters.

I picked up the binoculars again, and zeroed in on the fence, just up from where the first, smaller building was. If I went in through there, adjacent to the very furthest edge of the property, the CCTV cameras wouldn't be able to pick me up. None of them were trained on that part of the compound, which gave me a relatively free run down to the building. Once I was inside, I'd have to figure out my next move. It would depend on *what* was inside—or who was waiting for me.

I glanced at the glove compartment again.

Jason's gun was also in there.

As I looked at it, I thought of the bullet I had encased in glass in the spare room of my house, and then—further back—to the day I'd first removed it from the bloodstained streets of a South African township. I'd been so young then, so utterly fearless, which was probably the reason the newspaper sent me, and I'd wondered many times since about how much of that person remained. The smell of burning rubber. The crackle of gunfire. The sun melting the tarmac beneath our feet. I could smell those streets, *hear* them, like it was yesterday. And, when I looked down the road, toward the dormant farm, I saw something of the same.

It was colder here, quieter.

On the surface, at least, more benign.

But, on the inside of these walls, just like on the streets of South Africa in the years before the elections, there was a war going on. People were losing their lives for a cause, just the same. The only difference was there were no factions here. There were no tribes breaching each other's territory, no government vehicles flattening shacks or firing indiscriminately. There was no black or white.

There was them.

And there was me.

39

The smaller building had an old cottage-style look to it: pale red windowsills and frames, trays of dead flowers—and a plaque next to the door that said BETHANY.

I came in diagonally from the hole I'd cut in the fence, using the empty barns as cover. There was a second door at the back of Bethany, blistered and old. I slid the gun into my belt, and pushed. The door shuddered and creaked open.

Immediately inside was a kitchen.

The sink was missing taps and parts of its plumbing, and some cupboards had been dismantled and removed. A table had been chopped into pieces and left in the middle of the room. Off the kitchen were two doors: one to a pantry, the second to a living room without any furniture. In the living room were the stairs.

I headed up.

There were three doors on the landing but no carpet. The first was for a bedroom. An "A" was carved into the door. Inside, about halfway along, a square chimney flue ran from floor to ceiling, coming out of the wall about three feet. At the windows, there were no curtains, just sheets, moving in the breeze. No beds. No cupboards. Water trails ran down one of the walls, from holes in the ceiling.

I looked into the second bedroom, a "B" in the center of its door. This one was different. It was bigger, and the crumbling stone walls had thick cast-iron rings nailed into them, spaced out at intervals of three or four feet. From each of the rings, a set of handcuffs hung down. I moved forward, into the room. It was about forty feet long and smelled of vomit and shit. Exposed wooden floorboards, scarred and dirty, ran the length of it, and there were four windows, all covered by sheets. I turned and looked down at one of the rings closest to me, half-hidden behind the door. Above it, someone had gouged out a message in the damp walls.

Help me.

In the grooves of the letters were pieces of fingernail.

I backed out, and turned to face the third door. The bathroom. It had most of its fixtures, and a basin, toilet and bath. The bath was filthy—full of hair and broken pieces of tile—but the basin was clean, used recently, droplets of water next to the plughole. There was a mirror on the wall above. The bruising on my cheek had darkened, and the cuts from the thorns in the forest had started to dry. I had a little blood in my eye too, something that I hadn't noticed before. I leaned in even closer to the mirror to get a better look—and then spotted something.

I turned and looked back at the bath.

Its paneling doesn't fit properly.

Kneeling down beside it, I pushed at the panel, feeling it pop and wobble, and watched it regain its shape. I pushed again. This time the corners of the panel came away, and I could see the edges were slightly serrated, all the way around, as if the panel had been cut, and then fitted back in again. This time, I fed two of my fingers into the gap between the panel and its edge, and started to pull at it.

Without much effort, it came away completely.

Inside the bath, stacked around the half-oval shape of the tub, were hundreds of glass vials. They climbed as tall and as wide as the bath allowed, dark brown and identically labeled. Instructions for use were printed at the bottom of each vial, underneath a warning label: CAUTION: FOR VETERINARY USE ONLY.

The vials contained ketamine.

Snap.

A noise from outside.

I went to the window of the bathroom, and saw a woman coming up the track from the other building: pale, young, probably only twenty, her dark brown hair pulled back in a ponytail. She had on a pair of denims, a red top and a white ski jacket, and chunky, fur-lined boots. Loose pieces of gravel scattered beneath her feet as she made her way, before her footsteps deadened as she hit the snow.

I didn't have time to get out, so I put the panel back on the bath and padded through to Room B—the one with the rings on the walls. In behind the door, I backed all the way up against the wall, feeling the gun tucked into the back of my trousers. I reached around, my hands clammy despite the cold, and slid my fingers in around the grip, around the trigger. I had no idea if she was armed too.

I had no idea if I'd been spotted.

Were they on to me?

Was this a trap?

Footsteps sounded at the staircase. I had a narrow view between the door and the frame, enough to see her get to the top of the stairs. She had her phone in her hand now, and was checking something. She headed past me, to the bathroom.

I heard the squeak of the bath panel being removed.

Vials clinking together.

Quietly, she started humming to herself.

I moved out from behind the door, taking a big stride from the door of the bedroom to the door of the bathroom, and placed the gun at the back of her head.

"Good morning."

She jolted, as if a current had just cut her in two. Without moving, her eyes swiveled into the corners of her skull, looking back over her shoulder at me.

"Get up."

She stood slowly, leaving the vials on the floor, her hands up in front of her, telling me she wasn't going to be any trouble. As she half-turned toward me, I saw a flare of recognition in her face. She'd been briefed. She knew who I was.

"What's your name?"

"Sarah," she said quietly.

I gestured with the gun, indicating where I wanted her to head: Room B. She inched out of the bathroom, leaving the vials of ketamine on the bathroom floor, the panel discarded next to it. Inside Room B, I told her to kneel in front of the *help me* message, scrawled onto the wall.

"Can you read that, Sarah?"

She nodded.

Her breathing was short and sharp, scared.

"Good. So you speak English. Someone carved that message in the wall and left half their fingernails in there. You can see their fingernails, Sarah, can't you?"

She nodded again.

"Speak up, I can't hear you."

"Yes."

"Have you got any idea how painful that must have been? How *desperate* someone has got to be to carve a message in a wall like that using their fingers?"

She didn't move, didn't reply.

"Sarah?"

"Yes."

"Yes what?"

"Yes, I know."

"Good. Now I'm going to ask you some questions, and you're going to give me some answers. And if I get even as much as a whiff of a lie from you, Sarah, I'll be using your fingers to scratch a message in the wall next to that. Are we clear?"

She nodded.

I pulled her up and guided her out of the room.

I couldn't stand the smell any longer.

On the landing, I forced her to kneel down facing one of the walls. For a moment, I caught a glimpse of myself in the bathroom mirror, and didn't like the person that looked back. But things had changed now. *I* had changed. There was no going back to the man I'd been before, not now. They'd made certain of that.

"I don't want to hurt you," I said. She was kneeling down, one of her hands on the wall in front of her. "Everything will be fine if you just tell me the truth."

I paused, let her take it in.

She nodded.

"Okay. Did anyone see me arrive?"

She shook her head. "No."

"But you knew I'd get here eventually?"

"Yes. We were expecting you."

"Tilton called you?"

"Yes."

"How many of you are there here?"

"I don't know."

"Don't lie to me, Sarah."

"I'm not. I don't know. Honestly. Twenty-five. Maybe thirty."

I tried not to show my concern on my face.

Thirty people.

I looked into Room B. "What is the room with the rings used for?"

A hesitation, then: "Acclimatization."

"Which means what?"

"We bring them here to dry them out."

I thought of the teenager I'd found in the house in Bristol, the syringe on the floor next to him. "So this is a place for drug addicts? A rehabilitation clinic?"

She nodded again.

"We're not doing sign language any more. Yes or no?"

"Mostly, yes."

"What does 'mostly' mean?"

"It's mostly drug addicts. But there are others too."

"Others?"

"It's not . . ."

"Not what?"

"Not like a normal program."

I looked at the handcuffs, at the blood spatters, smelled the decay and the sickness in the air. "No kidding. So, what is it then?"

"It's a way to help people forget."

"Forget what?"

"The things they've seen. The things they've done."

"Like what?"

She didn't reply.

"Like *what*, Sarah?"

She paused, finally dropped her hand away from the wall, and turned her head slightly so she could get a better look at me. "I'm not sure you'd understand."

"I guess we'll see."

Another pause. "They've all suffered traumas."

"Like what?"

"Life-affecting traumas."

"*Specifics*," I said.

She'd looked away briefly, but finally her eyes fixed on mine again, moving across my face. I could see the fear I'd glimpsed after I'd surprised her. But now, somehow, it looked less convincing . . . as if she might be playing me; as if all of this—the scared little girl act—might be how she turned the game on its head.

"Life-affecting traumas like what?" I said.

She smiled a little, sadly. "Like Derryn."

I pushed the gun into the back of her head, forcing her against the wall. A puff of plaster spat out, into her face. She coughed.

"Don't try to get inside my head. Don't mention her name. Don't ever try to use her as a way to get at me. I hear you say her name again, I'll fucking kill you."

She nodded.

"Keep your eyes closed."

She frowned, as if she didn't understand.

"Keep your eyes closed."

She shut them.

"Specifics," I repeated. "Give me specifi—"

"Sarah?"

I paused, looking off along the landing.

"Sarah? Is everything okay?"

A man's voice, downstairs.

Someone else was inside the house.

40

I leaned in to Sarah. "Don't make a sound—got it?"

Her eyes snapped open again and she looked at me. I realized then why I'd asked her to close them in the first place. She wasn't classically beautiful but her eyes were incredible: as perfectly blue as an ocean without a single breath of wind on it. They were her weapons. They were what made her powerful. You looked into them and you dropped your guard. You lost yourself.

"Sarah?"

The man's voice again.

I covered her mouth and hauled her to her feet, then slowly backed up—her in front of me—into Room A.

"Sarah?"

A creak on the stairs.

I pushed her into the center of the room, so she was standing there alone, and moved back, behind the door. She looked at me; I looked right back at her.

Don't do anything stupid.

"Sarah?"

She turned to face the door.

"I'm up here."

I looked through the door jamb, toward the stairs. A head appeared, but slowly, as if—whoever it was—sensed something was up. "Are you okay?" he said.

"Yeah, fine."

"What are you doing?"

He's got an Eastern European accent.

He stopped short of the top of the stairs and looked around. I could see flashes of his face between the bars on the staircase, eyes darting between doors, and then he focused in on the ketamine vials, discarded on the bathroom floor.

"Sarah, what are you doing?"

He took another step.

When she didn't reply, I looked at her and gestured for her to reply.

"I . . . I thought, uh, that I heard a noise in here," she said. "I just came in to check it out."

I could see the man's face now.

Stefan Myzwik.

He was older than in the mugshots I'd seen, but leaner and more focused. He had a hand placed at the back of his trousers, clearly reaching for a weapon.

"It's warm in here."

I shot a look at Sarah.

She's just told him I'm here.

She stared back at me: didn't move, didn't say anything else. When I glanced back in Myzwik's direction, I could see his gun was up in front of him, aimed in the direction of the bedrooms. His eyes flicked left to the vials again, as he silently moved across the landing, knowing exactly where to place his feet. If I hadn't heard him calling Sarah's name, I'd never have heard him approach.

"Where?" he said.

"Room A," she replied.

Myzwik moved level with the door, looking in at Sarah—and, without her even having to say anything, he seemed to immediately know where I was.

I ducked as he fired twice through the door.

The noise shattered the silence, piercing the walls of the building and cracking across the fields outside. Wood splintered above me as bullets passed through the door, and a shower of plaster rained down into my hair and face.

I kicked the door closed.

It slammed shut, rattling in its frame.

Sarah glanced at me, then at the door, trying to work out if she could get out of the room before I got to her. But she didn't move for it. Instead, she turned, her hands up again, backing away. I raised the gun and pointed it at her, then darted across the room, grabbed her by the arm and brought her into me.

"Myzwik!" I shouted through the door.

Nothing.

No noise from the other side.

"I've got her and I'll k—"

A mobile phone started ringing on the other side of the door and, slowly, the door handle started turning. I pulled Sarah in closer to me, one arm around her neck, the other out over her shoulder, aiming the gun at the door.

It opened.

Myzwik stood with his gun down by his side and his mobile phone at his ear. His eyes were pale, almost the color of his skin, and he was growing a beard—jet black—which gave him an odd, alien appearance. He didn't take his eyes off me, he just stood there, listening to whoever had called him. I could hear the faint murmur of a voice, but not any clear sentences. It was an obvious ploy: him standing in the doorway, blocking my exit, telling me he didn't believe I would shoot him. In front of me, Sarah could probably feel my heart thumping against her spine. They probably both realized the truth now: that I fell short of the man I needed to be—because that man aimed his gun at Myzwik and pulled the trigger.

Finally, Myzwik said: "Yes, he has her."

"Put the phone down," I said.

He didn't. The voice continued, a constant barrage of instructions. There was a movement in his face. "Are you sure?"

"Put the *phone* down," I said.

This time I almost spat the words at him, and the change in tone seemed to surprise him. For the first time, he saw something of concern. Maybe not a killer, but a man determined enough to come right into their nest.

He flipped the phone shut.

"What are you doing here, David?" His accent had softened over time, but his voice remained hard, emotionless. "Have you got any idea what you're doin—"

"What the hell's going on here, Myzwik?"

"Why?"

"*Why?* Why do you think?"

He shrugged. "I feel sorry for you."

"Yeah? How's that?"

"You've no idea what you're doing."

I smiled. "You're all starting to sound the same—you know that?"

"Maybe it's because you're not listening properly."

"Or maybe it's because you haven't got an original thought in your heads. You're blinded, violent fanatics. I mean, *look* at this place. You're keeping people chained to the walls next door. You *seriously* think that's what belief is about?"

"Belief? What would you know about—"

"Save your breath."

He looked at me. "What do you want?"

"You're going to answer my questions, right here, right now. Because if you don't, I will kill her." I paused, feeling Sarah shift against me. She was panicked. I wasn't about to kill her—even now, even after what happened to me in the forest, I found the idea repellent—but Myzwik didn't need to know that. "If it's kill or be killed," I said to him, "you better believe I will put a bullet through her head."

Myzwik glanced at Sarah for the first time, eyes lingering on her, and then back at me, a shift in his face betraying him somehow. Sadness. Regret. Doubt.

Something's up.

And then I remembered what he'd asked at the end of his phone call: *Are you sure?* A moment of reluctance, as if someone had asked him to do something.

Oh shit.

A split second too late, I saw what.

"Wait a sec—"

He raised his gun—and shot Sarah in the chest.

The bullet entered high up, just above her left breast. She jerked back, her blood spitting into my face, and then fell away. In an automatic response, I tried to prevent her hitting the floor, tried to yank her back up toward me, but she folded completely. The transfer of weight was too much and too fast for me to cling on to. I stumbled back, dropping to my knee, laying her body on the ground, and by the time I looked up, Myzwik was almost on top of me, gun aimed at my head.

"*What the fuck have you just done?*"

"Get up," he said.

I glanced at Sarah. She was at my feet, clutching her chest, blood pumping out between her fingers. In her eyes some of the light had already disappeared.

"She's going to die."

"Get to your feet or you're next."

I stood. Sarah's eyes followed mine, but then she seemed to lose focus and her gaze drifted off. I wiped some of her blood from my face.

"She'll die, Stefan," I said to him, using his name as a way to get at his humanity. "She doesn't deserv—"

"Don't tell me what she deserves."

"I'll do whatever you want, just call her an ambulance."

He flicked a look at her for the first time.

I held up a hand. "Just call her an ambulance—before it's too late."

He seemed to waver for a moment: unbalanced, remote. But then he was back. He stepped forward and kicked my gun across the room, out of reach.

"She died for the cause," he said quietly.

I looked down at her again. Her life—maybe only twenty years of it—was running out over her hands, into her shirt, into her jacket, into the floorboards.

"You really believe that?" I said.

He didn't answer.

He just shoved the gun into my back, and forced me forward, out onto the landing—and we left her to die alone, in a room stained with pain and memories.

41

We headed down the track, toward the second building, an old slate farmhouse with an extension on the back. At the front was a veranda, exactly matching the one in the Polaroid of Alex, and a wooden sign, nailed to the inside of the railings.

It said LAZARUS.

The snow-covered grass, either side of the track, dropped away to the sea—heather scattered across it, spreading in all directions—and, beyond, fields were laid out in patches, unfurling north and south along the coast, like squares on the same chessboard. Inside the boundaries of the farm, I could see rectangles of grass had been dug up, spades, pickaxes and garden forks left out on the hard ground.

A hush settled across the farm, the only sound coming from a set of wind chimes, swinging gently in the breeze coming off the sea, and the grinding sound of metal against metal as a weathervane turned in the wind on top of the house. As the wind died down again, the weathervane settled back into place, and I saw what it was: an angel with a bow and arrow, string pulled back, eyes facing up.

Myzwik shoved me up, onto the veranda, and I looked in through a front window to my right. Alex had been in there once having his picture taken, frozen for a moment in time, framed by the window, the railings of the veranda and the blue of the sea and sky. What had happened to him? How had he ended up here?

"Open the door and go inside."

Myzwik brought me back into the moment.

I tried the door.

Like Bethany, Lazarus opened into a kitchen. It was small, dark, all three windows covered in black plastic sheeting. Two doors led from the kitchen. One was closed. The other was open, and I could see into a stark living room with a table in the center and a single chair pushed underneath it. On the walls of the kitchen were picture frames with Bible quotes in them, and shelves full of food.

Above the cooker was a newspaper cutting.

Boy, 10, found floating in the Thames.

It was the same one I'd seen in the flat in Brixton.

Myzwik flicked the lights on and closed the door. He grabbed my shoulder, pressed his gun into my spine and sat me in a chair at the kitchen table, facing away from the door. Behind me, I heard him open and close a drawer. The tear of duct tape. He started to wrap it around my chest and legs, securing me to the chair. When he was finished, he threw the duct tape onto the table and came around, standing in front of me, looking down at me. He touched a finger to one of my bruises. As I jolted away from him, he grabbed me more violently, fingers and thumb pressing hard into either cheek, and pulled me right in toward him.

"You're going to die," he whispered.

I wriggled free from his grip and stared at him.

He held my gaze for a moment, then turned away, removing his mobile phone. He flipped it open and speed-dialed a number. "Yeah, it's me. He's here."

He ended the call.

We paused there for a moment, staring at one another, and then he said: "You're not here to hurt people, is that right? You're here to—what?—liberate?"

I didn't reply.

He shook his head. "You were just pissing in the wind."

"You know that's not true," I said. "If I was pissing in the wind, two of your friends wouldn't have driven me to the middle of a forest to execute me."

His eyes narrowed.

He pulled out a chair and sat down, and—again—we looked at each other across the table, without saying anything. After a minute, maybe longer, he said: "I don't think we ever really clicked, Alex and I. A lot of us here tried to help him, but you've got to want to meet in the middle—and he couldn't do that."

"So, where is he?"

Myzwik shrugged. "Not here."

I glanced around the room, trying to come up with something: some plan, some way to get out. When I turned back to Myzwik, he seemed amused by me.

"I can hear your brain. *Tick, tock, tick, tock.*"

I stared at him.

"I'm sure his mother painted a beautiful picture for you," he said, "but Alex is a killer." He glanced at the newspaper cutting on the wall.

"He had nowhere else to turn, but we were there for him. Just like we've been there for everybody else."

"Like you were there for Sarah."

His eyes narrowed. "You don't understand."

"You just killed her in cold blood."

He shook his head. "You murdered her by turning up here."

"Even you don't believe that."

He didn't answer, fingers spread on the table in front of him. "She was your bargaining chip. You'd use her against us until you got exactly what you wanted."

"Don't you value life?"

"I value it greatly," he said. "I value it . . ."

He stopped.

Behind me, I heard the door open.

Myzwik looked over my shoulder and, suddenly—like a light switching off—his expression changed completely: everything fell away. His control, bravura.

He was scared.

In one of the picture frames in front of me, I could make out a reflection. A vague shape, a silhouette, standing close to my shoulder, slightly aback. I couldn't see his face and couldn't see whether he was looking at me, or looking at Myzwik.

But I could smell something.

A smell like decay.

Myzwik got to his feet, his eyes flicking between me and the man behind me, and then he edged away slightly, clearing his throat, as if he couldn't stand the smell. He slid along the kitchen counter, back toward the corner of the room.

Finally, in the reflection, I saw him.

Legion.

His mask was half-hidden in darkness—just an eyehole, a corner of the mouth, a horn. But there was something else: in his gloved hands was a needle.

I felt it plunge into my neck.

And then everything went black.

42

When I came round, I was sitting in the middle of a disused industrial fridge. There were no windows, and it was lit by the dull glow from a single strip light. Meat hooks hung from a long metal tube to my left. There were two doors, both of them closed: one seemed to be the entrance, dotted brown and orange with rust, and the second was some sort of side door, painted the same cream as the walls.

They'd placed me on an old wooden chair, but hadn't tied me to it. My feet were on the floor in front of me, exactly parallel to one another, and my elbows were flat to the arms of the chair. My shirt and trousers had been removed too, so I was just in my underwear, and they'd taken off my wedding ring and placed it on top of my left hand. I went to move my right hand, to pick up the ring, and felt my arm shift across my body toward it. Except, in reality, I hadn't moved at all.

It was just muscle memory.

The residual feeling of movement.

I was paralyzed.

When I tried moving my head, I had complete freedom. I could turn from side to side, look left and right, but my shoulders stayed exactly where they were.

So did my body.

Legs. Arms. Feet.

"What the hell have you done to me?"

My voice died instantly, replaced by the sound of something dripping, and my heart thumping in my ears. I tried to calm myself, closing my eyes, breathing.

Clunk.

The entrance door started opening.

A slow, grinding rumble as it forced its way out from the frame, and then a man filled the doorway. Not Legion. Another. He was massive: probably six foot four and eighteen stone. His blond hair was closely cropped, and he was dressed head to toe in black. He watched me for a moment, tilting his head slightly, as if vaguely amused, and then he stepped forward and brought his arms out from behind his back. There was something in his hands. At first I thought it was a belt.

But it wasn't a belt.

It was a scourge; a multi-thonged whip.

"What the hell have you done to me?"

The man didn't reply.

Instead, he reached back, into the darkness of the room beyond this one, and retrieved a chair from the shadows. He placed it down, just inside the fridge, pushed the door closed again, then came across and set it down in front of me.

"What have you done to me?" I said again.

Once more, he didn't reply. He just sat, placing the scourge on the floor beside him, and then shuffled his seat in closer, so our feet were almost touching. Still not making an effort to say anything, he looked me over, his eyes following the lines of my body, and ending up at the wedding ring, placed on top of my hand.

"That must be frustrating," he said quietly.

His voice matched his size: deep, heavy, forceful.

"My name is Andrew," he said eventually.

"What have you done?"

"It's good to finally meet you, David."

"What have you don—"

"In a lot of ways I admire you," he cut in, holding a finger up to me, telling me to be quiet. "My organization has managed to protect itself against people like you. On the rare occasions outsiders have got close to us before, we've managed to throw them off the scent. But not you, David. You're special. Until you came along, no one ever found out about what we have here. We made some mistakes, of course, but I think we underestimated you too." I glanced at the scourge, then back up at him. He hadn't taken his eyes away from me. I didn't even remember seeing him blink. "Everyone we take in here has made mistakes, some bigger than others, but we give people a chance to start again. In exchange, we require certain things. We require them to give themselves up to the program—completely. There are no half-measures." He paused, studied me. "And we require secrecy."

He stopped again, this time for longer.

"Are you listening to me? What I'm saying is we've worked too hard on this and gone too far for it to unravel because some no-note kid got lost in the ether."

He meant Alex.

We looked at each other for a moment, before he glanced at the ring again. "What you've never understood, David, is that our old lives don't exist any more. We don't have a space we can fit back into. We remove ourselves from society and we don't go back. If you took *one* of these kids out of the program because you thought you were saving them, where is it exactly that you think they might go?"

I glanced around the fridge. "Somewhere better than here."

He studied me, as if waiting for me to correct myself.

"Oh," he said. "I thought you were being facetious."

I just looked at him.

"Somewhere better than here," he repeated quietly.

Suddenly—just a blur of movement—he smashed his fist down onto the top of my right thigh. It was delivered with such power, I should have crumpled to a heap. Instead, my chair shifted back, and my leg levered away to the right.

But I felt nothing.

He grabbed his chair again, and moved in closer, so we were back, almost within touching distance. "It must be nice not feeling any pain," he said, looking down at my leg, at the rest of my body. "You, of all people, must be able to see the logic in that. I mean, can you imagine going the *rest of your life* without pain?"

I felt a twitch in one of my toes.

He tilted his head again. "Is the feeling coming back?"

I glanced from him, down to my toe.

"It will do," he went on. "See, we've drugged you. Well, actually, technically we've partially paralyzed you. A little homebrew we use when our students join the program. By the time they arrive here, they appreciate the lack of feeling. I mean, I'm sure you would have given a lot to feel *this* numb a year ago, correct?"

"You're insane."

He smiled again, a flash of darkness in his face for the first time. "Actually, I'm very lucid. *Think* about it, David. The only way you can change someone is by removing temptation from their life. Drugs. Sex. Violence." He paused, looking at my wedding ring. "*Grief.* The kids we bring here, especially the drug addicts, if we dried them out and returned them to society again, the temptation is still there."

I got a feeling in my toes again, stronger this time.

A shooting sensation.

He leaned in to me. "The temptation eats away at you, bit by bit, piece by piece, day by day. Rehabilitation only works when it takes you the whole way. You spend thirty days getting someone off drugs, and what are you left with, David?"

I didn't respond.

"A drug addict who hasn't taken drugs for thirty days. That's all. That's *it*. What you need to do is alter them. Not just their addictions but their whole *life*."

"So, you're imprisoning them here?"

He was incredulous. "*Imprisoning* them?"

"You think you're helping people by keeping them here?"

"I don't think. I know. We're offering shelter, food, support, family. We're giving them a place to belong to, a reason to get up in the morning. But, the most important thing of all, we're helping them to *forget*. Forget about their addiction. Forget about their past. I mean, do you honestly think any of them *want* to recall what they've done and what they've been through? One of the girls here stabbed a man in the chest after he raped her continuously for five years. Do you think she wants to recall what it feels like to have that man forcing himself inside her?"

"Are you saying you're erasing their memories?"

"We're helping them trade one life for another."

I looked at him, stunned. "You're wiping their mem—"

"No," he said, holding a finger up. "We're resurrecting them into a new life, one more deserving." He paused, leaning in to me, as if about to impart some sort of secret. "Stefan told me that you discovered our ketamine stash up in Bethany."

"What if they don't want to forget?"

"They do, believe me."

"What if they don't?"

"They *do*." He paused, eyeing me, clearly trying to calm himself. "Do you know what ketamine users say about the high? It's like reaching another state of consciousness. Like seeing the world as God sees it. You come out of your body, and you look down, and you see yourself there—this pathetic creature, lying there, unable to move—while this new part of you moves around, free, no longer tethered to what has gone before. They say it's the closest thing to dying. Users call it the 'K-hole.' We mix it with dimethyltryptamine and call it a resurrection."

"You're crazy."

"Once they've been through that symbolic resurrection," he continued, ignoring me, "we keep them on a program of drugs, which includes ketamine, just in lower doses, and over time our students begin to break off the chains that bound them, and emerge into this new existence— one free of pain and regret."

"You're destroying them."

He laughed, and looked down at my body.

I had feeling all the way up to my knees, but he'd trapped my legs between his. He'd stripped me down to my pants to make me feel weaker, to humiliate me, and he'd placed my wedding band on my hand to taunt me, and because—once I got feeling back in my hands and arms—I was a threat to him again. When my hand started twitching, when the ring fell away, he'd know I was back to full power.

"You saw that boy down in Bristol, correct?"

He meant the kid on the sofa.

"Correct, David?"

I nodded.

"What memories do you think he has that he wants to keep?" He leaned in, his face about a foot from mine. "He's seventeen. He's spent two years on heroin, and the ten years before that being molested by his father. So, go on David: tell me *exactly* what memories you think that boy will want to keep from this life?"

"It doesn't make it right."

He grunted. "How would you know what's right?"

"You're forcing them."

"We ease their pain."

"You're forcing drugs into them."

"*We're helping them build a new life!*"

More sensation: in my thighs, my groin, my stomach.

"I've spent a long time building this place, David. I've spent a long time getting the right people into the right positions to help me. Surely you understand the need for me to protect what is important." He glanced at the wedding band on the top of my hand. "You'd protect what was important to you—wouldn't you?"

"The right people?"

He nodded.

"Like that freak in the mask?"

He didn't move, didn't reply.

"What's right about him?"

"He does what is necessary to secure our survival. We had problems at the beginning, and he helped us with those problems. In return, we helped him."

"Was he helping you when he came for me in my home?"

He didn't comment, his eyes dropping to my waist, where I could feel the bottom of my ribcage shifting. "You're pushing it out of your system impressively fast," he said. "I wanted to see what kind of a dose it would take to knock you out."

I frowned. "What are you talking about?"

"Let's just say, we need to know how much to give you."

I tried to move my elbows off the arm of the chair, imagined grabbing him by the throat, could even *feel* my arms going there, doing it, my fingers crushing his larynx into paste. Instead, they didn't going anywhere. They were disabled.

"Where's Alex?"

He laughed. "Don't you know when to give up?"

"Where is he?"

His eyes lingered on me, a hint of conflict in them. "Alex was different. He came to me just over a year ago after a long time in the wilderness. I didn't go out and find him. He was given to me by Michael." A pause. "He was . . . different."

"Different how?"

Andrew's eyes moved from my face, to the wedding ring.

"When I first started the farm, I suppose I expected every kid I took in to respond to what we were doing. They had problems, we were offering them a way out—and for a while it worked beautifully. We turned the first batch into clean-living people; people we could use. I got Zack off drugs, and he became a recruiter for me. I gave Jade her dignity back after years of abuse and she contributed to our operations down in London." He leaned back in his chair. It creaked under his weight. "But then things got more difficult. Zack found this heroin addict down in Bristol, who was working as a prostitute. We started her on a detox program. But then, one night, she told me she didn't want to be here. I told her she had made her choice and now she had to stick to it." His body sank a little. "So, she pulled out a pair of scissors—and she stabbed one of my best people in the chest."

I watched him: a flicker of sadness, of anguish.

The first genuine emotion I'd seen.

"I hit her," he said. "And then I hit her again and again and again. And when I finished, she wasn't moving any more. She pleaded with us to help her, so we brought her here with the promise of a new life. And she repaid us, repaid me, by stabbing one of my best friends." He stopped again, drifting, but then snapped back into the moment. "I had an epiphany after that. A watershed moment. When others fought us like she did, threw everything we offered them back in our faces, I realized we had to deal with them. We'd taken them out of society, given them a roof over their head. We'd made sacrifices for them—so, they'd make a sacrifice for us. They'd become martyrs. They'd help us by cementing the resurrection."

I frowned, unsure of what he was saying.

But then it hit me: he was talking about the people who had died *instead* of Alex, of Jade, of Myzwik, of everyone else here who had been assimilated into the program. It wasn't Alex who had died in the car crash, or Jade who had been brutally murdered in her home, or Myzwik who had washed up on the shores of the reservoir, but it was still people from the farm—failures, rebels, runaways.

The ones who didn't want to forget.

Who didn't want to erase every memory.

"That's why you brought Legion in," I said.

"Yes," he replied, and then, unexpectedly, got to his feet. "We'd been in the army together. He had some unique skills. You see how a man values existence when you're on a battlefield, David. You see how quickly he's prepared to turn life into death. Most soldiers, most people, don't want to have to kill. They have a line that they don't ever want to cross." I followed him as he picked up the chair and placed it behind him, returning for the scourge. Once he'd scooped it up, he started running his fingers through the thongs. "But, for him, there *was* no line."

"I thought this was a mission from God?"

"It is."

"You ever read the Ten Commandments?"

He smiled. "I was protecting the project."

"You brought in a murdering psychopath."

"You will never understand, David."

"You're right about that."

"You've never had a cause to fight for." He looked briefly at the wedding band. "Other than the memory of your dead wife. And what sort of cause is that?"

He smiled again as he saw the anger burning in me.

"We have people in useful places. In the hospital system. In the police. We secure our supplies through them, and we ensure any potential lines of inquiry are cut off as soon as possible. Our men and women on the inside, they've experienced redemption. They're like Zack, and Jade, and Stephen. Once broken, now repaired. They give others that same chance by protecting what we have."

"Whose body did you use for Alex?"

He shrugged. "Does it matter?"

"It matters to the people who love him."

He watched me for a moment. "You don't know anything, David. Most of their families don't care if they're dead or alive."

"You think Mary cares whether Alex is alive?"

"She does now she's seen him."

"She did anyway."

"Like I said, I didn't have a choice with Alex—"

Suddenly, my whole body spasmed.

Andrew smiled, and stepped in.

And, finally, my wedding ring fell from my hand, pinging against the floor of the fridge and rolling away. We both watched it until it came to a stop against the wall, and then Andrew shifted the chair and leaned in closer.

I could move my arms.

Not much, but I could move them.

"After I left the army, I got into some trouble," he said. "I couldn't find work. I missed the routine the military had brought to my life. The discipline. So, I resorted to stealing, and I hurt people. After that, I deservedly went to prison."

He glanced behind me, eyes lingering on something.

I tried to turn, to see what had got his attention, but he reached out and grabbed my face, straightening it, forcing me to look ahead. The power he had in his fingers brought it home to me: I could move my arms—but I was still weak.

"After I got out, I found God. Eventually, I even managed to get to the Via Dolorosa in Jerusalem. I saw the path Jesus walked on his way to the crucifixion. You gain an appreciation of what he had to endure when you visit those places—and, afterward, you look at people differently. You look at *yourself* differently. You realize, if people could experience even a little of what he had to go through, they might have a greater appreciation of what they've been given in this life."

He looked behind me again.

"Legion brought an idea to me one day. At first I thought it was a little . . . medieval. But then when I considered it some more I realized the kids we took in were exactly the sort of people I was thinking about when I visited Israel. Like me, they never appreciated what they'd been given in their first lives: the drugs, and the promiscuity, and the violence. All these opportunities, all that life had to bring us and offer us, and we choose to ruin it with those things. But if they could get a taste of what Jesus went through, if they could carry around with them a reminder of that, maybe they'd appreciate life a lot more the second time round."

He grabbed my chair, and started moving me.

And I saw what was behind me.

Legion.

He was standing in a double doorway, the room behind him black, with his mask on top of his head. It was the same man who had come up to me in the pub in Cornwall, except now he looked more manic, more frantic, as if on the cusp of something exciting. Something he had been desperate to do for a long time. He glanced at Andrew and back to me and smiled—his teeth small, uneven, yellow.

And I could see his tongue.

It's forked.

He reached out to something on the wall inside the room behind him—a light switch—and, in an instant, the room filled with low-level light.

Through the double doors was a small space, probably fifteen feet squared, with very high ceilings. It was another fridge, but the walls were painted black. In the center of the room, half in shadow—almost touching the ceiling—was a huge structure made from two railway ties. One was horizontal, the other vertical.

It was a crucifix.

Legion reached for the mask on top of his head and pulled it down over his face. And—as I desperately tried to move, tried to will myself to fight back—I felt Andrew disturb the air to my left, and a needle enter my neck for a second time.

Black.

43

I opened my eyes.

My head was forward, against my chest. Gravity had forced it there. I was handcuffed to the cross, five feet off the floor, my toes touching a footrest a third of the way up the vertical tie, my hands cuffed to either end of the horizontal piece. I was still in my underwear, but despite the feeling being restored to my body, there was now something else to contend with: the cold of the room. It was freezing—almost sub-zero. As I wriggled my fingers, unable to move my wrists in toward me, I felt my circulation kick into life, and a shiver at the top of my spine.

A gentle squeak.

Behind me, slightly to the left.

I turned on the cross and looked down. I couldn't see much, but I could see enough. There was a metal trolley in view—the type used in operating theaters.

Legion, dressed in an apron, was beside it, looking up.

He had the mask on.

I tried to face him down, to keep my composure, but my eyes drifted to the instruments he had laid out in front of him. Individual metal plates containing a scalpel and a hammer—and a set of pencil-sized nails. I couldn't prevent my face from showing what I felt this time, and the change amused him. He smiled inside the mask, teeth showing through the mouth slit, feeding off my fear, my distress.

Nails.

My stomach clenched as something Andrew had said earlier came back to me: *Let's just say, we need to know how much to give you.* I understood now.

It wasn't just drugs. They were only a part of it; a second stage in this so-called resurrection. The drugs emulated the sensation of dying, of leaving your body. But before that, there was this—the first stage— what you looked down on before it began: your body, hoisted up onto a tie, dying the way Jesus had.

Nailed to a cross.

"Wait a second," I said, guts churning.

But he ignored me and disappeared from view.

I tried to follow him, panicking now, and then—once he was behind me—pulled at the handcuffs, straining every muscle, every sinew, trying to tear them away from the tie. When I failed, I looked for him again, and he appeared on the other side, carrying an aluminum stepladder, and the scourge Andrew had been holding. He laid the scourge on top of the ladder and returned to his trolley.

"Don't do this," I said.

He continued straightening the instruments on the trolley, as if he hadn't even heard me, and then he crossed back to the stepladder, and readjusted it, so it was directly beneath my left arm. He looked up. His eyes moved back and forth across my body, his tongue making a scratching sound against the inside of the mask, and then he climbed to the second step of the ladder, and leaned in at me.

He was less than a foot away.

I could hear him breathing.

I could smell him.

He picked up the scourge, fingers moving through the thongs, and then he shifted closer to me, so I could see them. There were traces of wet blood on them.

"That's your blood," he said.

I looked from the scourge to his eyes—menacing, cruel—showing through the holes on the mask. Was this a trick? Another lie? I shook my head at him.

"I whipped you with it."

I felt no pain anywhere. "No."

"Yes. We've heavily anesthetized the area around your lower back, so you won't feel it for a while." He leaned even closer. I could feel his breath on my face now. "But you'll have some beautiful scars to prove it. Down there . . ." He paused, and looked along the horizontal tie to my left hand. "As well as in your fingers."

He was right.

I can't feel anything in my lower back.

"It's amazing how much punishment the body can take," he said, a shiver passing through me, a revulsion, as he touched his fingers to my arm, sweeping from shoulder to wrist, "the lengths it will go to in order to survive, the reservoirs of strength. After they scourged Jesus, reducing his back to *shreds*, he still carried his cross all the way to Calvary. But then he *was* the son of God. You're . . . *what* exactly?" His eyes narrowed, obviously disgusted by the sight of me. "You're less than worthless. You're a parasite, a *cockroach*, scuttling around in the darkness."

He climbed back down and went to the trolley.

I felt nauseous, weak, scared.

"The hand's a very complex piece of anatomy," he continued, selecting a nail from the tray. He held it up, examining it, turning it. "Twenty-seven bones, including eight in the wrist alone. Muscles, tendons, ligaments, cartilage, veins, arteries, nerves . . . You've got to make sure you don't hit anything important."

He picked up the rest of the nails.

There were five.

One for each finger.

"No!" I shouted, and struggled against the handcuffs again—again, again—knowing, somewhere deep down, that it was futile, a worthless gesture, but trying all the same, desperately fighting what was coming. But when I stopped, I saw he was beneath me looking up—fascinated— like he was watching a dying animal.

He rolled his neck. *Click.*

"Don't worry, I've become quite an expert at this," he said, a horrible smile opening up like a cut inside the mask. "I mean, if I put a nail through the palm of the hand, what use is a person? How can they dig fields, or plant seeds? How can they eat, drink, piss, shit? But if I put one in their *fingers*, after a time they can still operate their hand—and they get to experience a little of what it was like two thousand years ago, up there on that hill in Calvary. What a *privilege* for them—"

Suddenly, an alarm started.

I looked at Legion, and then he disappeared beneath my arm. I was facing the back wall of the room, unable to see out through the double doors behind me, into the disused fridge that Andrew and I had occupied, but I could hear him: his quick footsteps; the sound of the doors opening; the alarm getting louder, almost ear-piercing. *It's coming from somewhere beyond this room; beyond the fridge.*

"What's that?"

Legion's voice: calm, but concerned.

He doesn't know why it's gone off.

I couldn't hear anyone reply to him—but then the sound became subdued again, the door closing. Outside, the alarm continued whirring. Inside, I saw him pass beneath my right arm, dump the nails on the trolley, and then slide a hand into the front pocket of his apron. He brought out a syringe. Removing the plastic sleeve from the needle and throwing it across the room, he started climbing up.

"We'll have to do this back to front," he said, leaning in to me. He came so close, I felt the mask touch my cheek, felt his breath in my mouth. "We have no use for you. You're *pathetic*. But I want you to experience what it's like to die."

His eyes flicked to my arm, trying to find a vein.

"And then I'll nail you to this—and then I'll kill you for real."

I started moving, violently shaking, whipping my arms back and forth, the crucifix wobbling on the base they'd built for it. He clamped a hand to my arm, as much to prevent himself falling as to stop me, and I made a movement with my head toward him, feeling my skull glance the mask. He rocked, unsteady—but, then, he recovered. As he came back toward me, he moved fast: he dropped the syringe into the apron pocket, and whipped out a knife, raising it to my throat.

The tip of the blade nicked my chin.

The alarm still going off, slowly he reached into his apron with his other hand and took out the syringe. I tried moving my arm, tried to make it impossible for him to find a vein, but he'd boxed me in. If I moved too much, the blade would sink into my larynx. All I could do was watch as he leaned forward, elbow at the crook of my arm, pressing hard, my veins rising to the surface like cords of string.

He brought the syringe around.

"I'll come back for you," I said.

He smiled. "Not in this life you won't."

And then he sunk the syringe into my arm.

I died.

All objects were swallowed up, light turned to darkness, and then, quickly, the darkness became something else. A haze, a fuzz, indistinct and confusing. In some distant part of my consciousness, I could hear the alarm. But it didn't *sound* like an alarm: it was an incredibly slow series of pops, like camera bulbs going off, and, with every one, it felt like I jolted further forward, moving toward someone.

It was me.

Suddenly, I was above myself, my near-naked body frozen on the cross, my wrists handcuffed. I could see Legion, standing at the bottom of the ladder, but he wasn't moving. I wasn't even sure if it was him, or if he was real. I couldn't process what I was seeing: the eyes, mouth, horns. They seemed melded to him.

The plastic had fused with his scalp.

The mask had become his face.

I could feel the wooden tie against the back of my arms, the numbness at my back, and my inner voice telling me, over and over, that I wasn't dead yet.

But then something shifted.

A feeling washed over me, like the control I'd had left was slipping away, and—as that went—scenes from my life began to play out. Standing on a beach with my mum, aged eight. Shooting targets with my dad. Sitting beside his bed after he'd died. Meeting Derryn. The day I asked her to marry me. The day we got told we couldn't have kids. The day she told me to find that first missing girl.

The day of her funeral.

It's perfect for you, David.

Her voice again, saying those words on repeat; and, after her voice faded, a different kind of darkness moved in, devouring everything, consuming it, until all that was left were echoes of images and voices: people I'd loved, people I'd buried.

And beyond that, waves crashing on top of one another.

Over and over, on and on.

The sound of the sea.

44

"What's that?"

"The Red Room alarm."

"Why's it going off?"

"Because someone's *set* it off."

"I'm finishing this."

"Later."

"No, Andrew. We don't let Raker go again."

"*Later.* You sweep the compound and *then* you finish with him."

"Who gives a shit about the Red Room?"

"I give a shit about it. Let's go."

In the darkness, there was only sound. There was nothing to see. And yet, I could feel myself slowly moving to something, a star being drawn to a black hole, shifting closer and closer as a deafening, relentless alarm got louder and louder.

Suddenly, there was a door.

I was standing right in front of it, light on the other side. It was startlingly bright, burning through the keyhole, the cracks in the wood, a knot about halfway up that had pinprick-sized holes in it. I shifted even closer to it, looking down at the handle, and felt myself reach out for it. I couldn't see my arms, didn't reach for it with my fingers, but I could feel my hands *on* it, and sense it was turning.

Then I stopped.

Behind me, I felt someone move in close to me.

As they did, the sound of the alarm faded out, revealing another noise behind it—gentle, comforting. I let go of the door handle, still unable to see my arms, and realized the sound was the sea: waves crashing endlessly on a shore.

I know this sound.

Somehow, I felt the person behind me nod.

I know why I'm hearing it. This was the night I asked Derryn to marry me. We were staying with my parents on the farm, and we'd walked down into the village and sat on the sea wall, and we'd watched the sun start to go down.

I felt the person nod again.

Is that you behind me now?

No reply this time.

I want to see you.

I tried to turn but, as I did, I felt the person drift away.

I want to see my wife. Please, let me see you—

"David?"

I opened my eyes.

Below me a man was looking up: stained, mismatched clothes, skin smeared with dirt, the hood up on his jacket, an unkempt beard that consumed his face. At first, I wasn't even sure if he was real or not. I was drifting in and out of consciousness so fast and so often, I was finding it hard to tell the two apart.

He took a step closer.

"David," he said again, more firmly.

Something flickered in me, the smallest fire of recognition, and then it was gone again. But as he took another step closer to the ladder, I clawed at the memory and it came to me. *The man who had broken into my car. The man I'd lost outside Angel's. The man I'd seen outside my house.* I knew who he was now.

I knew him all along.

It was Alex.

Family

There were four in a group, digging flowerbeds in the earth outside Bethany. Across from them, a man and a woman watched. He was forgetting so much now—dates, faces, conversations he'd vowed never to lose—but he remembered their names. The man was Stephen, the first person he'd met when he arrived on the farm; and the woman was Maggie. He didn't remember much about her. He wasn't sure he had ever spoken to her. But he knew her face. In the darkness at the back of his mind, where he stored the memories that he was determined they would never ever take, he had a clear memory of her, clamping his mouth open.

She'd been the one that had taken his teeth.

Beneath his feet, the earth was wet. It was early spring. He scooped up a pile of soil and tossed it aside, and—as he came up again—he saw Rose, the girl who had been in the room with the rings, forty yards down the slope from him.

They'd spent three days in that room together until she'd been taken away. She'd talked to him a little during that time, telling him things about the farm, about the people who ran it—or, at least, as much as she could remember—and then she was moved on to the next part of the program, and she was never the same. She looked better now—less gray, more color—but she barely seemed to recognize his face. She looked through him. Sometimes he would pass her and he could see her big, bright eyes lingering on him, her brain firing as she tried to remember where she'd seen him, or what they had talked about. But most times, she just looked past him, as if he were a ghost among these fields.

He pounded the shovel down into the ground and felt it reverberate up the handle. The fingers of his hands throbbed for a moment, and then the pain faded into a dull ache. He turned his left hand over, examining it. At the ends of his fingers, where once he'd traced creases and lifelines, there were patches of smooth, white skin. Wounds: half an inch across and vaguely circular in shape.

That was where the devil had put the nails in.

When he turned his hand over, he could see the same wound, replicated beneath the veneer of his fingernails. They'd mostly grown back over, but the injuries were visible beneath, trapped there, like a hole beneath a sheet of ice.

The crucifixion. The drugs.

The last stage of the program.

He'd worked out what this place was doing even before he'd been put on that cross, partly from observing, partly from what Rose had told him. He knew the program destroyed and rebuilt them, ready for this new life; a life free from the memories of addiction, and rape, and violence. But free, as well, from the memories of anything else they'd once done. Any places they'd been. Any people they'd loved. By the time the program was over, they had no history.

Only now.

Only this.

Except he was different.

He slid a hand into his pocket and touched the top of the Polaroid. He didn't need to take it out. He knew what it looked like, every inch of it. And he knew what he was going to do with it if he ever got the chance. He'd fought the program all the way through, right from the start—and the memories he'd managed to cling on to, in his pocket and in his head, they would never get to. They could fight him, and hurt him, and hunt him from the corners of the room.

But they would never get everything.

These memories were his.

Always.

He pulls up to the curb and switches off the engine. There's a crack in the windshield, from left to right. In the corner, over the steering wheel, he can see blood.

A lot of blood.

He gets out and locks the doors.

At the front of the car, the grille above the bumper is broken, one of the headlights has smashed and there's blood across the hood, splashed like paint.

Panicked, he heads to the house.

Through the window, he can see his dad.

He moves quickly up the path, onto the porch and opens the front door. The house smells of fried food. In the kitchen he can see his dad, standing over a frying pan, moving the handle, two steaks shifting around in oil. His dad doesn't notice him at first, but then he seems to sense someone is watching, and turns.

His dad startles. "Oh, you frightened me," he says, and then looks his son up and down. "Are you okay? What's the matter?"

"I did it, Dad."

"Did what?"

"Uncle Al."

"What about him?"

"I took care of him."

His dad nods, smiles. "You talked to him?"

"No. No. I mean I took care of him. Like we said."

A frown. "What are you talking about?"

"We can keep the money."

No reply this time.

"The money," he says, a little more desperate now. "We can *keep* it. We can do what we want with it. Al's gone, Dad. I took care of him for you. He's gone."

"What do you mean, 'gone'?"

"You know."

"No, I don't know. What do you mean, 'gone'?"

"Gone," he says quietly. "Dead."

His dad's face drops. "*What?*"

"I did what you asked."

"You *killed* him?"

"Yes."

"Wha—why?"

He frowns. "The money."

"The money?"

"Remember we talked about it. About keeping it."

"You killed him for the *money?*"

"For us."

"I never told you to *kill* him!"

"Dad . . ."

"Don't you make me a part of this."

"But Dad . . ."

"Don't you *dare* make me a part of this."

"But you wanted to keep the money. To take care of Al."

"You offered to talk to him, not *kill* him."

"Dad, I thought that's what you wanted."

"*No*," his dad says. "Why the hell would I want that? I wanted you to *talk* to him, to reason with him."

"But you told me—"

"I told you to talk to him."

"You told me to kill him."

"What? Are you out of your mind?"

"You told me to do it."

"What the hell were you thinking?"

"I was the one who said I didn't want him dead."

"What the fuck were you thinking?"

"You wanted him dead, Dad. I did this because you wanted it done. I did this for *you*, not for me. Don't do this. Don't try to deny you ever said it to me."

"I never told you to murder him."

"You di—"

"*No!* Just shut up for a minute and think about what you've done." His dad stops, massaging his forehead. "Have you any idea what you've done? I mean . . . *shit*. You shouldn't even *be* here. You should be running for the bloody hills."

"What?"

"Where's Al?"

"Is that what you want?"

"Where's Al?"

"Is that what you want—for me to run for the hills?"

"*Where's Al?*"

"In the car park."

"At the strip club?"

"You want me to run away?"

"At the strip club?"

"Yes."

"You just left him there?"

"Of course I left him there."

"*Shit*. What have you done?"

"You want me to run?"

His dad doesn't answer.

"Dad?"

"What do you suggest?"

He looks at his dad, then backs away, out of the kitchen and into the living room. "You're just going to turn your back on me, Dad? You're going to do this?"

"Find a place to stay."

"That's it?"

"Lay low for a while."

"Lay low?"

"Let it blow ov—"

"Why should I lay *low*? This is bullshit! You're as much a part of this as me. You talked about wanting him dead. You talked about taking the money. Why do you think I did this? I did this to save you and Mum. I did this to save our family."

"What you did was wrong."

"You're turning your back on me?"

"What do you expect?"

"What do I *expect*?"

"You killed someone."

He still has the car keys in his hands. He feels for them, runs a finger along the ignition key, feels the grooves against his skin. Now all he has left is the car.

"I won't come back," he says.

"Just let it blow over."

"No, Dad. If I go, I don't come back."

His dad looks at him.

"That's it?"

"What do you expect me to say, son?"

He turns and heads for the front door, then he remembers something. He looks back over his shoulder at his dad, standing in the doorway to the kitchen.

"Al told me something tonight."

"You need to go," his dad says.

"Were you ever going to tell me?"

"Tell you what?"

"Were you ever going to tell me?"

"Tell you *what*?"

"Tell me that I had a brother."

They stay like that for a while, Malcolm staring into space, eyes glistening in the light from the kitchen; and Alex opposite him, a tear rolling down his face.

Then, finally, Alex turns and leaves.

And they never see each other again.

PART FIVE

45

The alarm hadn't stopped.

Against the wall of sound, I watched a dead man move beneath me, going to the stepladder, picking it up, and setting it down beneath my left arm. *Alex.* He looked past me, out to the double doors, and then climbed up the steps. As I started to pull myself further out of the funk, my hearing kicked in and the alarm seemed to become louder than ever, as if it were wired directly into my eardrums.

I winced.

My head thumped. My back hurt.

I felt nauseous.

They'd drugged me and numbed me, and yet I could feel myself returning to the surface: as my hearing came back, my vision lost its haze, and I could see detail on the wall in front of me, and the grime on Alex's face as he looked at me.

"You have to trust me, okay?"

I swallowed and tried to speak.

Instead, I erupted into a coughing fit.

By the time I was done, I could see he'd unzipped his coat and had a pair of bolt cutters in his hand. He placed the teeth on the cuffs and snapped them shut.

My arm fell away from the tie.

He caught it as it dropped, but the movement still unbalanced me, and I wobbled on the footrest, the crucifix vibrating as I leaned forward. But Alex had anticipated it: he pressed a hand flat to my stomach and managed to steady me.

Slowly, he guided my arm down to my side.

He moved down the stepladder, picked it up and placed it under my right arm. Every passing second, I felt more alive, but with it came sensation: there was pain in my lower spine, fading in fast, and as I thought back, I saw a moment before Legion injected me, his words in my head: *I whipped you. We've heavily anesthetized the area around your lower back, so you won't feel it for a while.*

"My back," I said.

Alex nodded. "It's okay."

His voice was soft—almost soothing—a complete contrast to the way he looked. Placing a hand around my lower arm, he snapped through the handcuffs, watching them fall to the floor, and used his hand to pin my body to the crucifix.

"Are you steady?" he said.

I was in pain. I still wasn't one hundred percent.

But I nodded.

"Are you sure?"

I nodded again. "Yes."

He let go of me, and I rocked briefly. But then he started to help me off the footrest, guiding me down the steps and onto the floor. I knelt down, sucking in air. The cold of the room helped, clearing my head, the fog, the drug.

"What have they done to my back?" I said.

My voice was soft, hoarse.

"He's whipped you," Alex replied, looking at my back, and then he removed some bandaging from his jacket. "I've been where you are," he said, looking out at the double doors, at the disused fridge, checking we were still alone. "*Everyone* here has been where you are. You have wounds at your lower back. Whip marks. They'll scar, but they'll hurt until they do. I can't give you a painkiller yet because of the drugs he's just put in your body. You've been out for twenty-five minutes."

Less than half an hour.

But it had felt like days.

He tore the plastic wrapping away from the bandaging, and then started to circle me, binding it. It helped. My lower back was starting to feel like it was on fire, but the tighter he wound the bandage, the more the feeling was suppressed.

"Why?" I said to him, once he was done.

"Why what?"

He hauled me to my feet.

"Why are you doing this?"

He looked through the double doors, into the fridge, and then threaded an arm through mine. "Because someone has to pay."

That was when the alarm stopped.

46

Immediately outside the crucifixion room was a long, thin, partially lit corridor. It looked like a military compound or a bomb shelter. There were no windows, just arrows on the wall pointing left, and the word SURFACE. We were underground.

Alex led me along the corridor, in the direction of the arrows. Every step I took seemed to bring my body alive even more: the strength returned to my legs and arms, my head cleared. But, at the same time, my back got worse. I couldn't feel open wounds, because I couldn't feel blood, but it was raw and hurt like hell.

The whole place reeked of damp; a musty, enclosed smell. On the walls, rust ran in strips, and naked lightbulbs dangled on cords above us. Every so often we passed other doors. Most were closed, but a couple were open. I glanced in at one of the rooms. It was small, plain, with two bunk beds inside.

Alex stopped about halfway down and listened. Somewhere above us there were voices—muffled, echoing slightly. It was hard to make out words, hard even to tell whether the voices were male or female. And then we were moving forward again, eventually reaching a set of doors. We pushed through them. On the other side was an anteroom with two further doors. One on the left had a glass window in it and was marked MEDICAL. Inside I could make out whitewashed walls, a dentist's chair, a panel of switches above the headboard of a bed, an oxygen tank, and a trolley like the one Legion had used, full of scalpels, chisels, scissors and clamps. The door on the right wasn't marked but also had a glass window— it was mostly dark, except for one strip light, dull and creamy in the blackness beyond.

Alex pushed through the right-hand door.

On the other side, it was barely lit—only the strip light I'd glimpsed, and two identical ones further down, spaced about fifteen feet apart. They buzzed above us as we walked. This corridor was shorter than the last, with two doors on either side, and a further one, standing open, at the end, revealing a set of stairs.

At the top of the stairs was daylight.

Alex looked at me. "We need to get you dressed."

Suddenly, silhouettes started forming in the light.

Alex yanked me forward and through the door closest to us. Inside, it was similar to the room I'd seen before: two bunk beds and a table. He closed the door and switched on the light. On the back of the door hung four green training tops with hoods, four pairs of green tracksuit trousers, and four pairs of boots.

"What size shoe are you?" he whispered.

"Eleven."

He started looking through the boots, and picked out a pair from the middle. "These will fit," he said, handing them to me. "Put the clothes on too."

He glanced at his watch.

I looked at him as I pulled on the clothes and the boots. He was incredibly focused—decisive, driven—so different from the person I imagined him being.

When I raised my arms, the marks from the scourge burned. I paused for a moment, letting the pain dull a little, and then fed my arms through the sleeves and pulled it down over my body. "Those are standard issue," he said, and then quieted again as voices passed the door. When they were gone, he turned back to me and looked at his watch again. "The alarm will go off again in sixty seconds."

"And then?"

"And then we make a break for it."

I nodded. He removed his jeans and pulled on a pair of tracksuit trousers and then relaced the boots he'd been wearing. Shrugging off his coat and jumper and leaving them on the floor, he pulled on a training top and flipped the hood.

"Are you okay?" he said quietly.

I pulled up my hood too. "Yeah."

"Good. Let's go."

47

Almost on cue, the alarm burst into life again.

This time it sounded different to before: a long drawn-out wail rather than the short, staccato beeps of the first time around.

We moved out into the corridor and toward the stairs. At the bottom, I looked up. In the block of light, more shapes began to form: others, dressed like us, coming down the steps. Three of them. They glanced at us as we passed, their eyes firing as they tried to recall who we were and what part of the farm they might have seen us in, and when I looked back over my shoulder, I could see one of them—a woman—stop on the steps. She was staring at Alex as we headed up.

"She recognizes you," I said, warning him.

"Just keep moving."

"She *recognizes* you."

"Even if she does," he replied, "she doesn't know why."

He meant they'd robbed her of her memories. Her past, a life she'd once lived—they were gone now.

At the top of the stairs, emerging into hazy gray light, I quickly got my bearings. Off to my right, at the top of the track, I could see the side of Bethany, half-disguised behind the barns in between: there was the A-shape of the roof, the bathroom window under it, flowerbeds beneath that. There were people next to the flowerbeds too, also dressed like us. They were continuing to dig up earth—ten, maybe twelve of them— seemingly oblivious to the alarm that was still going off. To my left, I could see the fields of heather running all the way down to the beach— and, directly behind me, the rear side of Lazarus: dilapidated, run-down.

"What *is* this place?" I asked.

Alex was behind me, further back in the shadows. "It used to be a training facility for the army in the 50s. A local guy converted it into a farm in the 70s."

I glanced at the people digging. "And them?"

"Students."

"Yeah, but what are they doing?"

"Turning over the soil."

"Why aren't they following the others down here?"

"I don't know. All of them should return here when the alarm goes off." A flicker of concern in his face, and then he glanced at his watch again. "The first alarm was because someone broke the locks on the Red Room."

"The Red Room?"

"Where they keep all the memories. That's where all your stuff is: your car keys, wallet, the photos of your wife. Your wedding ring." He looked at his watch again, and then up the slope. "*I* was the one that broke the locks on that room."

"To create a diversion."

He nodded. "Right."

"And this alarm?"

He listened to the second alarm for a moment. "This one's the compound alarm; the one for down here. It goes off if there's a security breach in the tunnels—or if someone leaves the door to Calvary open for more than five minutes."

"What's Calvary?"

"The crucifixion room." He looked at the diggers, a few of them glancing toward us. An army of faces in their late teens and early twenties. "Follow me."

We angled left, out of the darkness and into the light.

It was freezing cold, snow still on the ground. I looked up at the sky as we moved, trying to gauge the position of the sun. It must have been late afternoon.

The mouth of the compound was built into the extension I'd seen on the side of Lazarus. We moved past a blacked-out window. Then a second. Finally, we reached a door at the back of the house, painted red, next to a small car port. The car port wrapped around the side of the farmhouse and joined up with the main track running back up toward Bethany. Parked underneath was a Shogun.

Alex had split the lock to the Red Room with a chisel.

The door hung open, moving slightly in the breeze coming off the water. As we edged closer, I started to be able to make out the inside: a storage room, probably ten foot square, with floor-to-ceiling shelving on three sides and dull red walls. On the shelves were shoeboxes, stacked one after the other, *rows* of them, covering almost all the space. Countless surnames were scribbled on their fronts.

Some I recognized: Myzwik, O'Connell, Towne.

Most, though, I didn't.

I took Alex's down and looked inside.

"There's nothing in there," he said.

"How come?"

"I had nothing when I came back."

"Came back? Came back from where?"

He glanced out through a small gap in the door.

"Alex?"

"I'll tell you, but not now. We haven't got time. Get your things."

I looked for my belongings. Further along the middle shelf I saw a box with *Mitchell* on it. I leaned in closer. Underneath the surname was a first name.

Simon.

Simon Mitchell.

I glanced at Alex, and his expression confirmed that I was right: his friend, the one that had lived with him; the one that had struggled with drug addiction.

He'd disappeared.

"He came here too?" I said.

A noise outside.

Gently, I pushed the door to, leaving only a sliver of a gap to see through—and then watched as someone approached the Shogun, car keys in their hands.

Myzwik.

He opened the car, reached into the backseat, and removed a jacket, and as he pulled it on, his eyes moved back up the slope, past the door. They stopped.

He was looking at the Red Room now.

I felt Alex shift behind me, and the movement disturbed the air, the door jolting away from the frame a fraction. Immediately, Myzwik reacted. He reached around to the back of his belt and removed a gun— and then started toward us.

Shit.

I looked around the storage room for something to arm myself with, Alex doing the same. When I looked back at Myzwik, he was ten feet away, his eyes narrowed, his weapon out in front of him. There was nothing to fight back with.

We were sitting targets.

I glanced at Myzwik again and saw him reaching out for the door handle with his spare hand. *Do something.* As the door began to fan out, I kicked at it.

It whipped back.

A thump.

Myzwik was stumbling away, clutching the top of his face. I made a move for him, closing the space between us, and aimed a punch at his wrist. The gun ejected instantly, clattering against the frozen grass. As he recovered, he tried to throw a punch back, but I ducked and drove into him, forcing him back against the Shogun. We hit it hard, my body protected against his. My back twinged, and then flared up, like a fire catching light—but Myzwik was worse: he was dazed, doubled over, gripping the bonnet of the Shogun as he tried to recover himself.

As quickly as I could, I picked up his gun, flipped it around, and thrashed the butt across the side of his head. He blacked out instantly and hit the grass.

I looked behind me.

We were protected from view by the edges of Lazarus, but I wasn't about to take any chances. Calling Alex over, we each grabbed a leg and dragged Myzwik back to the Red Room. Once he was inside, I located my shoebox on the shelves.

Inside it was my life.

The car keys. My wallet. The photos of Derryn I kept there. The wedding ring I thought I'd lost forever when I'd watched it roll away, across the floor of the fridge. I slipped it on, pocketed the wallet and the car keys, and slid Myzwik's gun into the belt at the back of my trousers. When I turned, Alex was knelt beside Myzwik's prone body, going through his pockets.

"What are you doing?"

"Trying to find a key," he said.

"For what?"

He didn't reply, just kept searching. Eventually, he stood and looked at me—frustrated, his face etched with unease—and gestured in a northerly direction.

"What?" I said.

"He doesn't have a key."

"A key for what?"

"The gates; a way out of here."

"I cut a hole in the fence—we can go back out that way."

"The electricity's on."

"Electricity?"

"In the fencing."

I looked out at the wire mesh fencing that ran in a gentle curve from the top entrance, all the way down the slope at either side of the property boundary, before tethering together again at the edge of the beach. When the wind dropped away, and the waves quietened, I could hear it: the buzz of the electrical charge.

"When the alarm goes off," Alex said, "the electricity comes on, and stays on for thirty minutes. You can only switch it off from inside the compound, but we're not going back in there. So the little hole you crawled through to get in here? That's no longer an option, unless you want to risk being fried to death. The only other way to get out is to find one of the master keys and use it to unlock the main gate. That isn't electrified, it's just codelocked. But I haven't got one of those."

"So, who has?"

"The instructors."

I saw where he was going with this. "No way."

"We join the group working up the slope, outside Bethany, and wait for one of the instructors to come back. Once they do, we spring them and take the key."

"I'm at least fifteen years older than anyone else up there."

"We haven't got a choice."

"The minute one of the instructors sees me, our cover is blown."

"Not if you keep your head down."

"And the students? They're going to know I'm not part of the program. What's to stop one of them finding someone in charge and raising the alarm?"

"They won't," he replied.

"Because?"

"Because they're too deep into the program to remember if we're part of the farm or not. They won't care about the age difference either." He looked at his watch, at me. "When you've got no memory, you can't be sure about anything."

I looked at him, unconvinced.

But what other choice was there?

"We need to go," he said, more frantic now. "Andrew will be securing the compound, room by room, making sure everything's as it should be. He'll get to Calvary last, which means we've got about a minute before he and his attack dog discover that you're not nailed to that cross any more. Are you ready, David?"

I eyed him—and then nodded.

We headed out.

48

The ground beneath our feet was uneven, the track rising through fields of snow, up toward the group gathered in front of Bethany. I let Alex lead the way, falling in behind him, my head down, trying to disguise my face from view. Every time I looked up, expecting to see the group staring at us, they were unchanged from the last time, shovels, spades and forks in their hands, their attention at the ground.

I glanced back down the slope, to the extension, to Lazarus, but there was no sign of Andrew, of Legion. They were still inside, checking rooms. Something wasn't right here, though. I could feel it. It bugged me that the group ahead of us hadn't returned to the compound with the other students. If that was the rule, why had they disobeyed it? And, if they were waiting for an instructor to tell them what to do, that was even worse: if we disguised ourselves within the group and an instructor returned and told us all to head back to the compound, what then?

My back flared up again, and I sucked in a breath.

"Are you okay?" Alex said, speaking through the side of his mouth, his eyes still on the group. I didn't reply, trying to settle myself. "David? Are you okay?"

"Is this all they do all day?" I replied, changing the subject.

"No. Some work locally too."

We continued moving, edging closer and closer.

"The locals are in on this as well?"

"Only the ones that used to work here. When someone breaches security, or gets too close, Andrew swaps everyone around. There'll be new people working out of Angel's now, someone else managing the flat in Brixton. The people down in London will be in Bristol; the people in Bristol will be up here—on the farm or in the villages somewhere. The project owns a couple of shops along the coast."

Every time a hole opened up, they closed it.

"What do they do in the villages?" I said.

"The same as they do here. Tilling the soil, planting, fetching, carrying, maybe standing behind a counter and serving. Menial tasks. Andrew argues it's a purer, untarnished existence. But the truth is, by the time they've finished with you here, you're not good for much else."

We stopped talking when we got within twenty feet of the group. A few of the faces were visible beneath the hoods, staring down the hill toward us. They looked normal, even healthy, until you watched their eyes, darting between us, desperately trying to fit memories together like broken pieces of a jigsaw puzzle.

As we reached them, a couple looked up: a teenaged girl, a man in his mid-twenties. In front of them, cracks and fissures in the frozen earth were gradually being levered open; fingers, wrapped around the shovels, were red with cold.

There were four shovels propped against the wall behind the group. Alex and I grabbed one each and settled into a space in the middle of the group, pretending to dig, hoods still up to disguise our faces, but with a clear sight of the compound. A couple of the group continued to watch us, especially Alex—but then, as we started to dig away, they gradually turned their attention back to their own work.

Shortly after, from the mouth of the compound, they came.

There were two of them. One I recognized immediately as Andrew; the other was smaller, maybe female, and had the hood up on her top. As soon as they emerged from the darkness of the compound, they were looking right to left, their eyes adjusting to the late afternoon light. It was four, perhaps half-past. In the time we'd been outside, the sun had begun to melt away beyond the horizon.

They both looked up toward us and studied the group.

They knew we were on the farm somewhere.

It was just a question of where.

We continued our slow, rhythmic digging of the earth, the sound of the shovels chinging against the mud, the wind blowing in from the mountains and the sea. A thought came to me: *what if they'd done a head count before we joined the group?* I looked at Alex, he shot a glance back. Was he thinking the same?

This plan is going to get us killed.

Out of the corner of my eye, I saw Andrew head toward the veranda on the front of Lazarus. The woman started making her way toward us.

Alex and I turned away from her slightly, and began digging properly. It took her about sixty seconds to get from the mouth of the compound to the edges of the group. She was wearing heavy-duty boots, the steel toe-caps scuffing against the gravel and the snow that had settled on the track. Apart from Andrew, the instructors dressed like the students—hooded tops, tracksuit trousers, boots—only in blue instead of green. With my back half-turned, I couldn't make out her face clearly, and as she got closer to the group I turned away from her even more.

I bent double, keeping her at the periphery of my vision.

I dug the shovel into the earth and removed a slab of mud, and when I jammed the shovel down again, into the ground, I felt a twinge in my back. I tried not to make my pain obvious, centralizing it, pushing it away from my face, and watched as she started circling the group, eyes flicking between the students. The alarm stopped, and the silence was like a ringing in my ears. The sudden switch put a pause in the woman's stride too, and she came to a halt at a pile of earth.

A minute passed.

When I glanced again at her, she'd moved around, closer to Bethany. She was bent over, watching one of the women brush away some of the earth at her feet. Then the instructor moved again, finally disappearing from my line of sight.

I flicked a glance at Alex.

He was at the opposite angle to me, facing the other way, but I was able to watch his eyes follow the path of the instructor as she came around behind me.

We continued digging.

Thirty seconds later I saw Alex glance up at the woman again, and worked out that she was directly behind me. We hadn't agreed anything, hadn't made any sort of plan, but I gripped the handle of the shovel, my knuckles whitening, and flicked a look, back across my shoulder. She was less than six feet away from me.

I looked back at the patch I was digging, and then again at the woman, as a sudden gust of wind swept up the hill, lifting the hood from her face. It fell away.

My heart dropped.

It was Evelyn.

Through the corner of her eye she must have seen me staring at her. She turned and fully faced me, her eyes narrowing—and then she realized who it was beneath the hood. For a second, she must have thought she could reason with me. We had history. We'd got on, laughed, talked—even been drawn to each other in some way. But then she remembered what she'd been a part of down in Bristol.

She'd let them take me out to the forest.

"I'm sorry, Evelyn," I said.

She started to call out for help.

I swung the shovel at her, dirt spitting off as it arced, and caught her in the left hip. The impact reverberated along the handle, into my hands. She stumbled sideways and fell to her knees, and—as she scrabbled around in the dirt—I took out Myzwik's gun and whipped it against her head. She collapsed onto her belly.

The rest of the group looked up.

Alex glanced between me and the others, and back down toward the farm. No sign of anybody else. He dropped his shovel to the ground and moved across to Evelyn, who I hadn't been able to knock out completely. She was shifting around, drifting in and out. He covered her mouth with his hand to keep her quiet, and started to go through her pockets. Eventually, he found a keyring in her trousers.

Two keys.

One brass. One silver.

Alex selected the silver one and held it up to me.

And then his whole face collapsed.

The color drained out of him, and he lost his balance, falling against Evelyn. As he started scrambling backward, I followed his gaze, out behind me.

"We have something to finish," one of the students said.

Except it wasn't a student.

It was Legion.

49

He'd been working beside us the whole time, wearing the same clothes, hood up, digging the same ground. As he came forward, across the frozen ground, some of the students looked up, saw who it was and cowered. He pushed between them, knocking one of them over, his hands at his side. In his left, he was carrying a small gun.

His eyes switched from me to Alex.

The wind moved up the slope again, fierce and raw, and panic began to set in among the students. They parted around him, dropping their shovels and stepping away, some inching out into the snow and the track, some backing up against Bethany. Legion didn't move, his feet planted in a square of freshly dug earth, like a specter rising from a grave. Inside the hood, he didn't have the mask on, but I could see its band around his ears, and knew it was on top of his head.

"We have something to finish, David," he said again, but he wasn't looking at me. His eyes were still on Alex, his lips turned up in an expression of disgust.

"No," I said, and aimed Myzwik's gun at him.

This time he looked at me, his body perfectly still, only his head moving. It was like looking at a ventriloquist's dummy—all the movement was in his neck.

He glanced at the gun. "Are you going to shoot me?"

"Maybe."

He nodded once, but didn't say anything, looking downwards, examining the ground between where he stood and where Alex was, about three feet to his left. Alex was standing now.

"Put the gun down," he said to me.

He still hadn't raised his from his side.

"Put the gun down, or I'll kill Alex where he stands."

I glanced at Alex, but he seemed strangely unaffected by the threat. "That's not true, David," he said. "Don't listen. Don't put the gun down. He can't kill me."

I frowned, glancing at him. "What?"

"Put the gun down," Legion said.

Alex shook his head. "Don't do it."

"What's going on, Alex?"

"I'll kill him," Legion said.

"No. No. You need to listen to me, David. They can't kill m—"

In a flash of movement, Legion jabbed the barrel of the gun forward, right into the center of Alex's forehead. Alex lurched backward, falling like a sack of cement—no grace, no arms out, no reactions at all—and hit the ground. He was unconscious, bleeding from a cut in the middle of his face. By the time I realized, Legion had bridged the gap between us with a long stride. He was four feet away.

"Stop," I said.

"We need to finish what we started."

I looked down at the gun, locked to his side, my heart bashing against the inside of my ribs. He didn't believe I'd kill him—not facing him here, not in cold blood. What I'd done to Zack and Jason, it was self-defense. This was different.

"This is over," he hissed.

Take this chance, David.

Her voice in my head, suddenly, unexpectedly. Legion noticed something in my face—a flicker—and, for the first time, some of the bravado dropped away.

I felt sweat on my fingers, my adrenalin flowing, my heart pumping in my ears. I glanced down at the gun again and then back up at the man in front of me.

Take this chance, David.

I aimed low, and fired into his leg.

He staggered back against one of the others in the group, clutching the top of his thigh. One of the group screamed. A shovel clanged to the earth. I glanced at Alex—and then I made a break for it, heading up the track, toward Bethany.

Snow crunched behind me.

The devil was coming.

I kicked open the back door, immediately realizing I'd led myself into a trap. Half-inside the kitchen, I turned—thinking about heading back the way I'd come, about some other plan—and saw his silhouette pass across the windows.

It was too late.

Swiveling, I sprinted through to the living room—dark now, as daylight began to fade—and toward the stairs. I glanced back. From the semi-darkness of the kitchen he came, leg dragging behind him. His hood was still up, but the mask was down—the eyes moving inside the holes; the mouth wide and leering.

I headed upstairs.

Bullets fizzed into the wall behind me, old brickwork spitting out dust and debris, the ping of a ricochet. I heard the scrape of his leg beneath me as he moved across the living room, broken tiles under his feet. At the top of the landing, I paused, looking at the three doors—the three rooms—trying to figure out which was going to keep me alive the longest, and then made a beeline for Room A.

I could hear him on the stairs.

Sliding in behind the chimney flue, I turned as quickly as I could, raised the gun, and faced along the landing, waiting for him to appear. But he didn't.

There was no one on the stairs.

No one on the landing.

Where is he?

The flue came about three feet out from the wall, and ran floor to ceiling. It was deep enough to provide cover. It was the smart thing to do, the best way for me to gain an advantage. He couldn't hit me through brick, but I could hit back.

Except I didn't know where he was.

I'd seen him coming after me outside. I'd heard him in the living room below me, dragging his injured leg through the tiles. I'd *heard* him on the stairs.

So where the hell was he?

My teeth throbbed. My eyes watered. My back was on fire. I listened for Legion, for any sign of movement inside the house, but there was nothing. The more I willed myself to hear, the more I became aware of the sounds beyond the walls; the commotion at the front; students—scared, unsettled. Maybe Evelyn.

Maybe Alex.

It was getting dark fast too, closing in like a shroud. Every second I waited, the shadows got longer: on the stairs, on the landing, filling in at the windows.

The gun started to feel heavy.

My whole *body* felt heavy.

I looked along the landing, and then out into the empty room. What did I have left? What choices were there now? I thought I'd been reducing the chances of me being hit. I'd seen the flue as a place of safety. But it was the total opposite.

I'd backed myself into a corner.

My guts churned and I began to feel nauseous again. *He's got all the cards. He's a soldier. He's been trained to use silence and time to his advantage.* When I swallowed, my saliva felt like glass. I tried to calm myself, to settle my nerves.

But it was too late for that.

I looked down at my left hand, at my silver wedding band glinting dully in the diminishing light. Would I have found that first girl if I'd known it would turn out like this? Would I have let Derryn talk me around if I'd glimpsed the future, the reality—cowering in the corner of a room, waiting to die? Missing people had brought routine to my life. I'd needed that, had fed off it for a year. They gave me substance and momentum. Without them, I'd have fallen away a long time ago.

So what are you going to do?

I peered along the landing again, tightening my grip on the gun. Outside, there was no noise from the group now, just the whine of the wind in the house.

I took a long breath.

Then, slowly, I edged out from the flue.

50

A shiver hit me, cold air passing in through cracks in the wall—except it wasn't the weather that was affecting me. It was the fear. My nerves were fried. I could hardly walk straight. Tremors passed along my arms, into my fingers, as I got to the doorway and paused. To my right, the bathroom was empty, cleared of the ketamine vials that had been left on the floor, the bath panel replaced. Ahead of me, the stairs were almost dark, but I could see enough: there was no one there.

I turned my attention to Room B.

Gripping the gun, I inched forward, and—out of the night—came tiny zig-zags of snow, compacted. *They'd fallen away from his shoes.* The snow formed a rough trail, across the landing and into Room B. Was that where he was hiding?

Or was this a trick?

Keeping the gun up and in front of me, I edged around in a semi-circle, so I was facing the doorway to Room B from the side the stairs were on. The idea was to give myself a clearer view of the room, the back of it, but it was hard to see anything. A brief, crippling panic hit me: what if he could see me *right now*?

I backed up again, closer to the stairs.

And a smell hit me.

His smell.

I glanced behind me, at the stairs, thinking for a moment that it might be because he was approaching from there, unseen—but there was no one there. *At least I don't think so.* Every minute, the place was getting darker, harder to navigate.

I sniffed the air again.

It's definitely him. That smell of decay, of mold and grime; of unwashed clothes—or maybe washed clothes, but a body he could no longer scrub clean. It was like an animal scent, trailing him; a warning. It was like he was telling me not to come any closer—except, if I was ever going to leave the farm alive, I had to.

I leaned into the door jamb.

Through the gap, I could just about make out the ends of the room, rings all along the wall. Something twitched at the back. Was that him? Was he wait—

Out of nowhere, it felt like I got hit by a train.

It took a split second for my brain to catch up—and, by that time, I was lurching sideways, back toward Room A, feet barely touching the floor. I hit the ground hard, winded myself, and managed to half-roll over—enough time to see Andrew, armed with a length of wood, approaching me, looming out of the dark.

I hadn't seen him coming.

I hadn't heard him; even *thought* of him.

Still gripping Myzwik's gun, I lifted it off the ground, aiming it roughly in his direction, and went to pull the trigger. But he was fast. The length of wood crashed against my fingers, my clenched fist springing open, and the gun hit the floorboards with a clunk. Before I'd even had a chance to react, a second blow hit me in the ribs—not the wood this time, but his boot. The air hissed out of me, my ribs shifting, one of them cracking. I yelled out in pain, an agonizing hum rippling across my ribcage. As I tried to move again, tried to drag myself up onto all fours, he pushed me down with the flat of his hand, bearing all his weight at my back.

I screamed again, harder this time.

"I understand," he said as my cries died down, his knee in the center of my back, his bulk pinning me to the floor. "I understand how you must feel. I get it, David. I do. That desperation to get her back, it consumes your every thought."

He shifted slightly, but as he took some of his weight away, he pressed the end of the length of the wood into the base of my skull, pushing my face down.

"After I got out of prison," he said quietly, bending down toward me again, closer to my ear, "my parole officer found me a job teaching kids to play football at a youth club. He knew the guy who ran it. The first evening I turned up there, the guy in charge pulled me aside and said, 'I know you've got a record. You're just a favor for a friend, so if you mess up once, even if it's to tell me we're out of orange squash, you're finished.' I got twenty-five pounds cash in hand, and was claiming dole every week as well. When Sunday came round, I had nothing. The temptation for more cash, the temptation to steal, whoever I hurt, was immense."

The only thing I could move were my eyes. I scoured my surroundings for anything I could make an attempt for, but the gun was out of reach. There were some bits of old tiles, shards scattered on the bathroom floor. Even if they weren't out of reach, even if he'd instantly stop me going for them, they'd be worthless.

I had nowhere else to go.

I was done.

"Prison was tough," he continued, his voice soft, almost mournful. "So, I didn't want to go back. And, anyway, about five months after I started there, at that youth club, everything changed. I got talking to the mum of one of the boys. He'd had leukemia, but it was in remission. And the way she spoke about him, about the love she had for him, it just absolutely stopped me dead. When I found out she was on her own, I asked her out—even before I knew what her name was. She was the one who first took me to a church. She was how I found my faith."

Unexpectedly, he stood, his weight shifting off me.

"Charlotte," he said. There was a long pause as he stared down at me. "We'd been seeing each other for about two years when her son's leukemia came back. I'd moved in with them by then. I had a job. Everything in my life was perfect. But when Charlotte found out the disease had come back, something just turned off in her—as if she knew, this time, it wasn't going until it took her boy with it."

I rolled over, onto my back, eyes shifting out into the shadows either side of me. He saw the movement and shook his head, placing the end of the length of wood to my throat. I swallowed, watching something painful move in his eyes.

"I came home three months after he passed away and she was in the bath. She'd overdosed on sleeping pills. That was when I came up with the idea for this place. A place to help people start again, to leave behind memories—everything they wish they could forget. I went to the bank and they turned me down on the spot. But eventually, a few months later, someone cared enough to help me out."

I just looked up at him.

"This place was built for people like you, David. You must understand that, surely?" He paused, but it wasn't a question. "I'm not going to let you destroy it."

He brought the length of wood back up toward him, gripping it tighter—and, as I saw the end coming, the final blow, a strange kind of peace settled on me. I thought back to the moments on the cross, feeling Derryn behind me, waiting.

And I closed my eyes.

Except the blow never came.

51

A dull thud sounded.

Andrew staggered sideways, clutching his head, blood dripping from above his eye: dazed, disoriented, off balance. It took me a moment to put it together.

But, then, in the darkness, I saw Alex.

He came forward, teeth clenched, armed with a chunk of wood, and struck again. This time he caught Andrew in the ribs. A howl of pain, like another alarm ringing out, but—before he could gather himself—the club was in his stomach.

Again, again.

Andrew hit the wall with a thump, and collapsed.

I hauled myself up off the floor, my own head swimming. "Alex," I said, but my voice hardly registered, and Alex didn't hear it. He wasn't hearing anything. He just kept striking Andrew—face, legs, arms, anything that was close—hitting him so hard, chunks of wood were breaking off and spinning out across the floorboards. There was no reaction from Andrew now: no movement, no grunts.

Nothing.

"Alex!"

He stopped, panting heavily, cloaked in the shadows, and looked around toward me. In the silence, his act seemed to dawn on him. He glanced at Andrew, back to me, then to Andrew again, and I saw tears shimmer in his eyes.

Click.

A noise from the room with the rings.

I hauled myself up, pain everywhere, and then tried to refocus. Grabbing Myzwik's gun off the floor, I waved Alex toward me and then pointed at Room B.

Legion, I mouthed.

A flicker of fear in Alex's face.

He's in there.

I raised the gun, gestured for Alex to fall in behind me, and then started inching toward the open door. But then I felt Alex's hand grab at my shoulder.

I turned. *What?*

He leaned into my ear. "Use me."

What?

He leaned in again. "Use me. Pretend you're going to kill me." He shifted in front of me, and said: "Use me as a shield."

I frowned. "What the hell are you talking about?"

"They can't kill me."

"They can."

"They can't."

"They can *kill* you, Alex. Now stop messing—"

He grabbed me by the arm, a new determination to him, an unwillingness to back down. "Do it," he said, looking me square in the eyes. "Do it, and trust me."

"You're out of your fucking mind."

But then I remembered what he'd said out front, in the moments after we discovered Legion among us. *You need to listen to me, David. They can't kill me.*

He turned his back to me and faced down the doorway to Room B. For a moment, I hesitated. It was suicide. I was walking him in there as a dead man.

And, yet, there wasn't one hint of doubt in him.

I inched close to him, so Legion wouldn't have a clear shot at me, and then we began to move forward. The boards creaked beneath us, Alex's shoes kicking up splintered wood and shattered pieces of glass, and then we were inside, the layout revealing itself little by little, every footstep feeling heavier in my muscles.

At the end of the room, it was pitch black.

"I'll kill him," I said, staring into the darkness.

I shuffled Alex forward another step, hoping the light might change subtly, showing what it hid, but I couldn't see a thing. The flue in the next room created an uneven kink in the wall to the left, in turn casting long shadows, side to side.

"If it's him or me, I swear I'll kill him."

A half-step toward the center of the room.

"I swear."

There was no reply. No movement.

"Are you listening to me?"

My eyes adjusted a little more, shapes starting to emerge from the far end of the room. An uneven floorboard; a solitary, broken chair. To my left, I could see the hole in the wall with the *Help me* message, the rings lined up, the water running down brickwork in between them, glistening like the skin of a reptile. On the right, a sheet at one of the windows bellowed slightly in a breeze coming in.

"Answer me," I said.

A memory surfaced, there and then gone: when we were outside, disguised among the group of students, I'd looked up at Bethany—but I hadn't noticed a window being open on the front. *Or had I?* I slowed, uncertain, trying to recall.

And there was something else too.

His smell has changed.

"Answer me," I repeated, but my thoughts were racing.

Click.

That was when I knew for sure: the window *hadn't* been open—and his smell hadn't changed either. It just wasn't coming from in front of me any more.

It was coming from behind.

I felt a gun at the back of my head.

"Cockroach," a voice said quietly.

52

The end of the barrel pushed in against the top of my spine. He'd tricked us. He'd come in here, and then gone out through the window, double-backing on us. The windows had all been secured with padlocks when I'd been into Room B the first time, but Legion would have had a set of keys. He had free run of the place. He'd opened the window, got out onto the flat roof, come around—and then waited.

Shit.

"I'll kill him," I said.

He pushed the gun in harder. "No, you won't."

"Put your gun down," I said pushing back against the muzzle.

"No."

"Put it down."

"No."

"Put your gun *down.*"

In an instant, his head was at my ear. I could feel the mask brush against the side of my face and his warm breath passing through the holes in the plastic.

"No," he said again.

The gun pressed harder against the back of my head, digging in against the curve of my skull. "You've got three seconds," I said, doubts flashing through my head—*He's wrong, Alex is wrong, this plan will fail*—"or I blow his brains out."

The gun didn't move.

"One."

Nothing.

"Two."

I cocked the gun, heart pounding.

"Thr—"

With one last push of the barrel, he shoved us both forward, and then I heard glass crunch beneath his feet as he stepped back, the gun going with him.

I swiveled, so hard Alex almost stumbled.

Legion was standing in the doorway.

I felt Alex freeze, drawing in a breath at the sight of him: the gun was at his side, a second, smaller one in his belt, his sleeves rolled up, revealing the tattoo. His eyes were fixed on me, peering through the eyeholes, but it was hard to make out the rest of his face, even though—in the quiet of the house—I could hear his breath, whistling through the gaps on the mask. The top of his thigh, where I'd shot him, was awash in blood, the leg out in front of him and bent slightly, as if uncomfortable. But, if it hurt, if it was affecting him somehow, it was hard to tell.

"Put them on the floor," I said, nodding to both guns.

He looked at me, at Alex, then back to me. Maybe he didn't believe I would kill Alex. If you're a killer, you wear it—like a cut that doesn't heal. But he'd have heard enough about me, about what I'd done to Zack and Jason in the forest. So he knew, if I had to, I *could* do it. If it came to that, it would be them before me.

"On the floor," I repeated.

His eyes narrowed, and then he opened his hand and dropped the gun he'd been holding to the floor. Chips of glass scattered as it turned and came to rest.

"Now the other one."

He paused, placed a hand on it, his fingers closing around the grip like the legs of an insect. I could see dirt and blood under his nails. Drawing it out from his belt, he held it there—right out in front of him—as if refusing to let go of it.

But then he did.

It hit the ground with a clunk.

"I can taste your fear," he said.

I nodded as if I'd barely heard him, but the truth was different: every word out of his mouth was like the end of a knife blade. He lived off this, fed on it. Even with both his guns on the floor, he was still dangerous; in a weird way, it still felt like he was in control—and the minute he stopped believing I might kill Alex, he would be. I pressed a hand down onto Alex's shoulder, pushing him to his knees in front of me, and then leveled the gun at the back of his head. He looked up at me, the right amount of fear in his face: I wasn't sure if he really believed I would do it or not, especially after coming all this way—but there was a flicker of doubt.

Legion looked between us.

"Kick the guns over here," I said.

I expected to have to repeat myself, just like before, but this time he did it straight away. Instantly, I started to worry. Everything else had been a struggle. Now he was sending his weapons across to me, out of reach of himself, without even pausing for thought. I looked between the weapons and him. What was going on?

"Put your hands behind your head."

He snorted and, instead, moved his hands up to his mask and slowly lifted it away from his face. I saw Alex flinch a little in front of me. The devil tossed his mask away. He blinked, his eyes fixed on me, and ran a hand across the top of his shaved head, stubble bristling against his palm. And then he smiled, his mouth widening, tongue pushing through his lips, running across them, tasting them.

"I wonder what you would taste like?" he said.

It sounded absurd, *looked* absurd, his tongue rolling across his bottom lip. But it was hard not to be unsettled by him: he was bizarre, vicious, barbaric.

"Put your hands behind your head."

He smiled again, but did what I asked, sliding his hands behind his head, linking them together. *Too easy again.* Something was definitely up. I'd forgotten something. Missed something. What had I missed? I looked from him, to Alex.

"Turn around," I said.

Legion picked up on something in my voice.

Another smile broke out on his face. "What's the matter?"

"Turn around."

"You scared?"

"Turn around."

His eyes widened, like huge holes opening inside his head, sucking in the darkness from the room. I felt my control of the situation beginning to unravel.

What had I missed?

"You scared, cockroach?" he said quietly, menacingly.

"Shut up and turn arou—"

He darted forward then, a sudden bloom of movement, pulling a knife out from somewhere behind his back. The handle was small, but the blade was long, slightly curved, glinting even in the gloom. We were seven feet from one another but he crossed the ground like it was no distance at all, bringing the knife out in front of him, a blur that moved from the height of his shoulders to his waist, and slashed across Alex's chest. Alex stumbled backward, knocking me off balance.

I fired accidentally, the bullet lodging in the ceiling, and then the gun spilled from my grasp.

By the time I was back in control of myself, Legion had flipped the knife—blade facing down and away from us—and jabbed the butt into Alex's temple. He staggered sideways, his legs giving way, and I could see a long, thin, shallow tear in his clothes. There was no blood, but it had slashed through his top like paper.

Legion moved in a third and final time and punched the knife's handle into Alex's head on the opposite side. Alex lost his footing completely and tumbled to his left—but not before pulling me down with him. I couldn't understand why he'd done it to start with, why he'd made such a conscious effort to grab me. But then, as he crashed to the floor and rolled over on top of me, I could see what he was doing. *He's protecting me.* Legion couldn't go through him.

The devil came toward us.

I was still too close to Alex for him to get careless, so he stabbed the blade into the floor next to my ear, trying to force a reaction movement from me, away from Alex. But I couldn't move. I was trapped beneath Alex. Realizing it, he then rammed a foot into Alex's face and the back of Alex's head hit my nose—a force like a hammer blow. White light flashed in my eyes. Blurring. Soundless blurring. As noise returned, Legion was rolling Alex off me, onto the floor. Alex was dazed.

I looked for Myzwik's gun, and found it: out of reach.

And then I was back in the moment.

Legion was bent over, foot dragging beneath him, hauling Alex across the room, woozy, semi-conscious. In a flash, I saw how everything had gone south so fast: on the rear of Legion's top, criss-crossing between his shoulder blades, were two lengths of gaffer tape in an X. He'd taped the knife to his back—out of sight.

When he had Alex far enough away, he turned back to me, eyes flashing, and limped back across the room toward me. I scrambled onto all fours, wincing at the pain in my back, and started to move toward his smaller gun, the closest weapon to where I was. But then he hit me hard, coming at me from a low angle: his knee jammed into the small of my back, and he pinned me to the floorboards.

I struggled, trying to release myself, trying to do something, *do something, do something, do something*—but, out of the corner of my eye, all I could see was him raising the knife above his head, blade glinting, ready to drive it downwards.

The final act.

But then he stopped, frozen.

When I looked again, up and back across my shoulder, I saw Alex behind him, one eye puffy, blinking furiously as he tried to regain his composure.

He had a gun at Legion's head.

"What are you doing?"

"Let*sssh* him go," Alex said, stunned, his words slurred.

"What are you doing, *Alex*?"

One side of my face was flat to the floor. I could feel shards of glass under my cheek but, as I tried to lift myself up off the floor and shake them off, Legion looked down at me and pushed his knee harder into my back, tightening his grip.

His fingers wriggled at my neck.

"Let*sssh* him go," Alex said again.

"You can't even speak properly."

My eyes darted across the room. I had a narrow field of vision, but I could see the smaller gun a foot away, level with my face. When Legion had launched himself into my back, he'd pushed us both across the floor and closer toward it.

"You should have been dead a long time ago," he said to Alex, and he half-turned his body toward Alex, his head going the whole way, staring him down.

I moved my hand an inch away from my body and waited for a reaction from Legion. When none came, I moved another inch, and then another.

"What I would have given to see you suffer."

I carried on moving my arm in an arc, slowly sweeping through the debris. Sooner or later, I expected the movement of my body to register with him, but—for the first time—Legion had started to lose control of himself. He *hated* Alex.

"I'm going to cut you."

I moved even closer to the gun.

"I'm going to slice you into pieces."

My fingers touched the weapon, the rough texture of its grip, and pulled it toward me, praying it didn't make a sound.

A second later, I had it in my hand.

"You're a worthless piece of *shit*," Legion said, almost spitting the words back across his shoulder at Alex. "You're a *fucking cockroach*, just like this—"

He looked down at me. I raised the gun off the ground, bending my arm as far back as it would go, and pushed it into the folds of his top.

I fired.

He fell off me, his grip instantly releasing, and I rolled over and saw his hand clutching a space just under the ribcage. He was doubled over, barely able to stand, blood spilling out over his fingers. He brought the knife up—still in his hand—and swung it in my direction, but the power had gone from his arms, and the motion unbalanced him: he swiped again, lost his footing, and hit the wall.

His eyes darkened, like the gates of hell had opened for him.

And then, finally, the devil was still.

53

I brought the Shogun up the track to Bethany, and Alex and I carried Legion out, and dumped his body in the back of the car. We stood there for a moment, staring in at him, the night thick around us. Even as death claimed his body, his eyes still looked out at us, as powerful as when they blinked and moved behind the mask.

Next, we got Andrew.

He was bigger, heavier, more difficult. We carried him down the hill, his body broken, the bones shifting and moving inside his skin, his face reduced to its own bloodied mask. When we got to the Shogun, we dropped him into the back, and then Alex asked me to turn Andrew's face away from him. He'd killed a man, we both had, but he was having a harder time processing it, perhaps because—in Andrew—there had been some grain of humanity left; a glimpse of the man he'd once been, before this farm, before it had corrupted and twisted him. Legion—or whatever his real name was—was different: I wasn't sure there had *ever* been any good in him; and, if I hadn't pulled the trigger, I wouldn't still be breathing.

Evelyn and Myzwik were gone.

All the instructors were.

The property had been abandoned like a sinking ship, and if we drove to the next village—where the tendrils of the organization spread—I knew that they wouldn't be there either. They were on the run now, reduced to fugitives, perhaps understanding some of the desperation that the students on the farm felt. I found a security suite inside the compound, close to where the cross was, a bank of six monitors showing CCTV feeds of different corners of the property. I spent fifteen minutes erasing the last twenty-four hours from the hard drive, wiping my arrival from existence, and then reset the software, so that the feed kicked in at seven the next morning.

Our next act on the farm was to round up the students we could find—the drug addicts and victims of abuse that had come to the farm with the promise of a better life—and lead them to the living room in Lazarus, where it was warmer.

There were twenty-two of them in all.

Most were the same—healthy, yet virtual amnesiacs—but a few of them at the beginning of the program were still strung out on whatever drugs they'd been forced to take. We made them hot drinks and grabbed blankets from the compound, but as I handed them out, I looked at their faces and wondered what sort of life these kids could ever hope to live now. Every time I told them it was going to be all right, they eyed me with suspicion, and I realized how empty my words were to them. They'd been tied to rings in rooms that smelled of death, terrified by a killer who watched them from the dark. They bore scars on their backs and in their fingers. Their memories might have gone—but they weren't stupid.

They knew this existence wasn't the one Michael, Zack, Jade and all the others had promised them. It was a prison where they slowly drifted into a void.

Once the students were settled, Alex and I drove out along the coast to a cove about four miles away. Majestic cliffs rose out of the sea for three hundred feet, waves crashed on the shore below, their sound swallowed up by the wind.

At the edge of the cliff, we tied a concrete block to Legion and then to Andrew—and then we pushed both bodies off the side. They turned in the air as they dropped, and quickly disappeared in the spray. When they came into view again, it was about thirty feet out and they were fading into the depths of the sea.

We waited with the students overnight, all of them eventually falling asleep, and before they stirred the next morning, we left the farm through the main gates and headed back along the road to my hire car. My back was sore, right down to the bones, but my ribs weren't broken, as I feared they might be, and everything else was just bruising. Those would heal over the coming days, but the scourge marks were a part of me now. I'd looked in the mirror the previous night and seen them for the first time, a mesh of red lines. All the other people here had the same: four or five whip marks that acted like a brand, a fingerprint, a reminder of this place and of who the students were the property of.

The only difference between the students and me was that I was supposed to be in the ground now. The whipping, the crucifix, the nails, my "death," Andrew and Legion wanted me to experience it all before they murdered me, but for very different reasons: Andrew, because he was so consumed by the program, by the concept of the farm, its ideals, that he seemed to think, somehow, I'd become convinced by what it was they were doing if he could show me the process, the so-called resurrection. Legion was different: he was a killer, and he enjoyed killing.

Nothing more, nothing less.

Ten minutes down the road, I stopped at a payphone and called the police, telling them they needed to send a team to the farm. They asked for my name.

That was when I hung up.

54

We stopped at a service station outside Manchester.

The temperature readout inside the building said it was $-3°C$, and as we sat at a table by one of the windows, looking out at a children's play park, we both nursed coffees and said nothing. My back hurt, my ribs too; Alex's face was bruised on both sides where Legion had smashed him with the butt of a gun.

In the glass, I could see people staring at us, their eyes being drawn to the damaged men in the corner, so I told him to bring his coffee, and we headed out.

Snow started falling about twenty minutes later, coming out of a pale sky. I turned to Alex. He was looking out of the window, his coffee steaming in the car's cup holder, his eyes on the vehicles blurring past. For a moment, I was reminded of driving Jade to Strawberry's, of her face being the same: distant, reflected back at me.

"How did you know about me?" I asked him.

He shrugged. "I broke into Mum and Dad's home and found your name in among Mum's things. That's what I'd become: a fugitive." He glanced at me; shrugged again. "I wanted Mum to see me that day. I let her follow me to that library so she would believe enough, and then I prayed she would go to someone. I used to watch her when she came into London after that: follow her from the train to her work, hope that one day she might stop somewhere and ask for help—and eventually she did. She asked you. I didn't know anything about you, couldn't find you in the Yellow Pages, even online. That was why I finally went back to Mum and Dad's." He stopped again, half-smiling. "You need to get a website."

I returned the smile, and then pushed on: "How did you escape?"

"From the farm?"

I nodded.

He picked up his coffee and sipped at it. "I'd been there a few months when I heard a voice I recognized, passing in the corridor outside my bunk room. Not one of the instructors, not Andrew, not that . . . freak. Not any of the students either. We weren't allowed up past half past nine in the evening, and if we bent the rules, we were punished. So I knew it had to be someone they'd brought from outside. Someone new." He paused, glancing at me. "I got up, went to the door."

"Who was it?"

"Simon."

"Your friend Simon? The drug addict?"

"Yeah. I couldn't believe it was him. I hadn't seen him for *years* and then, all of a sudden, he was there, on that farm, at the same time as me. It was him. But they treated him . . . I'd never seen them treat anyone like that. They had a neck strap on him, a leash, and were pulling him around like an animal."

"Did you follow them?"

"No," he said. "No, no, no. I was too scared. I was still pretty new then. I was absolutely terrified of what they'd do to me, of what the devil would do. I used to stay awake half the night thinking he was watching me in the bunk room, just like he used to at the start." He stopped, swallowed. "So, no, I didn't follow them, but seeing Simon like that—being *treated* like that—it stayed with me, and seven, eight months later, I heard someone else brought in at night. I didn't recognize them this time, but they were on a leash too. I'd had enough of the farm by then."

"So you followed them this time?"

"Yes. I left the room and started following them. I expected to be stopped straight away, but I got to the end of the corridor and no one came after me. There was no one around. I knew they'd try to stop me once they saw me on CCTV—except they didn't. It was like the whole place had been abandoned. Normally you couldn't breathe without someone hearing you, but I managed to walk out of the compound, up to the surface."

"Did you find the person they'd brought in?"

"No. I was too far behind him . . ." He trailed off, glanced at me, regret and guilt in his face. "And I guess I forgot about them as soon as I got to the surface."

"Why?"

"Because the entrance had been left open."

"The main gate?"

"Yes. It was open enough to allow me to escape. My heart was telling me to make a break for it, but my brain was holding me back. They *never* left it open."

"Was it some kind of trap?"

"That was my first thought. It was a trap. It *had* to be. But, after a couple of minutes, no one came for me, so I decided to start walking up toward the gate."

"And that was it—you just went through?"

"No. When I got to the top . . . Andrew was there."

"Waiting for you?"

"Just there. In the shadows. I was about four feet from the open gate, close enough to run for it if he tried to grab me—but he didn't. He just stood there."

I looked at him. "And did what?"

"And did nothing. He just stayed like that. And then, when I finally made a move toward the other side, he said, 'Bringing you here was a mistake. We never wanted you, Alex. None of us. I'm sick of fighting you; of not being able to give you the drugs I need to. If you were *really* a part of this program, we would have sacrificed you a long time ago. We wouldn't have let you live after all the trouble you've caused us. But you're not— never will be—and I'm willing to take whatever consequences come my way. I don't want to see your face any more.'"

"That's what he said?"

Alex nodded. "It still felt like a trap, but when I stepped through the gate, onto the road, I realized it wasn't. I looked back and watched him push the gate shut behind me. Then he said, 'If things get bad, if you try to do anything to us, or tell anyone about us, we'll hunt you down and we'll make you suffer. Your past won't be able to protect you any more.' After that, he headed back to the farm."

"What did he mean by 'your past won't protect you'?"

"I don't know. I just know they can't kill me."

We drove for a little while without speaking, both of us thinking about the night that Alex had described. My mind was racing, trying to put things together.

Something didn't add up.

"Did they say anything else to you?"

"No. I ran and didn't look back. I hitched a lift to the first station I could find, and then got on the train down to London. I hid in the toilets the whole way. I didn't have any money, but it wasn't just that—I was too scared to go out in case they'd tricked me; in case they were waiting. They weren't waiting for me, and it wasn't a trick, but I couldn't get that place out of my head: the horrendous things that had gone on there, and the things . . ." He paused, holding up his hand, the fingers scarred, the nails disfigured. "The things they did to me; to all of us there."

"That was why you let Mary see you."

"Yes. I had to get someone to go to that place."

We drove for a while in silence, snow continuing to fall. The motorway was slow, cars traveling at reduced speeds, headlights smudges against a white wall.

"What about Al?" I asked eventually.

He looked at me. "You know about him?"

I nodded.

"I've had a lot of time to think about what I did."

"What *did* you do?"

He took a long breath. "I spent a lot of months, after I left the farm, scared about dying: that it *was* a trick after all, that they *were* coming back for me. And, then recently, I started thinking about what they would do to me if I came back."

"What's that got to do with Al?"

"I don't know. Maybe I hoped that, by coming back here, by exposing the farm for what it was, corrupt, violent, I might be able to make up for what I did."

I didn't say anything.

"Dad and Al," he continued, "they went way back. They grew up on the same street, they were at school together, but while Dad was the one with the brains, Al was the one with all the balls. Dad got the grades and went to university—and ended up in a succession of dead end jobs, doing the books for local businesses; Al left school an abject failure—I don't think he passed one exam—and ended up opening electronics stores all across the city. Eventually, I think Al felt sorry for Dad, so he offered him a full-time job doing his books." Alex stopped, swirling the dregs of his coffee around in its cup. "That was when our life started to change."

"Change how?"

"We never had any money, *ever,* but as soon as Dad started working for Al, suddenly we got a new TV, a new kitchen, went on a nice holiday to the south of France. I mean, you might not understand just how *big* that was, but we literally *never* went on holiday, because we could never afford it—and then, *bang,* there we were, in a hotel in Nice. It was great. You didn't see Mum and I complaining."

He stopped, thoughts drifting for a moment, and I could sense what was coming: a *but*, a reversal of their fortunes, a realization that something was a lie.

"Thing was," he said eventually, his voice dropping away, "everything Mum and I thought we owned, Dad knew differently. Because Al really owned it all."

"What do you mean?"

"He'd loaned Dad money for just about everything, told him he never had to pay it back because we were like family to him. He'd never married. He didn't have kids. He spent weekends with us, meal times—sometimes it was easy to forget that he didn't actually *live* with us. When Dad took that money, he took it reluctantly, because he was a proud man—but he took it because he believed Al."

"So what changed?"

"Like that—" He clicked his fingers "—Al flipped. Just . . . flipped; completely transformed. Dad came home one night, white as a sheet, and told me Al wanted everything back, everything he'd paid for: furniture, holidays, everything. There was no way in hell we could do that. We didn't *have* thousands of pounds just sitting there in a bank account, and if we sold all the furniture, what then? We'd have nothing. Dad said that Al had even paid off a chunk of the mortgage for us. The house itself, everything in it, it wasn't Dad's, or Mum's, or mine. It was Al's."

"Why would he suddenly turn like that?"

"I don't know, but it just got worse and worse. Dad managed to keep most of it away from Mum, but she could see he wasn't eating. He was losing weight, he couldn't concentrate on anything. He begged me not to tell her—that stupid pride of his coming out again—promising that he'd sort it out, and so one night he invited Al round to the house when Mum was out, to try and talk him around."

"What happened?"

"It was a disaster."

"Why?"

"They went down into the basement, and Al just lost his head. He punched Dad square in the face. When Mum asked what had happened, we told her he'd had a fall while we were out at the lake, fishing. Dad couldn't bring himself to tell her—even after he'd been assaulted—because he couldn't bring himself to tell her that everything he'd ever bought for her, the life he had created for her, for all of us, was about to fall apart; that our home and everything in it would be gone."

Alex looked out of the window. "This went on for a few months," he said, "and then Dad came up with an idea: we'd pay Al back with his own money. Dad reckoned he could fiddle Al's books quite easily. Al had three stores, each making a lot of cash—that was when we first got talking about the five hundred grand."

"Five hundred grand?"

"The money we would take from him." He glanced at me, guilt in his face. "It started off as fifty grand—just enough to cover some of what we owed Al. But then it escalated. The more we talked about it, the more Dad became convinced that he could pass bigger chunks of money in and out of the business, without Al ever noticing. And then . . . and then it just sort of spiraled out of control, and we were suddenly talking about stopping Al. Like, *stopping* him. With him out of the way, we didn't have to pay back any of the money. We got to keep it—and more."

"You came up with a plan to murder him."

"We just got swept along by it, corrupted by the idea . . ." He seemed to fade a little then. "In the end, I did it. But, that night, I never set out to. The closer we got to the idea, the less certain we both became, until eventually I said to Dad it might be better for me to go and talk to Al. We were scared shitless so he agreed."

We passed under a set of signs.

Eighty miles to London.

"I went to meet Al at that strip club in Harrow. He was drunk by the time I got there, sitting next to the stage, letting these strippers rub their tits in his face. He wasn't in a fit state to talk. He wasn't in a fit state to do anything. But I gave it a shot. Except, every time I tried to reason with him, he turned his back on me and told me I didn't know what I was talking about. I tried to give him a chance, tried to let him *give* me a chance, but in the end I lost it. I told him to stay the hell away from my family, to stop threatening us, my dad, my mum. The more composure I lost, the worse it got. I told him if he ever came near us again, I would kill him."

He stopped. We both knew what came next.

"I told him I would kill him," Alex said gently, "and that's exactly what I did. Mum had the car that night. She was out with friends. I guess I could have got the train, but it was an hour and a half, I'd have to change twice, and I don't know . . . maybe a part of me just knew already; just knew that I didn't want to get caught on camera, on the streets of Harrow, waiting for a train on a platform. I honestly didn't go there to kill him and, yet, my actions, the things I did before I ended up at that strip club, the thought must have been there. With a car, I just drove right into the car park, unseen. With a *hire* car, I could lie on the form, distance myself from the vehicle entirely. I looked around all the rental places in town, and found this really small one, staffed by a young kid, clearly only doing the job part-time. I showed him my ID, and then filled out the form, and everything I put on it was a lie. He didn't compare the two, the ID and the form. I took advantage of that, of him. But that was why no one ever traced the vehicle to me—at least until you came along."

"How did Al end up dead outside the club?"

He nodded, clearly still pained by the memory of what he'd done. "I came out of the bar and headed back to the car, and he came after me. He was so drunk he could hardly stand up, let alone walk in a straight line, but he charged over to me and started pointing at me; jabbing his finger into the center of my chest. He started telling me what a piece of shit my dad was. There were a couple of people standing outside the bar, smoking—but, as soon as they went in, I hit him. He was so drunk he didn't see it coming. I just snapped. I don't even recognize that person. When he was on the floor . . . I broke his nose with the heel of my shoe."

The lights from the motorway flashed in his eyes.

"When he finally got up, he was a mess, could hardly speak properly. But he said, 'You just made a big fucking mistake, Alex. I was trying to *help* you. I was trying to help your mum. You came down here for your dad, right? Your *fantastic* dad. Well, why don't you go and ask him about his dirty secret in Wembley?'"

"What did he mean by that?"

Something glistened in his eyes. "I got in the car and tried to calm myself, but then he started again. He was spitting blood all over the hood, telling me to go fuck myself, telling me he'd make a special journey to watch Dad being kicked out onto the streets. And then, before he headed back into the club, he looked at me through the windshield and said, 'Go and ask your dad about your brother in Wembley.'"

I glanced at him. "Your *brother*?"

He nodded. There were tears on his face now. "I put my foot to the floor, and went straight through him. He hit the middle of the car and just flew off the side, like he was nothing; just a cardboard cutout. And I left him there. When I looked in the mirror, he was lying in a puddle, and he was still. Absolutely still."

I gave him a moment. "You've got a brother?"

He nodded. "I went straight home and told Dad what had happened, but he was in shock. He just . . . let me go. He didn't know what to say to me—just told me to disappear, to lay low. I got angry, blaming him for what had happened, and I said to him, 'Were you ever going to tell me about your secret up in Wembley? About my *brother*?' But he just looked at me. I'm not sure he even knew where to begin, and I realized, the longer I waited there, with that car outside—smashed up, covered in blood—the more I put myself at risk. So I said good-bye . . . and left."

"You never asked your dad anything else?"

He shook his head. "I don't even know my brother's name."

"Al called it a 'dirty little secret,' right?"

"Right."

"So the likelihood is, Mary doesn't know either?"

A long, forlorn pause.

"Yeah," he said finally. "Yeah, that's right."

55

"Where did you go after you left home?"

It was dark, almost nine o'clock, and we were ten miles from my house, stuck in traffic on the edge of London. Alex looked at me and said, "France. I took my bank card, withdrew the maximum amount of money they would let me take in one day, and headed down to Dover. I dumped the car in long-term parking there, and then found a three-man trawler willing to take me across the Channel. I didn't have my passport so I paid them whatever it took to get me across there."

"What did you do in France?"

"Worked some crappy jobs, cleaning toilets, waiting tables at cafés. I just tried to keep my head down. I didn't spend more than three months in each job."

"In case the police were on to you?"

"Right."

"So what brought you back?"

"I got homesick. I ended up hating everything about my life there. The jobs were terrible, the places I lived in were worse. I spent five years doing that, and every day ground me down more. So I hung around the port in Le Havre, until I finally found a boat that would bring me back—and then I went and saw Michael."

"You knew him from before?"

"Yeah," Alex said. "He used to be a friend. A good one. Back when I lived with Mum and Dad, he worked at our local church. He called himself Mat back then—Michael Anthony Tilton—until he went traveling. When he got back, he took that job in east London, and I started noticing small changes in him. Like, he never talked about his family any more, and he got uncomfortable when I still called him Mat, as if he'd left that stage of his life behind. Andrew was changing him too, I suppose, just not with the drugs and torture and fear. He was doing it more subtly; brainwashing him, altering his DNA. I went and visited him at the church a few times before I disappeared. The last time was just before I killed Al."

"That was when you bought the birthday card for Kathy?"

He nodded.

"Why did you go to Michael after you came back from France?"

"I thought he would know what to do, that I could trust him. I couldn't go to Dad, I definitely couldn't go to Mum. I couldn't go to John, because of his job, and I didn't want to drag Kathy into my mess. But I thought Michael might help me, that he might understand me and forgive me. He was shocked when I turned up at the church but, when he gathered himself, he told me I'd made the right choice coming to him. After that, he made a few calls and, next thing I knew, I was being driven up to the farm, and—when I arrived there—it felt like it was all going to be okay. They took a picture of me on this old Polaroid they had, they let me keep it, talked to me, joked, told me everything was going to be okay. They said I was with family and that no one could hurt me now. But it took half a day."

"Before what?"

"Before I realized it was all a façade. I was sitting around with Michael and Stephen, and I happened to turn my back on them for a second, and they knocked me out. I woke up in this room with just a bed and a bucket—and they kept me there for days. Weeks. Maybe a month. I don't really know. And then they tried to take my memory away. They put me onto the program and, after a while, I could feel my body pleading for the drugs, but I had some fight in me. I managed to cling onto something. So, even in the darkest times, I could see the outline of the people I loved. I could see Dad, before everything went wrong. I could hear things Mum had said to me. I saw places I'd been with Kath. I used that as a way to focus my attention, and to compartmentalize things that were important to me."

He looked out at the edges of the city.

"You remember I said I saw Simon that night at the farm?" he asked.

"Yeah."

"I realized, eventually, why they treated him so badly, like an animal." He turned to me, but I'd already skipped ahead of him, and with a nod of the head he acknowledged that I was right: "Simon was the body in the car crash. He was me."

"Why did they choose him?"

"We had the same blood type. I remember that from when we used to give blood at university. I think maybe Andrew and some of the others on the farm, they liked the symmetry of it too: one friend making the ultimate sacrifice for the other. But I think the main reason was that

Simon had once been a part of the program too, just like me—and he'd fought it. They'd fed him drugs, but he kicked out, over and over, fighting them on everything. In the end he kicked back too hard. One night, when one of the women came in to tell him it was lights out, he launched himself at her. She didn't die, but he broke her ribs, her arm."

"How do you know all this?"

"When we were coming out of the compound last night, there was a woman that passed us on the stairs. You saw her. You said she recognized me, and I said that it didn't matter if she did. She wouldn't know my name. That was Rose. She was with me for a while in the room with the rings. They were punishing her, like they were punishing me. She wouldn't speak at night, because of Legion. She knew, at night, he watched us. But, in the day, before she started to lose herself into the program, she would talk to me a little and tell me things she'd heard."

We didn't speak after that.

I'd look over occasionally and see him playing with his gums. He had a set of false teeth in, which—later on—he told me he'd had fitted by a dentist, for cash, in the months between escaping the farm and passing Mary in the street. I saw the scars on his fingers, the bruises on his face, the bruises on mine, and the full gravity of what had gone on at the farm started to hit me; and then I spent the final few minutes of our journey just staring ahead of the car, watching it eat away at the last of the miles, unable to think of a single worthwhile thing to say.

I pulled into a parking bay at a train station about a mile from my house and gave Alex enough money for a ticket, somewhere to stay for a while, and some extra cash to get some new clothes and clean himself up. He got out of the car and shook my hand, and—as I held on to it—I said to him: "It's 11 p.m., Alex. Why don't you just crash at my place for the night?"

"I can't."

"Where are you going to go?"

"I don't know," he said. "But I think the less time you spend with me, and the less you know about where I'm going and what I'm doing, the better it'll be."

He got ready to go, but then turned back.

"Are you okay?" I said.

"Do you know what the last thing I heard was?"

I looked at him. "What are you talking about?"

"The drugs they give you."

"What about them?"

"Do you know what I heard when I died on that cross?"

I shook my head. "No. What?"

"It's different for everyone. That's what Andrew said."

"What did you hear?"

"I heard the sea."

I looked at him, a little stunned. He didn't know that was what I'd heard as well, because I hadn't told him. "The last thing I heard was the sea," he went on. "Waves crashing, sand washing away. Seagulls squawking. If that's the last sound I hear in this life, it won't matter, because that sound is everything to me."

It reminds him of Carcondrock.

It reminded him of being with Kathy.

After that, he turned around and disappeared into the crowds.

56

Twelve days after she'd first come to me, I headed to Mary's for the final time. It was late afternoon, snow still on the ground, mini Christmas trees and snowmen on front lawns, fairy lights winking in windows. It had been thirty-six hours since we'd left the farm, and it was already all over the news. From reports, it was hard to tell if anything that had been left behind connected either Alex or me to what had happened there. We'd been careful, exhaustive in our cleaning up, but that didn't mean we were one hundred percent insulated. The students had seen us there, in the living room of the farmhouse with them, although it was going to be hard for investigators to rely on them as witnesses: their memories had been wiped, and—even if they were able to give descriptions of what we looked like—as far as the wider world was concerned, Alex had been dead thirteen months, and any profile that was painted of me, could just as easily be confused with a fugitive instructor.

As I parked up and got out, I tried not to think too hard about what the fallout would be when, and if, any of the instructors were found by police: in one way, I *wanted* them found, because they deserved to face justice; on the other, if they were found, they would probably name me—and then I would be dragged back in.

At the door, as I waited for Mary to answer, I touched my back, pressing at the bumps there. It still hurt, but it had been bandaged properly now, and the pain was slowly beginning to fade as the reminders of the scourge began to scab over.

The door opened.

Mary saw it was me, and smiled. "David."

"Hello, Mary."

"Come in," she said, backing away from the door. She looked at me, at the bruises on my face. "Whatever happened?" she asked, concerned. "Are you okay?"

"It looks worse than it is."

I stepped past her, into the house.

"Have you seen a doctor?" she asked.

"Yes," I lied. "Everything's fine."

I hadn't seen a doctor, because with a doctor came more questions, but it seemed to placate her, and she told me she would fix me a drink. I waited in the living room, looking out of the windows into the back garden. The snow was still perfect here: no footprints, bird tracks or leaves, like a tract of unexplored land.

Mary came through with two cups of coffee, and we sat.

"Where's Malcolm?" I asked.

"Upstairs."

She shrugged; a sad smile. "Some days are better than others."

On the table in front of her I placed the envelope she had given to me with the rest of her money in it. She looked down at it, studied it, but didn't reach for it. Instead, her eyes flicked back to me and she said: "You don't need any more?"

"No," I replied. "That's most of what you paid me."

There was little emotion in her face, and I wondered whether she'd already talked herself into believing it had all been a mistake. "Uh, what do you mean?"

"He's alive."

"Alex is?"

"Yes."

Her mouth opened a little and her eyes began to fill—all the doubt, all the times she'd told herself she must have been seeing things. She went to speak, but the words got lost, so she cleared her throat and tried again: "Where is he now?"

"He's in Scotland," I said, but it was hard to look her in the eyes.

This was the plan I'd agreed with Alex on the drive down from Scotland. He'd said he needed time to get his head straight, to decide what he was going to do. He'd told me he desperately wanted to see his parents, but—by coming back—he was putting himself at risk again, not from the people on the farm this time, but from the police. There was still the murder of Leyton Alan Green in his past, a crime he'd now directly been tied to via the fingerprints he'd left on the Polaroid.

In a strange way, it was easier for Alex to re-enter the world of the living, because he had something to anchor him to his past, memories he'd refused to let go. The other students had nothing, just a blank. No memories of their former lives, no space to fit back into. And, yet, Alex had to contend with something else. Something just as big.

A murder, and his culpability.

"Did you talk to him?" Mary said.

"Yes. On the phone."

"How did he sound?"

"He sounded good," I said, attempting a smile. It felt awkward on my face, false, and I hoped she couldn't tell. "After he left home, he went to France," I went on, edging away from details of how Alex had been. *Homeless. On the run. Scared.* "That's where he was for those five years, until he came back to the UK."

"Why did he go there?"

I looked at her and thought of Al, and then of Malcolm, of the son that he had fathered with someone else. In the end, he and Alex had been the same, both burying secrets in their past. I started to feel drawn to Mary, uncomfortable with feeding her another lie, of adding to the deceit that had torn this family apart. But I'd promised Alex. So I made a pledge: if Alex didn't return within two weeks, and tell his mother everything, I was going to tell her myself. She deserved that much.

She deserved the truth.

"Why did he go to France?" she repeated.

I looked at her. "I don't know, Mary."

She broke down after that, crying into the sleeve of her cardigan, using her arm to cover her face. Briefly, I started to construct another lie; a way to comfort her. It was a lie about the friend of mine who just decided one day that he needed to break away—even if it was just for a short time—to clear his head and decide what he wanted to do with his life. But, in the end, I stopped myself. The deeper I dug, the further away from safety I got, and I didn't want Mary catching me out.

"What did Alex do in France?" she asked, after she'd recovered a little.

"Just worked some jobs there."

"Good jobs?"

I smiled. "He'd probably say not."

She nodded, rubbing her palms together. Her hands were small, the nails bitten. She reached to where her coffee sat beside her and placed her fingers over the top of the mug, as if trying to warm them. "How can he still be alive, David?"

I knew she'd ask.

I just didn't want to answer.

"We never got that far," I said. "All I know is that he misses you, and he will phone you. He promised me he would. If he doesn't, I will find out the reasons."

Above us, floorboards creaked.

"He just needs a little time, that's all."

Mary nodded, and her eyes went to the roof. Malcolm was moving around up there. "I better go and see if everything's all right. Will you wait here a second?"

I told her I would.

A few minutes later, she brought Malcolm down. He looked at me blankly, and then started telling her he was hungry. She settled him in front of the TV, and he asked her again about food. Calmly, she told him he'd eaten an hour ago, and that they would be having dinner in a couple of hours. He seemed to accept it, and sunk into the sofa, eyes on the television, colors blinking in his face. He looked old and tired, barely reacting to the images he was watching, and as Mary headed off to the sideboard in the living room, going through its drawers, I thought about how many conversations were trapped behind Malcolm's eyes, never to escape.

I felt desperately sorry for him.

For Mary, for Alex.

Mary returned from the sideboard with a bag of sweets.

"Do you want one of these, Malc?" she asked.

The minute detail in his face had become important to her. When a part of his mouth twitched, she took that as a yes, taking out a sweet and unwrapping it.

"Here we are," she said, slipping it into his mouth.

She held the bag of sweets against her and watched him sucking on it. He seemed to enjoy it, a snapshot of normality that she took some pleasure from.

"Would you like a sweet, David?"

She held out the bag to me.

"Sure," I said, taking one.

We headed to the front door and she said quietly, "I know it must seem so stupid, but the sweets are one of the only ways he'll interact with me these days."

We walked onto the porch and down the driveway toward my car. I could see her hanging on the back of that last sentence, pained by it. Again, I felt such a strong compulsion to give her the truth, to give her *anything* substantial—and, again, I resolved to tell her everything inside two weeks if Alex didn't call first.

As I flipped the locks on the car, a fierce winter wind ripped up the road, cutting right through us both. "I can't wait for the summer," I said.

Mary smiled.

And then, distantly, something registered with me—a noise I recognized—and I looked back at the house.

"Is everything okay, David?"

I listened.

"David?"

I nodded. "Yeah, it's fine."

I got into the car and pulled the door shut, buzzing down the windows. As Mary stepped in closer, I unwrapped the sweet and popped it into my mouth.

"Thank you for all your help, David," she said.

"It will come together, Mary."

"Okay."

"He promised he would call."

She smiled again, but it was flat, humorless.

"You were right," I said, "right to come to me, right to force me to believe you. Alex is alive—that's the important bit. Now he has to figure out a few things. And I promise you: if he doesn't call you, if he doesn't tell you everything, I will. I will drive up there myself, I will get all the answers from him. I will get the truth."

"Thank you."

Wind roared up the road again, pressing at the car windows, so hard they creaked. Mary stepped sideways, pushed by the wind—and then the same noise.

The one I recognized.

I looked past Mary to the house again, hanging baskets swaying, the front door swinging gently on its hinges, snow powder being scattered like a fine dust.

"What's the matter, David?" she asked again.

"That noise . . ."

Then I saw it.

On top of the house, almost a silhouette in the late afternoon light: a weathervane. The wind buffeted it, spinning it around—and, as the wind settled down again, the weathervane continued turning, squeaking gently as it did, as if a part of it had come loose. *Metal against metal.* It was a noise I'd heard before.

On the farm.

The weathervane was an angel.

"Where did you get that?" I asked her, pointing at it.

She looked back at the house—and, as she did, a second reaction hit me, even more powerful than the first.

My mouth.

". . . alcolm bought it from a shop before he got Alzheim . . ."

But I wasn't listening to her now.

At the tip of my ear, I could feel someone's breath, warm and saccharine like the smell of boiled sweets. The night down in Bristol, before they'd taken me out to the woods to kill me, they'd tied me to a chair in the remains of a factory, and the man in charge had tried to find out what I knew. I'd recognized his voice.

I thought it had been Legion.

Once I got to the farm and met him, maybe even Andrew.

But it wasn't either of them.

I looked at Mary, at the weathervane, at the house.

It was Malcolm.

57

I opened the door of the car and headed up the path.

Behind me, I heard Mary saying my name, asking me a question, but I was already at the house, pushing at the front door. On the sofa, across the room from me, Malcolm had changed positions, his back to me now.

"Malcolm."

He almost fell off the sofa.

He turned around and, when he saw who it was, surprised at the sound of my voice, he held up a hand, made a noise; a grunt. Fear darted across his eyes.

"Is this all an act?"

He shifted position on the sofa, moving across to where he'd been before. His eyes darted left to right, frightened, confused. "Don't hurt me," he moaned.

"It was you in Bristol."

"Where's Mary?"

I took a step closer. "You remember her now?"

"Mary!" he yelled, looking beyond me.

"Malcolm," I said again. "Are you listening to me?"

"Where's Ma—"

"I know about you."

He was up on his feet now, over on the other side of the sofa, in front of the window that looked out over the garden. He glanced over my shoulder again.

"Mary!"

"You tried to kill me."

"Mary!" he screamed again.

"You tried to *kill* me."

Tears filled his eyes, color draining from his face. He genuinely looked terrified now, small, weak, sick, and it made me hesitate. Had I called it wrong?

"David?"

I turned. Mary was in the doorway.

"David, what the hell are you doing?"

Her eyes darted from me to Malcolm, then back again.

"Mary, I—"

"*What the hell do you think you're doing?*" she said, and came toward me, to my side, looking at me. There were tears in her eyes, but she was strong now, fierce, protecting her husband. I looked from her to Malcolm. What had I done?

"Take whatever you want," Malcolm said, weakly.

I studied him.

No. No, I'm right. I have to be right.

"You tried to kill me, Malcolm."

Mary took a sharp breath. "*What?*"

"Take whatever you want!" he shouted.

"You know I'm not here for that."

"Take it all!"

"Are you listening, Malcolm? *You tried to kill me.*"

"There's money in the kitchen!"

I paused. "You remember where Mary keeps the money now?"

He realized what he'd said before he'd even finished the sentence. I could see him wince, like the air had been punched out of him. The shield fragmented.

"Malcolm?" Mary said.

He glanced at his wife as the cracks began to open up, piece by piece. After a few seconds, his body relaxed, straightened. He smiled and held out his hands.

"You got me, David," he said.

This time his voice was different.

The same one I'd heard in Bristol.

"Malcolm?" Mary said again, words trembling. She'd dropped back behind me, hand covering her mouth, eyes wide. The physical change in her husband was extraordinary: in just a few seconds, he seemed to fill out, his face changing, his physicality. He ran a hand through his hair, the fading shell of a man gone now.

"You're the reason they couldn't kill Alex."

He didn't say anything, but I could see I was right.

"That's how you were all onto me from the beginning."

He shrugged, glancing at Mary and then back to me. "The first time you came here, I spoke to Andrew and told him it might come to this. That was why he sent that . . . freak down to visit you in Cornwall. We wanted to see what kind of a man you were. When Legion told us about the photo you had of Alex, I knew we might have to fight you. We were protecting a secret, and part of the secret was with you. By the time you made it down to Bristol, to the house we had down there, I thought decisive action was needed. I needed to sort things out myself."

I ran a hand across my face.

Bruised, battered.

"How did you get to Bristol without Mary knowing?"

"Mary's a nurse. She works shifts. The people she gets in here to look after me . . ." A pause; a shrug. "They're monkeys. Useless. That night I came to see you . . . I drugged them." He brushed himself down, like he was blowing dust away from an old book cover. "I wanted to see first hand what we were dealing with."

I had so many questions. "How did you become involved?"

"*Involved?* I didn't become involved, David. I ran the fucking thing."

"The farm?"

"Everything. Where do you think Al's money went?"

"You took the five hundred grand?"

"I took more than that."

"How much?"

"It doesn't matter. It's untraceable. The money's been through the system and back out again. Al threatened us, threatened all of us. I took what was mine."

"You murdered Al."

"What?" Mary's voice from behind me.

"No, I didn't," he said.

"Malc?"

He glanced at her, then back at me.

"It was your idea," I said to him. "You wanted it done—but you didn't have the balls. You manipulated Alex—your own *son*—into doing what you wanted, and then turned your back on him when he returned here asking for your help."

"I never asked him to do anything."

"That's a lie."

"How do you know?"

"Because he told me."

He glanced at Mary again, I did too, and I hoped she could see what

I was telling her: *I made a promise to Alex. I made a promise to him that he could tell you himself what had gone on.* "But I didn't know about Malcolm," I said to her. "I swear."

She just looked at me, at her husband.

Lost.

I turned back to him, even angrier now, fueled by the pain in Mary's face: "You put the seed of an idea in his head, worked on it, hoped and prayed he would do it—and then, when he did, you turned your back on him. Have you any idea what you did to him?"

He shook his head. "You amuse me, David. You've no idea what it's like to raise a child. No idea. I loved Alex, *loved* him—but he was reckless. What he did was stupid. Talking about it and doing it are two entirely different things. He offered to *talk* to Al, not to drive a car through him. When he came to me after, he expected me to support him in what he'd done. But what he'd done was wrong. I told him to go somewhere and lay low. It ripped the heart out of me, but it was the best way to protect him. I didn't expect him to vanish for five fucking years."

"You were protecting yourself."

"I was protecting our son."

"*Protecting* him? How were you protecting him when he came back last year? By agreeing with Michael to send him to that *farm*? You're insane. Have you got any *idea* what they were doing to people up there? It was a slaughterhouse."

"You don't understand."

"*What* don't I understand?"

"He turns up on Michael's doorstep after five years—it wasn't going to be long before he started leaving a trail all the way back to Al. I wanted him away from the places that could hurt him. I didn't want him having to go to prison."

"You tried to erase his memory."

"You've got it all wrong, David. I protected myself at the beginning. I had to. The car Alex had hired turned up in Dover with Al's blood all over it, and the cops came here and asked me questions about Al because I was the person who probably knew him best. We'd been friends for decades. But by then I'd already decided to use this disease as cover, which made it difficult for them. Mary answered most of their questions. She could handle that. They were generic questions. I could tell they didn't have a clue where to start, or who had been driving that hire car. But it wasn't them I was worried about. They were the front line. If it got any further, they would bring out their best soldiers. That was what I was really worried about. But, as it turned out, we never heard from the police again. And by that stage I'd chosen to go down this route."

"And this was going to be it?"

He didn't reply.

But I could see the answer in his face.

This wasn't it—lying to the police, to the world, to his wife. *It* was going to be Mary waking up one day, in a month, in a year, and finding he was gone.

And only then would she know.

Everything in her life had been a lie.

58

"No one wanted Alex on the farm," Malcolm continued. "No one. Andrew fought against me, so did Legion, even Michael didn't know if it was a good idea. *Michael.* This was a boy I'd known since he attended the church down the road, a boy who watched his brother get stabbed to death dealing ecstasy. A boy who tried to get away, go traveling, but came back because he had nothing here and nothing out there. His parents were dead. And I took him in, told him about what we were doing and what a difference he could make to our cause. I changed his life. *I* turned him around. And when I asked for one thing, he fought me on it."

"Malcolm?" Mary said from behind us again.

He didn't acknowledge her. "You don't understand."

"You knew what they would do to Alex up there."

"I knew because they told me," he said. "After he left, I thought about Alex every day for five years. I thought he was dead. Then when he came back, when he went to see Michael, I knew the next stage of his life might be even harder for us than the last. Because I had to learn to know my son again through other people; through Michael and Andrew and the others on the farm. And Alex had to forget in order to get on with the process of living. It was painful for me, but I helped him out. I gave him a way out, an exit. But he couldn't know the farm was mine. He couldn't know I knew about him. It would have been too hard for him."

He took a long breath, and then sat down on the edge of the sofa. I heard Mary sniffing, caught movement as she wiped her nose with a handkerchief.

"Eight years ago," Malcolm said, quieter now, "May twenty-ninth, 2001— I was working for a bank, part-time, doing their books, and I got friendly with the branch manager there. After work, he told me about this guy who'd come in that day, wanting to set up a rehabilitation clinic for kids with problems; a place they could come and start again. This manager didn't know how the hell the loan would ever get repaid. This guy didn't know either, had no clue how he'd make money from it—plus he had a criminal record. So, of course, the bank turned him down. It would have been financial suicide to have said yes to him."

"Andrew," I said, remembering his story about the woman he'd dated after getting out of prison, the son she'd lost, and how he'd found her dead in the bath.

"Then I began to feel very strongly about the idea."

"Alex's brother."

For the first time he glanced at Mary. "Yes."

"What?" she asked from my side. "*What?*"

"I watched someone else I loved die young," Malcolm said, "this time with a needle in his arm, and I wasn't going to stand by and watch others do the same."

Suddenly, something else clicked into place.

"The boy in the photograph," I said.

I thought of the kid kicking a ball around in the picture Jade had showed me the night she'd died; the newspaper report about his death pinned to the wall of the flat in Brixton, and in Lazarus on the farm.

This is the reason we do it.

"The boy is yours."

Malcolm nodded.

Mary made little noise. That surprised me, but I didn't turn around to look at her. Malcolm was in full flow now, feeding off the fact he could finally say what he'd stored up, and I didn't want him distracted. I wanted to know everything.

"Whose son was he?"

"A stripper at Sinderella's," he said. "Al and I used to go there all the time. But at the end she was just a junkie, selling herself to fund her habit. The boy was wonderful, though. I tried to see him as often as I could. That was part of the reason why I took the job with Al—because Al's office was in Harrow and Robert lived in Wembley." He paused, looked at me. "But then Al found out about him."

"About the boy?"

"He saw me taking Robert to school one day."

"That was why he flipped."

"Yes. When he found out who Robert was, he wanted me to tell Mary. I refused. He said he'd tell her himself. So I threatened him, told him I'd kill him if he said anything. He said, if I didn't tell her, he'd take back everything that was his. I don't think he believed I would kill him. So it became a stand-off. The irony was, Mary hated Al—but, in the end, all Al was doing was trying to protect her."

"But Mary never found out."

"No. It had been going on for two months, Al threatening to tell her. I tried to close off all other avenues, like paying Robert's mother to keep her trap shut. But she ended up using the money to buy drugs. One day, I went round there and found a needle mark in his arm. He was ten years old. If I'd known that was going to happen, I would have killed her and brought him back here. I would have done that, without even pausing for thought. In the end, she was just a hooker. No one would have missed her. But, a couple of days later, she called me on the phone and told me he'd been found in the Thames. He'd overdosed. A ten-year-old boy."

Boy, 10, found floating in the Thames.

"Al didn't have anything on me then, not once the boy was dead, but all I felt was anger. All I wanted was to hit out at someone. I suggested to Alex we take his money. That was the first step. But that wasn't enough. It didn't quell anything. So I started thinking about killing Al, thought a lot about it. Then Alex really *did* kill him. When it happened, it suddenly seemed so huge. But after Alex had gone, I started to feel it again, eating away at me—this anger at Al, at the way he'd threatened me before he died. I couldn't suppress it, couldn't suppress the hatred I felt for him, even after he was buried—but, more than that, it was the anger I felt for Robert's mother. That fucking bitch showed nothing. No remorse."

He stopped, looking down into his hands. "I called up the bank manager I used to work for, and got the number for Andrew from him, and then I called Andrew to ask whether he'd ever got his business off the ground. He said he had, but it was small, and he had no money to fund it properly. So I said I would loan him the money to do it properly. *Al's* money. Andrew and I, we grew close, got on well, but the whole time—even when they bought the farm, and things started to come together—the anger just burned in me. That *bitch*, she'd forgotten Robert the moment we buried him. I think if she'd shown even a second's guilt, I would have let her live. But she didn't. She was pleased to be free of the responsibility."

"So you killed her?"

"I asked Andrew whether he knew anyone. He said he did, a guy he was in the army with, and that was when he sent Legion out to see her."

"As easy as that."

"Some things you regret. I don't regret that."

"What about all the kids you killed? Do you regret them?"

"We tried to save them."

"You murdered them."

"No one died who didn't deserve it."

"Did Simon deserve it?"

"*Simon*," he said, disgust in his face.

"Did he deserve it?"

"Simon became a problem."

"Because he refused to give up his memories?"

"*No!* Because he almost beat an instructor *to death*! I never wanted the violence. I only wanted Legion's help for that one thing. She killed that boy. She deserved it. But things happened up there, and I started to realize it was the only way we could protect ourselves. What we built and what we worked for *had* to be protected. And, in the end, utilizing Legion's skills allowed me to protect what I cared about most. It protected Alex—what happened to Simon protected Alex."

"But you *murdered* Simon."

"We gave him a chance, but he threw it back in our faces. Some of these kids were so fucking ungrateful. When they fought back, what the hell were we supposed to do with them? They couldn't go back. We couldn't put them back on the streets. They would have talked to people and we would have been found out and everything we built would have come tumbling down. They left us no choice."

"What about Alex?"

He paused for a moment. "Andrew and the others, they made mistakes with Alex. Terrible mistakes. Alex wasn't like the other kids we tried to help. He wasn't wheeled in on a trolley with a needle in his arm. He hadn't spent years being raped and abused. They were treating him differently, how he was meant to be treated. Not the same drugs. Not the same program. But then that freak didn't like it, and eventually neither did Andrew. They put Alex on the regular program when he shouldn't have been anywhere near it. They put him on it because they didn't think he deserved special treatment. *He was my fucking son!* He *deserved* special treatment! All I'd done for them, all the money I'd put into that project, and *that's* how they repaid me."

He paused, looking up at me, past me.

"Andrew used to call me when Mary was out and I listened to his reports about Alex, about what they were doing to him, and I knew it would go wrong. Putting him on the program just because he spoke to them in the wrong tone of voice? That was a misjudgment. But I was powerless to intervene. I knew Alex would fight the drugs, I knew he'd fight the containment. Alex was a fighter."

He looked at me; thought he saw something in my face.

"I don't give a fuck what you think," he said.

"You protected your son by sending him to a place where they'd make him forget about you like you pretended to forget about him. That wasn't for his sake."

I paused, thought I had him.

But I was wrong.

The smallest of smiles wormed its way across Malcolm's face, and— very gently—he reached into the pocket of his trousers and brought out a phone.

It was on.

He'd called someone, accessed the phone while it was in his pocket. Maybe they'd heard part of the conversation. Maybe they knew what was going on here.

Maybe they were close by.

The thought came to me too late. As I tried to imagine *how* close, I felt something at the side of my neck. *A knife.* I turned my head an inch to the left.

In the window, in its reflection, I saw who it was; saw him glance at me. He had Mary pulled in against him, her fingers wrapped around his arm, her mouth covered by his hand. It was the reason she'd suddenly gone so quiet.

Michael.

59

"I told you to walk the other way," Michael said. "I tried to help you. All I wanted to do was get back to helping those in need."

"You messed with the wrong people, David," Malcolm said, coming around the sofa. "The minute I found out Mary was going to you, I knew it would end like this. In violence, in bloodshed."

I glanced around me.

Nothing to pick up.

No weapons.

"You don't give up secrets worth protecting," he said. He moved up close to me, nose to nose. "Not without a fight, anyway. You've injured us, killed us and called in the police—but good will always triumph over evil."

Michael handed Malcolm the knife over my shoulder.

"I'm going to enjoy this," he said, taking it. It was a hunting knife, the blade about eight inches with a serrated spine. He turned it in his hand and held it up at me, the tip of the blade disturbing the air in front of my face. "I'm going to—"

Behind me, Mary tried to scream, as if she could see what was coming next—and Malcolm's eyes briefly pinged toward her.

I moved quickly.

I charged Malcolm and we flipped back over the sofa, my skull cracking against the side of the coffee table as we landed. For a moment I was dazed, head thumping, unable to get my bearings—and then I was back in the moment again.

Malcolm was scrambling to his feet, the knife still in his hand.

I looked back at Michael.

He'd picked up a fire poker and had pushed Mary aside: she was cowering beside one of the sofas, obviously still trying to process what she was seeing. Her husband. The man who had once been her son's friend. The knife. The violence. I looked back at Malcolm, a grimace in his face, the anger, the *hatred*, and then to Michael—gripping the iron fire poker—coming at me from the other side. I was outnumbered. I had nothing to fight back with. I had to gain myself some time.

Leaping to my feet, I made a break for the kitchen.

The basement door was open.

The lights were off.

I took the stairs so quickly I almost fell down them. Above me, I could hear movement, but not much. The occasional creak. A short whisper. I tried to force my eyes to adjust quicker to the darkness, but— unable to determine exactly what lay around me—I felt my way to the back wall instead, looking across the space at the stairs, knowing this gave me a small advantage. Light leaked down from the kitchen: I'd be able to see them from here, but they wouldn't be able to see me.

Then the lights came on.

I was blinded, everything a wall of white light. But then, as my eyes started to regulate, I saw them coming down the stairs, Malcolm taking two at a time, the knife out in front of him; Michael close behind him, two hands on the fire poker.

I looked around me.

About six feet to my right was a walking stick. It had a thin, breakable stem, but the handle was a hard ball of wood. I grabbed it, flipped it on its end.

At the bottom of the stairs, I saw Malcolm briefly, through a canyon of old boxes, reaching for a light switch. He looked back, eyes narrowing, knife flashing.

He flipped the lights.

Darkness.

Suddenly, sound became important. I heard shuffling. Readjustment. One of them said something quietly, but not quietly enough. It sounded like Malcolm.

The basement was a maze of pillars, of cardboard boxes stacked three and four high; of old pieces of furniture and storage cupboards. I couldn't navigate it in the dark, so I ducked right, heading for the corner of the room. In the stillness, I could hear wind passing through vents, coming down from the kitchen. I wasn't far from the stairs here—maybe twelve, fifteen feet—and I briefly thought about making a break for it, about getting to the kitchen and locking them down here.

But I didn't know if there was even a lock on the door.

Or how close to the stairs they are.

Then, as my eyes continued to adjust to the gloom, I saw movement directly ahead of me, between two towers of boxes. *Michael.* He was edging toward me without even knowing it, nervous, tentative, the poker out in front, like a sword.

He was way out of his depth.

I gripped the walking stick and slid down onto my haunches, using the wall behind me for support. He looked ahead of him, slightly off to my left, where some of the gardening equipment was stacked, then back in the direction he had come. *Keep coming.* He was still too far away.

Within seconds, something else caught my eye. Slightly behind him and to the right, between the stairs and a row of old furniture, I could see Malcolm. He was edging around, more slowly than Michael, more confidently, the knife at his side, almost against his leg. It was a smart move: he was trying to prevent the blade from catching any vague trace of light. As he got to the stairs, he stopped, conscious of being revealed by the glow from the kitchen, and he changed direction, disappearing from view.

Now I couldn't see him.

Just Michael.

I waited but Malcolm didn't reappear, and the longer I waited, the closer Michael got. Five feet. Four. *He's going to see me any second*—and then he did.

Before he had a chance to react, to bring the fire poker up, I went for him, using the wall as a springboard. I hit him twice: once in the side of his knee, the impact collapsing him, his leg giving way, his body dropping sideways; then a second time, in the top of the chest, winding him. He howled in pain, the poker spilling out of his grasp and clattering against the floor, and then he hit the deck.

I'd barely had time to process what was happening when Malcolm came at me from my right, angling around a tower of cardboard boxes. I jumped back, the knife passing through the space I'd occupied seconds before, and then I rocked on my heels and pushed forward, Malcolm's momentum carrying him toward me.

I grabbed his wrist, pushing the knife away from me, but I pushed too hard and too fast and the movement unbalanced both of us. We stumbled back, pinned to one another, into a series of boxes. The knife spun off, but I'd lost my grip on him, and he was in front of me now, on his feet, pushing boxes aside so I couldn't get at him. As I tried to get up, he heaved an old bookcase away from the wall, its shelves creaking, books sliding out, onto me—and then the bookcase came too.

It crashed against my body.

I was winded; stunned.

"I was prepared to give you a second chance, David," he said breathlessly, looking for his knife. "Do you remember that? We told you not to get involved."

He wiped some blood away from his nose.

"But I can't help you this time."

I tried to push the bookcase off me, but it was oak—heavy, cumbersome—and I could feel old injuries rising to the surface, locking me up, paralyzing me.

Come on. Come on.

I tried to heave it off.

Please. Not like this.

Come on.

He had his back to me, searching for the knife.

Then, in my hand, I felt something.

The walking stick.

I turned my head and, to my side, about four feet away, I saw Mary. She was huddled in the corner, partially lit by the light from upstairs, hidden from view behind a triangle of old paint cans. *She'd crept down into the basement.* Tears were running down her face, her eyes following Malcolm, and as she looked at me, I saw why she'd taken the risk: whatever came after, whatever happened to her husband, whatever the truth about her son, it had to be better than all of this.

She came out from behind cover, across to me, and began to push. I did the same. The bookcase shifted an inch, another, another, until it was far enough across my body for me to squeeze out from under it. It hit the floor with a thud.

Malcolm turned, bent down, picking up the knife.

I caught him across the back of the head. The impact sounded soft and hollow—and he went down as if every muscle in his body had stopped working. I waited for him to come at me again, to fight me again, but he didn't. He was still.

I turned to Mary. "Are you okay?"

She nodded.

"Thank you," I said.

But she didn't reply, her eyes fixed on her husband, out cold on the floor of the home they shared; a man she'd lived with and known for over thirty years.

A man she hadn't ever known at all.

60

I spoke to Mary about two weeks after the police led Malcolm, Michael and me away from the house. Understandably, she'd begun grieving. She'd lost her son, and now she had lost her husband as well—the man she'd spent years caring for. Every day she'd been by his side because every day she feared it might be his last.

I didn't tell her I knew how it felt.

Derryn would always be a part of me, her face and her voice so clear in my head. To Mary, Malcolm would only be a reflection obscured by ripples; a myth.

I looked at Malcolm as we left the house in handcuffs, and, in his eyes, I saw the trade. I wouldn't mention the girl who'd had his child, Simon, and all the others who died on the farm, or were sacrificed for it, and neither he nor Michael would mention my part in the deaths of Jason, Zack, Andrew or Legion. It was a better trade for them. While I remained silent, his son remained hidden, the truth about Leyton Alan Green's death too, and he and Michael got to blame everything on the farm—all the death, all the suffering on the people that had been left to run it. He'd claim he had no idea about what was going on; so would Michael.

It stuck in my throat, and it meant I had to convince Mary, as I talked to her on the phone, not to mention anything Malcolm had talked about at the end.

More deception, more fiction.

Liz sat with me during the interviews, mostly in silence, as it became obvious early on that the police weren't going to charge me with anything. They could see my injuries. They could see what sort of people they were dealing with. More difficult, though, than lying to the detectives about the things I'd done, was lying to her. I think, deep down, she knew I wasn't being entirely honest with her, but she never said anything—and a part of me liked her even more for that.

About ten days later, something good happened.

As winter sunlight broke through the trees, Mary got a phone call at the hospital. It was her first day back, and she was just finishing up a night shift. The caller was told that she was still on the ward, and that he could phone back or he could wait. He told the nurse that he would wait. Ten minutes later, once Mary returned to her station, she picked up the phone, thinking it would be the police.

But it wasn't.

It was Alex.

He was back in France—and he wanted her to come and meet him.

I drove back to Carcondrock about a fortnight after Malcolm and Michael had tried to kill me, and I buried the box full of photographs, because it seemed like the right thing to do. I called Kathy to tell her about some of the things I'd found out, and then I'd done the same for John Cary, but I stopped short of telling them Alex was alive. That, as with Mary, was down to Alex himself.

When I filled in the hole, after burying the box, there wasn't enough sand. The top of the hole sank in, making it look disturbed. I didn't want to leave it like that, and initially tried to cover it in, but then I started to think that there was a kind of resonance to it being like that. Because each of those memories in the box—every photograph, every line of the letter—had been disturbed a little as well.

61

The night I got back from Carcondrock, the house felt different. I couldn't explain it, wasn't even sure I was meant to, but something had changed. Or maybe I had.

I didn't put the TV on, like I always did when I got home. I forgot about it. I had a shower, got changed, and then stood there in the bedroom I'd once shared with my wife, and felt a strange compulsion to be here, among Derryn's things.

Sitting on the edge of the bed, I started going through the drawers of her dresser, the drawers of our bedside table, her wardrobe, the books lined up on the shelves, and the next time I really became lucid, clear about what I was doing, it was three o'clock in the morning, and I'd fallen asleep on our bed. I hadn't slept a single night on it for a year, but now I'd returned, I'd *slept*, not needing the sound of the television on mute, or the distance of the sofa from the bedroom, to settle.

And, as I went off again, my thoughts of Derryn, of her looking across at me from the rocking chair we used to keep out on the back porch, everything was suddenly so clear. I had a feeling wash over me, the feeling that this was the end of one stage of my life and the beginning of another.

I don't know how much time went by, but what started out as an abstract noise on the periphery quickly consumed me, then pulled me away with it. And as I fell away into the darkness of sleep, the darkness I wasn't scared of any more—the darkness that took me down below the surface—I finally realized what it was.

It was the sound of the sea.

Acknowledgments

There are a great many people who have helped with the writing of this book.

My agent Camilla Wray has been a constant source of guidance and encouragement, and is always armed to the teeth with incredible ideas and suggestions. A big thank you to everyone else at Darley Anderson too.

The team at Michael Joseph—and Penguin as a whole—are amazing, and I feel so fortunate to have had the opportunity to work with them. An extra special thanks to my editor Stefanie Bierwerth, whose eye for a story helped to massively improve the novel when it arrived on her desk. She was also kind enough to give me a say in other areas of publication when she really didn't have to. Thank you also to Rowland White in the UK, and to my US editor, Chris Russell, who has been such an incredible champion of the Raker series. The hard work of him, and the whole team at Viking Penguin, is just so appreciated.

For their faith and support: Mum and Dad, whose belief never wavered and who I have so much to thank for; my little sis Lucy; and my extended family, both in the UK and South Africa. And lastly, the two girls in my life: Erin, who I love more than anything in the world—even football. And my partner-in-crime, Sharlé, who had to put her evenings and weekends on hold for two years, but who has been there since before the book was even an idea, and who is, quite simply, the best.

The David Raker Mystery Series

The Dead Tracks

Seventeen-year-old Megan Carver was an unlikely runaway, a straight-A student from a happy home. Yet six months later, she still hasn't been found. Soon the conspiracy of silence leads David Raker towards a forest on the edge of the city, a place known as the Dead Tracks.

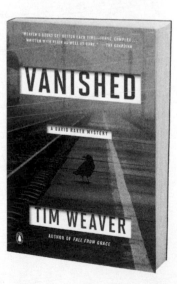

Vanished

For millions of Londoners, the morning of December 17 is just like any other. But not for Sam Wren. An hour after leaving home, he gets onto a tube train—and never gets off again. Sam's wife Julia hires David Raker to track him down, but in this case, the secrets go deeper than anyone imagined.

PENGUIN
BOOKS

The David Raker Mystery Series

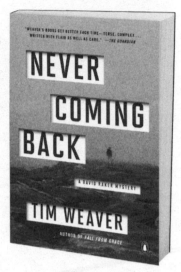

Never Coming Back

When Emily Kane arrives at her sister Carrie's house, she finds the front door unlocked. Dinner is in the oven—but Carrie, her husband, and their two daughters are gone. Emily enlists the help of David Raker, but as he gets closer to the truth, he begins to uncover evidence of a sinister cover-up, spanning decades and costing countless lives.

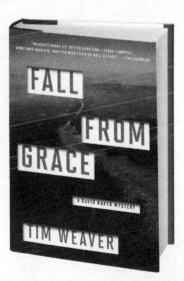

Fall From Grace

When ex-detective Leonard Franks and his wife retire to a secluded farmhouse, everything goes as expected, until the night that Leonard goes out to fetch firewood—and never returns. Leonard's daughter hires David Raker, but nothing can prepare him for what he's about to find—or for the devastating secret behind this disappearance.

PENGUIN
VIKING BOOKS